JEWS OF BABYLON

THE REMNANT RETURNS

REV. BILL AND FREDA BOWEN

Dorrance Publishing Co
585 Alpha Drive
Suite 103
Pittsburgh, PA 15238
Visit our website at *www.dorrancebookstore.com*

ISBN: 979-8-89027-159-4
eISBN: 979-8-89027-657-5

This book is dedicated to all people of the Middle East who have endured a lifetime of suffering. May it seem well unto GOD to grant them Leil Shimurim (Wiktionary Dictionary) a night of protection and security.

I would like to acknowledge all members of our families who have struggled through life to survive and make a living through hard work, love for family, and dedication unto GOD.

CONTENTS

PREFACE

THE COUNSELOR, RUACH HAKODESH

GOD has called many ministers and prophets in strange ways and has given them specific instructions to bring his word of truth to the people of flesh. Here are two of examples from Jeremiah and Ezekiel. I will start with Ezekiel chapter twelve. I have labeled it to be the prince behind the wall.

In chapter twelve of Ezekiel, GOD told Ezekiel to take stuff for removing and remove it in the sight of Israel and to place it on his shoulders and parade it through the streets so that people might see it. Then God said, "Take it to the wall and dig a hole. Take it with you and come up on the other side of the wall where the apple trees and other fruit trees, animals and gardens for food are growing." First, you need to know what GOD was referring to when he used the word "stuff."

We find the answer when we read about the story of Saul and how he was to become the first king over Israel. When the time came to crown Saul king, they could not find him. Then one stepped forth and said, "He is sitting among the stuff."

Stuff was the idols of gold and silver that had been collected and placed in the storehouse of treasure. Why was Saul sitting among the stuff or the statures of idols? These idols were manmade, little "g" gods and were a stink in GOD's nostril. "The idols of the heathen are silver and gold, the works of men's hands. They have mouths but they speak not, eyes but they see not. They that make them are like unto them, so is everyone, that trust in them" (Psa. 135:15-18 KJV). Saul was thinking about destroying these idols. Yet again, he had second thoughts because of their value. Even before he was king, he had a tough decision to make. Should he please GOD or should he please the flesh of man? The stuff was in reference to manmade.

Ezekiel was ready to follow GOD's instructions. He went to the storehouse of treasure and took one of the manufactured statues and set it upon his shoulders the same as a father would give his child a ride upon the shoulders.

When he did this the people followed him and made fun of him and the prophecy he would give. Here is the prophecy he gave:

"My dear people of Jerusalem, please listen to my words and follow the actions which I place before your eyes. GOD is getting ready to send the Great King of Babylon here to destroy our city of Jerusalem. Many that have worshipped the manufactured statues and have sought to please the flesh of man will die during the battle. When King Nebuchadnezzar comes, he will take your king captive, back into Babylon and he shall die the death of a thousand men. His sons will die before his eyes, and he will be blinded. However, you have seen me take this manmade idol to safety upon the other side of this wall. I will take the true seed from the loins of man into my safety net. He is more precious than the gold of Ophir. He shall grow up in Babylon captivity and become a nail in sure place for his people Israel."

I also mentioned Jeremiah. Here is a quick story about Jeremiah.

Jeremiah was known as the weeping prophet. He shed many tears because he would preach and offer the people good advice.

GOD said, "If you put your hand to the plough and then look back, you will not be worthy to enter into my Kingdom."

Jeremiah asks a question: "Is there no balm in Gilead? Is there no Physician there?" It was this conversation of getting everything that bothered him out in the opening, which would bring him back in line and in union with GOD. There is nothing better than being in union with the Lamb. Once Jeremiah realized that he could not kick against the pricks or ask GOD a question by saying, "What are you doing?" then and only then was he ready for the master's hand.

GOD broke him and threw him back on the potter's wheel to make him a vessel of honor that would suit GOD. Here is his story and what GOD wanted him to do and how he got Jeremiah to be an obedient servant. The first time that Nebuchadnezzar brought his army to Jerusalem, he left some of the people intact and did not destroy the whole city.

He also left one prophet behind to guide the people. That prophet was Jeremiah. Later, the King of Babylon headed back to Jerusalem. He was fascinated with gold and set his sight on finding the Holy Candelabra and the Ark of the Covenant. When Jeremiah got word of his returning, he knew his life would be taken so he headed to the mountains and made his way down into Egypt. After King Nebuchadnezzar left Jerusalem, he conquered Egypt. Jeremiah was sent to prison. After several years in prison, he was brought to the outer skirts of the prison and there he had more freedom. GOD had him in the right place at the right time. While here, Jeremiah found what GOD sent him to do. GOD had picked Jeremiah to discover and take possession of the title to land that was detrimental to the future of Israel and find a missing link in genealogy that would one day lead to the star out of Jacob. Here is the story of Jeremiah in the outer courts.

Jeremiah met up with his cousin, Hanameel. He held the title to Jeremiah's old home place. Prior to the invasion by Babylon the land was owned by Shallum, Jeremiah's uncle. The land had been in the family of Adonikam for generations. This land had once belonged to a Gentile named Ornan.

Ornan established a thriving business on this land. He had the perfect location for setting up a threshing floor and charging the people that came to his floor to separate the wheat from the chaff. Ornan charged them one penny for each measure of wheat and one penny for two measures of barley that they brought to him. The land surrounding the high ridge was known as Anathoth. The land had been in the family of Adonikam for generations, before the land was sold.

The ownership had changed hands many times during history of that land. Jeremiah knew the story of how David had purchased the land from Ornan for the full price. Jeremiah knew the value of paying the full price to GOD once you come into his knowledge and then you willfully sin or do something wrong pertaining to the Law of Moses as given by GOD. Jeremiah's thoughts were upon David.

King David had come to pay the full price. Ornan did not want to sell the land. He and his sons stood the ground against David. Then God sent two angels to stand one on either side of David. When Ornan saw this, he became afraid and told David he could just have the land for free. David knew he must pay the full price and use the land as a place where he could renew his fellowship with GOD.

After restoration David would begin a new way of life and he placed an immense value on this piece of land, with a high elevation. The highest in Israel. David developed this land and set it as a narrow six-hectare ridge. One hectare was 10,000 meters. It measured 60,000 square meters (Wikipedia). People could easily get to this parcel of land. David would begin to build a city here and it would be called the City of David. It was this history that made Jeremiah to purchase this land for the sake of Israel. With the title in hand, Jeremiah kept it in the safety of his bosom. The timing was right for Jeremiah to have an encounter of great importance.

The second magnificent event that GOD had chosen Jeremiah for was hidden in the genealogies, which no man could find.

In the outer courts Jeremiah had a supernatural visit from GOD. Jeremiah looked toward a lone window and saw a young boy looking from Egypt in the South toward Jerusalem. There appearing in full view from the stream of sun light was a perfect vision of a Star of David. The image stood still for a moment and began to fade to the light as GOD whispered into the Spiritual Ear of Jeremiah, "This is my native son, the holy seed." This seed was a third-generation descendant from the union of Daniel and a young girl named Sarah.

Immediately Jeremiah hired a runner to leave Egypt and to go down into Babylon, as one would run and escape from captivity (Ezek. 24:26-27 KJV). The runner delivered the title to the land into the hand of Ezekiel and brought him wonderful news that the holy seed was safe.

The Ruach HaKodesh (Encyclopedia), the Holy Ghost or the Great Counselor had come to teach his chosen, wonderful things. He reminds them of all he had spoken to them by the mouth of his prophets.

GOD called out to me, as the author, to speak the truth about his parables and riddles hidden within his Holy Bible.

I was not very cooperative. I wanted to kick against the prick as the Apostle Paul had done. My experience brought me back into line.

AN EXPERIENCE

I rebelled, as Jeremiah did, and I said to GOD, "I will speak for you no more." I was trying to fleece GOD like Gideon and the golden fleece. GOD was interested in getting me to the place he wanted me to be. He wanted me to follow him. He desired me to leave the people I worshipped with and go with him in another direction.

GOD called me on the carpet and said, "If you put your hand to the plough and look back, you will not be worthy of entering into my Kingdom. I will not leave you but will call to you in due season. What others will do they do for evil, but I will turn it for your good."

I did not want to speak for GOD. I did not want to be a minister. I only had a desire to teach school and coach football. I learned early on that you had better be careful of what you ask GOD, for he will give it to you just to show you that that is not where he wants you to go. Growing up and playing cow pasture football, I developed a love for football.

I was blessed of GOD to play football at Dobyns Bennett High School in Kingsport, Tennessee. Then I was to play in the Tennessee All-Star game. Funny how things turn out when you are in the hands of the Master Mark Mason, Y'shua (Jesus), the Conquering Lion of Judah.

One of the bigger boys on our team got a letter to play in the all-star game. He went to the coach with the letter and said, "I got this letter to play in the Tennessee All-Star football game. It came to my house, but it has Billy's name on it. What should I do?" Coach Bill Jasper said, "Give it to Billy. If his name is on it, the letter belongs to him."

I spent two weeks on campus in practice, getting ready for the game at Lees McRae College in Banner Elk, NC. The game was played in Bristol, Tennessee, in the Stone Castle. We won a victory over the Virginia All-Stars. Little did I know, it was GOD preparing me to go through various stages of growth as I worked my way back to him.

Coach Jasper, my high school coach, told me that Mr. W. B. Green wanted to talk to me about training to be a manager over the sports department at his store. I went to see Mr. Green.

Mr. Green introduced me to Hal, his son-in-law, and Hal would talk to me and get everything fixed up. Hal asked me what I wanted to do, and I told him I wanted to teach school and coach football. I knew that answer bypassed his desire to hire me as a manager trainee. Hal talked to me and told me to pursue my desire to teach and coach. I really did not know what to do or how to do it. Then I got a letter from Coach Fred I. Dickenson at Lees McRae College, and he offered me a football scholarship. He said I needed to come to Lees McRae soon, for football practice had started. He also stated that I needed to pay a $100 entrance fee. We did not have even ten dollars, let alone one hundred. One must remember that I am still in the hands of the Master Potter, who can remake us in the image he desires.

Next day my Aunt Maxie came to our house. Mom talked to her about my chance to go to college. She said, "All I have is $50 and I can let you have that. Do you know where you can get another fifty to go with it?" We could not produce an answer and suddenly I said, "I went to see Mr. Green about a job, and he seemed to be interested in me." Aunt Maxie put me in the car and drove to W. B. Green's store. She talked to Mr. Green about my needing another $50 to get into college. He took me next door to Dobyns Taylor Hardware Store. He introduced me to Mr. Dobyns. Mr. Green told me to go back home and that he would pick me up tomorrow at eleven o'clock.

At eleven o'clock he pulled up and I got in the car. He told me he was taking me to the Ridgefield Country Club to have lunch with the Kiwanis Club. He introduced me to the club and told them of my situation. He told me that I was to go to Lees McRae College tomorrow and not to worry about any financial needs I might have.

Mr. Green told me that he and the Kiwanis Club would take care of my entrance fee. He also asked if I had a way to school. I said my brother H. S. could take me.

H. S. took me to Banner Elk, NC, and the coach met me and took me to my room. I would stay in the basement apartment of Coach Lewis Hall. He told me that we would have a football game tomorrow and that I needed to come to the field house for practice that evening.

Gary Stacy, a former Marine, took me over to practice that evening.

The next morning, the day of the game, Coach Dickerson called out my name as a starter at free safety on defense. The same position I had started on the all-star team. I played some at quarterback because I already knew the offense.

I transferred to ETSU in Johnson City, Tennessee. Coach Star Wood said I could walk on. He let me stay in the dorm and gave me meals during our practice sessions. When school started, I was going back and forth from my home to ETSU. One evening Coach Hal Morris picked me up and gave me a ride. The next day Coach Wood called me and said he had a scholarship open for me.

Now what I wanted was to become a reality. I graduated and I entered the football coaching arena. I was in demand as a teacher and coach and every year I would have offers to come to one or two schools. I was blessed to coach at five different schools and in four different school systems. GOD was truly letting me get a taste of what I desired. Then He began to show me that what I wanted was not the best for me. He wanted me to step closer to Him and pay attention to what He was going to have me to do.

All the while he was saying, “My sheep hear my voice and a stranger they will not follow” (John 5:10 KJV). GOD was now becoming the Bell Sheep and I must follow him.

GOD held me captive and began to school me in the beauty of the old law and a fresh look at the Messiah from the Jewish standpoint of the law. The day I walked out of the church, I was in, after receiving the gift of the Holy Ghost, all that was within me belonged to GOD.

Rumor was that the church elders were going to bring me to council for speaking in tongues. They did not believe in this. One of the older elders called for me to come to his home. He gave me advice that might avoid a council meeting. He said, “Billy, if anyone says anything about what happened in church, you tell them what Apostle Paul said: ‘If strong meat makes my brother to offend, I will eat no meat while this world stands’” (1 Corinthians 8:13 KJV).

Some of the elders got together and brought me before the council. What they meant for evil, GOD meant for good. One of the most highly respected elders from Indiana came to the meeting and when the stones started to be thrown, he desired to claim the floor and speak. He said, "If this is of man it will come to naught; if it is of GOD it will stand. If it is from GOD, I am afraid to come against it." That was GOD's protection for me. I thought this would be the end of my troubled waters that I was in. The church ordained me as a deacon, indeed. Then they ordained me as an elder in the church. And finally, they elected me moderator of the oldest church in Wise County. Then after services one evening, a sister in church came in with steel braces used to hold her eyes open. The elder in charge of service that day said, "I am going to ask Elder Billy Bowen to lay his hands upon this sister and pray for her."

Surprise caught me! This was not a normal for the church. They did not practice laying hands on sick people and praying for them in the church. The sister came in front of me and suddenly, without any prior notice, I began to shake, and I stretched forth my hand and placed it on her forehead, and immediately I said five words in tongues, interpreted to mean "The Lord hath healed thee." It was as if shaken by a mighty wind. I realized what had taken place. All the world seemed to sit in silence. This sister came to the next meeting, and all was well, no braces on her eyes.

The association meeting was coming up and I was elected to be the director of the meeting. Our small church would only hold about thirty people and I knew I had to be creative for this meeting.

I went to Brother R. L. Crawford in Coeburn, Virginia. He had a large revival tent. I asked him what it would take to have the tent set up in a vacant field next to our church.

He countered with this. He said, "It will not cost you anything if you will let me hold a revival there for two weeks after your association is over."

Now we had a big tent that would easily hold two to three hundred people. I had to produce a way to feed the group when they came on Sunday.

I contacted the head of the J. I. Burton High School cafeteria, Ruth Hensley. Her mother had belonged to the church before she died. Ruth and her staff said they would fix the meals and deliver them to our meeting. I had ruffled feathers once again. Many of the elders from the three associations said they were not going to preach under a tent. They did not like the setup and the arrangements. They came and huddled in small groups to have their discussions. Meeting time came around and the first elder to open said, "We said we would not preach under a tent but here we are. GOD must be leading us." When time came for the business meeting, one of the elders took to the stand and brought before the group about my speaking in tongues.

A brother from our neighboring state of Kentucky came to my defense. Then, another brother said, "If you have an old stubborn mule, if you will just leave it alone sooner or later it will make you a good plow mule." I was in the very back of the tent. A few of the people felt I was doing this out of just being stubborn. They knew not the power of GOD. Members came to me and said, "Brother Billy, we are glad you are not up there taking part in this; GOD is on your side." Seemed like for the third time there was a charm. No one wanted to see me dismissed from the church. We had one of the most successful associations meetings ever held. We had over six hundred people in a three-day total coming to the big tent meeting. My travels were not yet over with these people.

There were some still looking for a catch-22 to have me dismissed from the church. GOD was using me in a situation of growth until I would come full circle and let him show me where he wanted me to go. The preaching committee called me, to preach the introductory sermon at the upcoming association meeting. I was told that I was one of the youngest elders ever picked to preach an introductory sermon at an association meeting.

My wife and I began going to the rest home for the sick and shut-in in Wise Virginia. Our reason for going was that a member of our church, Sister Pearl Ought, was in the rest home. After ministering on site for a while, I began to bring four sisters from the rest home to church with us. I would go up early on Sunday and load them up and bring them to our church. After church I had to take them back to the home.

It was a custom that after church those attending would sit and socialize. They did not like it because I did not stay with them and sit and talk.

Let me share with you what finally happened and how it all added up to the all-knowing GOD working out of the sight of men his wonders to perform. I will share with you my story of how I came to Appalachia, Virginia. My arrival in Appalachia took place a few years before I joined the church and became an ordained elder.

COMING INTO APPALACHIA

It was exceedingly early morning as I came through Appalachia. I did not see a sign that told me the name of the town. I did not know where I was exactly. As I rode through the one main street in the town, it was not hard to see that it was trash pickup day. A windstorm had blown over all the trashcans. Garbage and debris were scattered all over the street, from one side to the other. Stray dogs were enjoying some garbage leftovers. As I drove through the town, I said to myself, "I don't know what town this is, but I would not live here if they gave me the whole town." This was in 1974. Since that time, I try to be careful of what I say in front of the all-knowing, all-hearing and all-seeing GOD. About one year later, I came to Appalachia and was living right in the middle of town in the Old Mountain Manor Hotel. I was hired by the board of directors of the Appalachia Community Center as the new director.

The chairperson of the board said, "We cannot hire you unless you have an Appalachia address." She advised me to get a post office box so I would have an Appalachia address. I was director of a center that worked with underprivileged children. I began to form partnerships with all the agencies to help these children. I brought assembly programs of entertainment into the school for the children. I immediately applied for a grant and was funded to provide hot meals to eight recreation sites. I had established these sites in the outlying coal camps. I applied for and got Peace Corps volunteers to come to Appalachia. I had volunteers from New York and Connecticut. They stayed all summer. Families in the area kept them. These were my staff. One of the sites was in Keokee. After being asked if I had met the beautiful redhead from Keokee, I began asking everyone I knew if they had said that to me. I was on a mission to find out who had made that statement to me.

No one had said that. I thought I must have gotten a message from an angel. I formed an organization to work with and through parents and guardians of children who were victims of divorce or death. I had a meeting scheduled at the Keokee Baptist Church. That night as we were gathering to meet, I drove up to the church and got out of my car and looked around and there she came. The redhead, my wife-to-be. She and I both had been through some trying times. Her daddy was killed in the coalmines. Her mother died at an early age and left her as the head of the family to take care of other children at the age of thirteen. Her husband got killed in an accident as a brakeman on a train. Her little girl had gotten killed in a car accident at the age of fourteen. I met her and she had a young son who was nine years old. As my life began to gain an attachment in Appalachia and Keokee, she became my friend. A relative new government-funded program was taking applications for executive director for Wise County and Norton Head Start Program.

Many parents encouraged me to apply for the program. Many of the area teachers and at least one principal of a school was among the applicants. I did not think I had a chance at getting the job. I was still haunted by what I had said to the all-hearing ear of GOD. I said, "If you gave me the town, I would not have it." Now GOD was preparing me for my future marriage to Freda and for a job that would allow me to help even more underprivileged children and families for the next twenty-seven years. Unexpectedly I was hired as the executive director of a program, which I would help build into one of the best programs for head-start children in the area. We had no buses when I came. When I left, we had a fleet of buses and staff cars. We owned no buildings when I came. When I left, we had eight sites and a million-dollar complex for staff and children. When I came, we had a $98,000 budget. In my best year, we had an annual budget of over 5.5 million dollars, counting the state grant, the federal grant and local matching in-kind.

When I came, we had approximately twenty-one employees and when I left, we had a staff of 127 employees in our best year. I became a primary grants writer. We became a major employer in our area. I am writing this to let you know that it was not me at all, but it was the hand of GOD upon me. He was showing me, "If you let me fight your battles and trust in me, I will bring you through the storms of life." After Freda and I met and just before we got married, she told me of a dream she had. She was lying on her couch and suddenly muddy waters started rising in her room. Dark clouds of trouble began to surround her. She was in a great straight. She looked up and a great eagle came out of the East. The eagle was pushing the dark clouds out of her life and a bright light, brighter than the noonday sun, was brought to her by this eagle.

She said the eagle turned to look at her and when it did, my face was upon the eagle. The eagle was carrying an egg and the egg had a crack in it in the shape of the Star of David, and blood was dripping from the star.

If I had never met Freda, if I had never married her, I would never have been in the ministry and would never have written my first book. I would like to offer you this segment of our life that streams right back to the question of, why were we in Appalachia?

We were invited to leave the church we were associated with. We did not know what to do or where to go.

We were like two little orphans. We were without a home church. I was beginning to realize how cruel the church community could be.

Here is another open vision from Freda that will help your understanding of why we came to Appalachia. It is the story of the little white colt.

THE LITTLE WHITE COLT

Freda and I were leading a little white colt and the colt was pulling flatbed trailers hooked together with silver links of chain. The sun was shining bright and the reflection from the silver would almost blind you. The flatbed trailers were loaded with tons of hay. The trailers reached from the Big Stone Gap Straightaway all the way to Duffield, over thirty miles. This was enough to feed the flock of GOD for a long time. As we neared the turn off to go into Keokee, this was where we thought GOD wanted us to go. There blocking the turn off to keep us out of Keokee were two big horses.

A red horse and a black horse. They were big as a Clydesdale horse. They were pawing and kicking the little white colt. The little white colt fell under their big hooves. It was bleeding profusely. Billy and I began to cry. Billy picked up the little white colt, looked at its little lifeless body and said, "We are going to have to go another way; we cannot get through here."

Suddenly an angel appeared. It was a black man, with long black hair down to his shoulders. He was clothed in a flowing white garment. There was a heavenly glow all around about him. He had in his right hand a sickle and began to cut a pathway and bid to us that we should follow him. He was cutting coming and going. Billy still had the little white colt. We followed the pathway, and he stopped in the middle of Appalachia and the vision disappeared. Here is the meaning of the vision.

The little white colt was the beauty of the old law and signified the coming of freedom and a new birth of GOD's wisdom. The hay was the good news of the gospel, the power of GOD unto salvation unto them that believe. The silver links were the salvation that held the gospel diet close one to another. Now, just what were the horses?

The story about the horses will lead you back to my being separated from the church I was in.

I was brought before the church council for speaking in tongues and finally for preaching at the rest home and committing spiritual adultery. That is the act of leaving your church and preaching in another place. We were at the meeting. There were two elders in the church that took the platform and brought charges against Billy. My wife looked up and said, "Billy, there are these two horses of my dream. They do not want the Gospel as the power of GOD to come into Keokee, so they are kicking against your gift." Now GOD had sent an angel to show us an unusual way to go. A black minister, Rev. Roosevelt Jones, Pastor of Macedonia Baptist Church, took me under his wing. Rev. Jones was blind and had one leg off. I became a helping hand to him in the church. When he died, he left me his robe he ministered in. Macedonia helped us establish our storefront church. At our first meeting as the members left, they left a love offering on the altar of $11.38. We have been in Appalachia since 1983 and counting.

My wife had said when GOD shows us where to go, he will provide us a church. We did not have any financial support for our dream. A friend of Billy's had a space in a government building and let us have it for a church free of charge. We were there for a little over a year and some of our enemies complained and we were forced to move out of the building to separate the church-and-state rule. A man sent of GOD, Andy Taylor, let us have a great building for a modest rent of $200.00. Andy was a freemason and placed the Star of David on an awning he erected over our building. He told his family that when he died that the family was never to raise our rent. We have been in Andy's building for over thirty-six years and counting. We do not own membership from our congregation, and we do not solicit donations of money unless we have a visiting minister. Those that come give of their own free will.

We felt the presence of angels in our lives. Angels have always been watching over me. Here is my story about angels keeping watch.

ANGELS UNAWARES: AN INTRODUCTION

The Bible tells us that sometimes in our lives we will entertain an angel and not be aware that it is really an angel.

I began to think one day about angels and my thoughts turned to my wife Freda and the story she told me of her daughter Alfreda. Alfreda was fourteen years of age when her life was taken in a tragic automobile accident.

Freda said she was grieving and the burden she was carrying was so very heavy. She felt the hand of death was upon her. She wanted to know whereabouts of her lovely daughter after death.

She lay down upon the couch and she had no energy nor desire to go on living. Then the unexpected happened.

Alfreda suddenly walked into the room. She was dressed in a milky white dress, and it was moving in a constant rhythm as if the breath of GOD were breathing upon it.

Her skin was without flaw. It was pure and white as a fresh glass of white milk. Freda was so thrilled to see her and wanted to reach out and take her in her arms and hug and hold her tight.

Freda held out her arms as she walked toward Alfreda. Alfreda crossed her arms in front of her chest and began to wave them in a back-and-forth motion like the windshield wipers of an automobile in a rainstorm. The message was clear and simple. Alfreda was saying to her mother, "No, no, the flesh of the earth cannot touch the spiritual, heavenly body that belongs to GOD."

She was also letting her mother know she was all right and safe. She had walked into the room as an angel from GOD.

What a great reunion, prior to the resurrection. Can you imagine the love of GOD as he sends a loved one back to you after they have out stripped you and gone on? GOD sends his angels to us, letting us know that there is life after death and all is well. Mark 12:24-27 KJV tells us that after we die, we are as the angels in heaven.

Let me tell you of a couple of my experiences in life about my dad and then I will tell you about seeing my dad after his death.

MY DAD AT SCHOOL

Dad and I were never close. Due to a lot of factors, we had ten children in our family. There were five girls and five boys. All the boys accepted time with Dad.

My dad said, "Bill, good thing I met your mother when I did, or you would have been a redhead." Jokingly he was referring to one of the Fraley boys that used to like my mother when she was young.

On another occasion he said, "I wish I had twenty children and Molly was the mother of them all." This was a testimony of the love he had for Mother.

Although never close, it was trivial things that made me know that Dad loved his family. My dad could never read nor write, yet he always picked up a newspaper and looked it over with great intensity as if we were reading its every word. Here are two of my most remembered experiences about my dad and our relationship.

One was when I played football at Dobyns Bennett High School, and we had our annual father-and-son night. The other was when I was in the first grade at Lincoln Elementary School in Kingsport.

One evening I went to visit my nephew, Dewey Rasnick. Dewey lived directly across from Lincoln School. This visit was what triggered the recall memory about Dad.

My mother always walked me to school and then came to get me in the evening when school was out. As she took me to school one warm sunny morning, she told me that Dad would be there to get me in the evening. Dad had never been to my school, and I wondered if he would come.

When the bell rang at the end of the day and school was out, I watched as one by one all the children found their way to their waiting parents. After waiting awhile, the teacher said, "Billy, are you sure someone is coming to get you?" I said, "Yes, my dad is coming to get me." The teacher and I waited, and she kept looking and waiting.

Finally, I looked and saw him coming. He had taken the long walk around because he had never been to the school.

The picture of my dad coming to my rescue that day stuck to my mind. He had Kacie pants and a short-sleeved Kacie shirt on. He held my hand all the way home and I felt secure.

One day our heavenly father is going to walk with us home and we will be very secure. Our spirit goes back to GOD, who gave it unto us. And in the morning of the Great Resurrection the spirit will be reunited with the body. You will find this story in the writings of the Apostle Paul in I Corinthians, chapter 15. Now let me share with you the second time I had a great memory of my dad.

FATHER-AND-SON NIGHT

It was my senior year of playing football and this was our last game of the season. It was father-and-son night. I thought that my brother Otis would be at the game and sit in my dad's place.

The custom was that the father sat in a chair directly behind his son and wore his son's jersey number on his back. I told my brother Otis, and he said, "I'm going to take Dad to the game." My dad did not drive because he could not read nor write to take the test. He drove in the early forties until they started making people take a test to drive.

I said, "You know he will be drinking." My dad would work hard five days a week, then come the weekend he would drink and stay drunk until Sunday. On Sunday he would get sober to go back to work on Monday. He never missed a shift of work.

Otis said, "No, I am going to make sure he doesn't drink anything."

That night my dad showed great courage as he sat behind me. The night was cold and he was shaking and shivering. Someone started passing a bottle of liquor down the line.

The night was ice cold and each one took a drink as it came to them. When my dad got the bottle, he passed it up and refused to drink. He passed it by more times than one that night. We were playing Science Hill High School out of Johnson City.

Later in my coaching career, I would become the offensive back coach and the quarterback coach at Science Hill High School. Science Hill was a powerhouse of big linemen. We were on the 2-yard line and time for one play. The QB, Wally Bridewell, called my play. I said, "I can't make it; I'm beat all to pieces." My teammates said, "Yes, you can." I appreciated the confidence, but the QB would not change the play. I knew they were doing it for me and my dad. My 120-pound body could not push past big Johnson

City linemen. I was stopped short. The game ended in a 6-to-6 tie. Later, I would play in the Tennessee All-Star game and one of those big JC linemen on the team would be Roy Chapman.

The *Press Chronical* carried a picture of myself and Fuzz McDowell, from Ketron High School, standing under the outstretched arms of Roy. The picture was titled "The Big and Little of the Tennessee All-Star Team." Although the game ended in a 6-to-6 tie, my dad was proud to have been a part of the game. It was so cold, and my dad was wearing a thin sportscoat. After the game he was freezing so much that his whole body was shaking. I believe if I had had a bottle at that time, I would have offered him a drink and insisted that he drank it. Few would agree but that night my dad made a sacrifice for me. I never knew why my dad drank so much until later. Here is his story.

My dad worked in the coalmines for thirty years. He got paid five cents for digging a wheelbarrow full of coal. If it had slate in it, he had to dump it over a hillside and did not get paid for that load. He went back time after time. Sometimes he would make 35 or 40 cents for a day's work. He broke his back in a coalmining accident and was in a cast from his neck down to his waist. He was in this cast for six months. This was back in the mid- to late 1930s, before the medical field showed growth or advancement.

When the family came to Tennessee and Mom and Dad got a job at the Cotton Mill, our family moved into one of the company houses. This was one of the best houses the family ever lived in. Dad would work another thirty years in the mill. His body was never without pain. That was why he drank so much.

In my lifestyle, I have learned never to put down a person who drinks because you never know what made that person turn to the bottle for comfort.

I said I grew up watching my dad drinking liquor. My dad was a man of much sorrow.

He and my mother were baptized together at a tent revival on Wilcox Drive. He was striving to do better. The pain would not go away so he went back to drinking.

Dad was the first one in our family of twelve to die. He was eighty-six years old. My mom stood at the coffin, looked down upon him, and said,

"Hass, I have come as far as I can go with you. It will not be long, and I can join you." My mother was also eighty-six when she died. Here is my vision, I mentioned earlier about my father and life after death.

MY DAD – THE VISION

After Dad died the family was wondering if he went to heaven or hell. That was the least of my worries. Then came my open vision after my father was laid to rest.

I was at Mom's house at 113 W. Wanola Avenue. I was sitting in the swing on the front porch.

I looked across the street between two of the neighbors' houses. Here is what I saw. Dad was coming across the way. He was wrapped in heavy chains and his head had been cut off. He walked upon the porch. I went inside the house and said to Otis, my brother, "Otis, Dad is outside." Otis said, "Yes, I know!" We went outside.

There we looked and Dad was in a marble white coffin and two angels as men were dressed in white. They were sewing his head back onto his body. Then one of the angels said, "Don't worry, we do this all of the time."

The dream was a lifesaver for the family in distress. God told Daniel, "I, GOD, give the dreams and I also give the interpretation of the dreams." Here is the meaning of the dream that GOD gave unto me. My dad was a pilgrim of constant sorrow as he traveled the roads of this old life down here upon the earth. The load and the heavy burdens he carried were as heavy chains wrapped around about him. These burdens kept him separated from the head. However, in death he was joined back to the head. We must remember that GOD is the head, and we all are a part of the body. Death is just God's way of reuniting us back, in unity with Him.

You see, my dad was no different than you or I or any other living person upon this earth. The Bible tells us that we were all born in sin and brought forth in iniquity. "For all have sinned and come short of the glory of GOD" (Rom. 3:23 KJV). No matter who you are, eventually you will be confronted with situations in your life that will cause you to be separated from the love of GOD. There are only two ways to go: (1) You run toward GOD for help, or (2) you run toward drugs and alcohol or other things the world has to offer. When we get our thoughts upon GOD, that is when

Angels appear unto us. Another quote from the Bible is: "If I, the LORD GOD, have called you, I will visit you in visions and dreams."

In any situation we may receive a visit from angels. There are angels of light and there are powers and principalities of darkness. I like what Lou Holtz, the former football coach at Notre Dame, said: "There is never a right time to be wrong and there is never a wrong time that you can be right." In my travels of life, I came extremely near to turning and traveling down the wrong road of darkness. I can still hear my mother's voice, in prayer, calling and guiding me back to the right side of the tracks. More times than one her voice summoned angels to protect her family. When my brothers were in WWII they went through unbearable conditions.

MY BROTHERS

My two brothers, Ray and Garland, lied about their age to go into the Army and Navy, so that Mom might receive their check to feed the family. My brother Garland was in the 101st Airborne, the Screaming Eagles.

He made seventy-six jumps. He told of being in Germany and finding families, children, and adults. They were starving to death and dried upon the bone. There was no food. He said his commander ordered his men to do the only humane thing possible. Garland said he was forced to kill the whole family. Now, I understood Garland's drinking problem. Brother Ray went through troubles during the war. I heard Mom tell them when they came home how she prayed each night for their safety. Then there were special prayers said for my brother H. S., called Sam.

He was in the Korean War. He said one night he was on watch and one of his friends said, "Sam, would you trade watches with me and let me take your watch now and you take mine later on?"

Sam agreed. He told of how his friend was killed only a fleeting time after taking the watch. It could have been Sam that died. I overheard him and Mother talking, and she told him of how she prayed for him night after night.

One night I was invited to preach at Rev. Joe Goad's Church of GOD and Mom came to the meeting. As I ministered, I stopped and said, "Mom, I believe if we can hang on just a little longer GOD is going to bless our family. GOD has heard your voice and will honor each prayer you prayed for your family."

You see, GOD is a GOD of action. Here is the action GOD took on behalf of my brothers in answer to Mom's prayers.

Sam became a minister and pastored three different churches in the Kingsport, Tennessee, area. Now here is the story of Garland and Ray.

Garland and Ray, like Dad, had a drinking problem. Mother would get them dressed every morning. Garland and Ray always liked to dress up. They would go to town and clean up the pool hall for a drink of liquor and do other things to get liquor and then come home drunk and Mom would feed them and put them to bed. We were having a prayer meeting on the front porch and Mom had a bed on the screened-in back porch. A taxicab driver would pull in the driveway up to the back porch and help them out of the cab and into their bed. Even in their condition they would lie there and hear the preaching word that found its way into their innermost being.

I would go down to the house at times and Garland and Ray would be drunk and very talkative. In my mind's eye I could see no hope for them. Most of the time I became very mad. In the flesh I was operating outside of GOD and his realm of holiness. I had forgotten that GOD is love and he loves us despite the condition we get ourselves into a certain time. Here is the episode of the golden sponge.

THE GOLDEN SPONGE

I often wondered if they would ever quit drinking. As my wife Freda and I left to go home, Ray was still talkative, and Garland passed out in the bedroom.

When we got into the car, Freda said, "Bill, you don't have to worry about Garland anymore." I asked, "Why?" Then she gave me this answer: "I took my bottle of anointing oil and went into Garland's room and anointed him with oil. When I looked up, Jesus walked into the room. He took a golden sponge and began to bathe Garland. Gold was the glory of GOD, and the sponge was soaking up a lifetime of alcohol from Garland's system. Then Jesus took a container of pure water and poured it into Garland's navel, where his umbilical cord from his mother had been attached. A delivery and a new birth were taking place through this great visible miracle."

Later, I went back to the house and Garland said to me, "Billy, something happened to me while I was sleeping. I cannot begin to tell you what it was, but I do not drink anymore."

What could I say, but wow! Praise God. Later, my thoughts turned to Ray. I said in my doubt and unbelief, "You know Ray will get Garland back to drinking again." Then I justified my thoughts with a scripture from the Bible. I said, "An ox and ass cannot plough together." I criticized Ray for his drinking. We made another trip down to see Mother.

Ray met me at the door and said, "Billy, you have a brand-new brother. GOD brought me out of bed last night at the midnight hour and baptized me with the Holy Ghost and took drinking away from me." Then he started talking in tongues. We had a prayer meeting right there in the living room. Ray and Garland had no income and had never been sober enough to get on Social Security and their veterans pension. Finally, they got their monthly checks coming into the household.

Ray bought new suits and started going to church and paying his tithes. He became a member of the Church of GOD in Weber City. Rev. Raymond Hammond asked Ray to take charge and call each member every month and remind them to come to church. Ray loved doing this and enjoyed talking to everyone.

Mother had a stroke. Here is a helping way that GOD takes care of situations in our lives. Before she had the stroke, Mother took care of Ray and Garland all through their battle with alcohol. Now they stayed home and took care of Mother through her sickness.

One day Rev. Smith Ketner came down to the house and asked Garland, "Are you a Christian?" I thought he gave an answer that could only come from the heart.

Garland answered, "No, but I am not a hypocrite, neither." Then he continued, "I think GOD saw that Ray needed to go to church and I needed to stay home and take care of Mother."

I could tell you stories of angels and their involvement in our family and how my sisters and brothers all received visit from angels through my mother's prayers. Let me quickly tell you a story about my brother Otis. He had a tragic accident.

OTIS AND TRAGEDY

Otis was swinging at Lincoln School. He and H. S. were near age and big friends as were Garland and Ray. On this day Otis went too high in the swing and fell out and broke both of his arms. The bones shot through the skin. After he was stabilized at Holston Valley, they sent him to Knoxville, Tennessee, to a hospital for rehabilitation.

We were poor and we had no resources for Mom to go to Knoxville and visit Otis. I do not know how long Otis was in the hospital, but it was months. Mom prayed for GOD to make a way for her to see Otis. It was time for an angel to appear.

You guessed it. Mom had a visit and the angel told her to go to the Sluss house and ask if Mr. Sluss would take her to Knoxville. I walked with her to the Sluss home. They had a daughter named Jackie Sluss and she was a friend to Lula and Iva, my two sisters. They had a son about my age. His name was James and he and I were friends.

Upon arriving at the Sluss home, Mom told Mr. Sluss about the situation and he said, "Sure, I will take you on Sunday if you can help buy me gas." Boy, what great neighbors we had in the Borden Mill Village.

I never knew how Mom got the money, but she bought Otis three cartons of cigarettes and took him some cash money plus what she gave to Mr. Sluss. GOD always blessed Mom to be a money manager. She always tied some money in knots of a handkerchief and carried it in her bosom.

Here is a story about one of our trips to Knoxville.

KNOXVILLE

Mom and I walked up to the Sluss house. They had packed them a lunch and Mom had gotten some sandwiches ready for us. Mr. Sluss and his wife rode in the front. Mom, I, and James rode in the back seat. As we got close to Bean Station, Tennessee, just outside of Knoxville, we were crossing a bridge over the river. Cars were parked everywhere and people standing in groves looking toward the river. Mr. Sluss rolled the car window down and asked what happened. We were told that a preacher was baptizing a young girl of fourteen years of age and the rapid waves of the chest-high water swept her away and she drowned. As I got older, I learned that ministers do not always make the right decisions when it comes to interacting with other people. Common sense should have told him just by looking at the waters how dangerous it would be, especially after a hard rainfall. We continued our trip to Knoxville.

We got to the hospital, but we could not go to the patients' rooms. They brought my brother downstairs to see us. We could not stay long because Mr. Sluss and his wife had to get up early Monday morning to go to work at Borden Mill. Very quickly my thoughts returned to myself and angels, which we entertain without ever knowing of their presence. Here is the story of my travels.

MY TRAVELS

GOD has always intervened in my life and pulled me back in line, taking me in the right direction.

I am going to fast forward in my life and share with you a portion of my life that brought me into the ministry.

I had come to my wit's end. My heart was broken. I thought I was going to die. My health had failed quite a bit and I could not find an answer to my problems. Death would have been a welcome guest at my bedside. Then came an angel of light. My thoughts turned to just before I came to Appalachia. This is how GOD worked in my life, and he can work in your life also. He is no respecter of persons. I recall the words to an old song: "It is no secret what GOD can do. What he has done for others he will do for you. With arms wide open he will welcome you. It is no secret what GOD can do" (Stuart Hamblen). I was working as a professional fundraiser in the state of Kentucky. I started out in Louisville, Kentucky, and worked my way across the whole state.

I was in Pike County and headed toward the Ohio state line. I collaborated with schools to help raise money for needed projects. I always looked for school signs to get a lead on schools that I might have overlooked in the area. I was close to the Kentucky and Ohio line when I saw a sign. I could not see a school. I stopped and asked a gas station attendant. He answered, "Yes, there is a little old school up that holler down the road. You just passed it. All the children have something wrong with them."

I did not know what he meant. I went back and turned up the old graveled road and headed to the school. I could hardly believe my eyes as I looked upon the building they called a school. There was only one old car parked at the building. I parked my car and went to the door. It was an old one-room double-wide with an outdoor toilet.

As the door opened, I was welcomed in by an angel of light. I saw it in the face of the teacher that answered my knock. As the door opened, I saw a potbelly stove and buckets of coal and wood. The room was quite warm and the temperature outside was freezing. There were about twelve children all different ages with various handicapping conditions. There was no running water in the building. There was a handwashing bowl and a cake of soap with an old dirty towel where the children had washed their hands and dried them. I began to talk to the teacher. She told me of various special needs the children had. I could not believe what I was hearing. She said she had no help as she sat in a straight-back chair close to the stove and held a small girl about four years of age.

I asked, "What do you do for lunch?" In a bookcase she showed me cans of food and on the stove was cooked oatmeal left over from breakfast. What next? She asked one of the older boys to go outside and bring in a bucket of coal. I could barely hold back the tears. There was no outdoor play equipment. I ask about play period activities.

The teacher mentioned that they had one basketball for kickball and mostly the children would just run and chase one another. She said because the children were different no one ever came to see about them except for when a bus came at the end of the day to pick them up and shuttle them to split up and get on other buses to go home. I asked if I could give the children sports equipment and toys to play with. She said yes. I went to the car and cleared out my car trunk of prizes, balls and bats and other items I kept handing out to children at the schools I visited. I gave her flyers to have the children take home and get orders for a cleaning product. They would make some extra money to buy some things they needed. I said I would be back in three days, dressed as the Lone Ranger. She was overjoyed. Three days later the children were excited as I visited them as the Lone Ranger and brought a car trunk full of toys. I gave the teacher some money, gave her the product, and told her to keep what they collected. This experience almost burnt me out on school boards that refused to help the special-needs children. This would be my very last fundraising job. Thank

God the laws have eliminated situations like this. This was when I headed back to my mother's home. As I drove, I thought about the words a wise woman once said: "Billy, we are coming into a time of great awakenings.

GREAT AWAKENINGS IN THE FULLNESS OF TIME

The Holy Bible directs our attention to this time in Paul's writings. You can read about this dispensation of time in Ephesians, chapter one.

Paul says that in this time, we "should be holy and without blame before GOD, in love" (Eph. 1:4 KJV). We are to stand before GOD, naked (without the law), with a broken heart and a contrite spirit. This was just as David had done. He did not dance naked, without clothes, but without the scroll of the Torah, the laws. Why? He had sinned and was unworthy of GOD's favor. Why should we stand before the father this way? Because God has adopted us, the Gentile, for his own goodwill and pleasure. To be the praise of the glory of His grace, for he has accepted us through Y'shua or Jesus. Y'shua redeemed us through his blood and forgives our sins according to the riches of his grace.

He has thrown it toward us in all his wisdom and prudence. Now we must catch it and those that do catch it know that the ball is now in their possession. Are you holding the ball? One day in football practice at ETSU, the coach had me run a pass route. I ran into the end zone forty yards from where I started. I looked up and All-American QB Jim Baker threw the pass. As I turned the ball lodged between my helmet and my shoulder pad. I raised my arm slightly and caught the ball. The pass was perfect from someone that knew how to get the ball in my hands.

Had I been in a real game, I would not have caught the ball because there I was, 5'3" tall, and a defender would have always been bigger, would have knocked me and the ball down. Here is the point of this story.

After you have caught the ball of faith, you must work to hold on to it. The devil is almost certain to make you drop your faith. Why?

You are not battling against flesh and blood but against powers and principalities of darkness. Your flesh is no match for this type of setup. The only equalizer you can have for this situation is the Holy Ghost. If you have this the pass from the Master will be perfect. When will this happen for the Church? Look closely!

"That in the dispensation of the fullness of times He (GOD) might gather together in one all things in Christ both which are in heaven, and which are on earth even in him (GOD)", (Ephesians 1:10 KJV).

As you read on in this chapter, you will find that we as members of the body of Christ have obtained an inheritance according as it so pleases GOD, who worketh all things according to his own will. With the Holy Ghost we also become the praise of his glory as the Jew, who first trusted Christ.

It was through the Jew that we as Gentiles first heard the word of truth and the Gospel of salvation. Salvation is of the Jew and that Jew is Y'shua, Christ, the Messiah. Something happened after we heard the truth and believed. What was it?

I want to paraphrase Ephesians 1:12-14 KJV for you. I believe you will have a better understanding. We were sealed with the Holy Spirit of promise, which is our inheritance until we are redeemed and purchased with his Holy Possession of the Holy Ghost and become the praise of his glory. There is a difference in the Holy Spirit and the Holy Ghost; they are not the same.

HOLY SPIRIT VS. HOLY GHOST

To better understand this comparison, we will have to go back to when God first made man.

When GOD first made man and breathed into him and man became a living soul, within the breath that came from GOD into man was what GOD termed the spirit of man. GOD said, "The spirit of man is the candle of the Lord searching all the inward parts of the belly" (Prov. 20:27 KJV).

This was the Holy Spirit, and it is always searching to be lit. Only when it is lit does it become the Holy Ghost. The burning, consuming fire of GOD. The cloven tongues of fire like they had on Pentecost in the upper room.

The Holy Spirit or the breath of GOD is within all men. The spirit of GOD dwells in you", (1 Corinthians 3:16 KJV). It is the spirit that gives life to us. The Spirit of GOD is not lit in all people. Some people are dead, yet while they live, many people die never knowing of the light that could have been a part of their lives.

The story is told that one night on backstage of the Opry, Hank Williams wrote a song: "I Saw the Light." He said to Minnie Pearl, "You know, Minnie, I just can't see that light."

No wonder Elisha got such an odd answer from Elijah when he asked Elijah, "Can I go back to my home and stay while I bury my father?" Elijah answered, "Let the dead, who do not have candles lit, bury the dead. Your candle is lit, and it is searching so you need to come with me. If you see me go away, you can receive a double portion of the Holy Ghost power that is within me. You will receive it because you are obedient to the calling of GOD."

At the age of thirteen, Y'shua went to the leaper camp and said to his parents as he left, "I must be about my father's business." We all need to be about our father's business and that business is love one for another.

Many people are satisfied to have the breath of life or the Holy Spirit within them to keep them living from one minute to the next. They breathe, move and have a being in this world and do not know or even wonder why or where this life comes from.

It is like a bunch of hogs that eat the acorns that fall from the tree and never look up to see where they come from. Then there are others that put their hand to the plough and then look back. They are not worthy to enter the Kingdom. What is the Kingdom?

"The Kingdom is righteousness, and peace and joy in the Holy Ghost" (Rom. 14:17-19 KJV). This means your candle has been lit. There is light instead of darkness.

Here is the rule of thumb for using a Holy Ghost-lit candle under the dispensation of the fullness of time. It will lead and guide you into all truths.

FULLNESS OF TIME AND THE HOLY GHOST

"But the anointing which ye have received of him abideth in you, and ye need not that any man teaches you but as the same anointing teaches you of all things and is truth and is no lie and even as it hath taught you, ye abide in Him (GOD)" (I John 2:27 KJV). The oil is within you and the light is lit. That oil is Y'shua, or Jesus. He is the light that lights every man that comes into his Kingdom. Churches use the oil in diverse ways. For example, ministers still use the oil and make the sign of a cross on the forehead of those they anoint. Some make the sign of the Star of David by tracing two equilateral triangles on the forehead of those they pray for. Many people have unusual ways of anointing or using the oil.

When we first opened David's Tabernacle Church over thirty-nine years ago and still counting, my wife felt led to anoint everyone's right foot and march seven times around the sanctuary, which we did, and dedicated the building to the use for GOD's glory. We wanted to be like King David.

David was anointed king over Israel and Judah twice. Yet he said, "I shall be anointed with fresh oil." Fresh oil is like milk from Mother Wisdom's breast.

We need the sincere milk of Mother Jerusalem's breast to grow big and strong. Wisdom above is the mother of us all. Just as you have a natural mother and father of flesh to be born in this world, you must also have a mother and father to be born into GOD's Kingdom. The fifth commandment says: "Honor thy father and mother." This is a direct command not for the fleshly mother and father but to our spiritual parents, Mother Wisdom, and GOD, our heavenly father. Now let us look at a closing summary about oil.

Under the law the expensive oil was used to bathe the dead bodies of the rich, the high priests, and members of the royal family. The oil would saturate the skin and moisten the bones. Of the Messiah it was written: "His breast full of milk. His bones moistened with marrow" (Job 21:24-26 KJV). It became an embalming fluid and was poured upon linen cloth and wrapped about the body. We find this scripture: "Let it come like oil into his bones" (Psa. 109:18). While this Psalm was in reference to a wicked man, the bottom line was let him die and be bathed in oil so in the resurrection his sins he committed may have forgiven him. Recall the story of Lazarus; his sisters did not anoint his body because they had faith that Y'shua would come and raise him from the dead. The oil they had for Lazarus they kept until it was time to wash the feet of Y'shua. In the grace period the oil was used as a psychological visual aid to get the congregation in the right frame of mind. Many people came into the congregation carrying great burdens and many problems; they had a tough time mustering up faith and forgetting their troubles. The oil was used to break the yoke.

"The yoke on his neck shall be destroyed because of the anointing" (Isa. 10:27). Now we look forward to the new day dawning under the fullness of time.

THE FULLNESS OF TIME

In this dispensation we wait for the Jewish people to come and suck the milk of the Gentiles (Isa. 60:16-18 KJV). We await to eat the bread of life with the strong meat offering. Y'shua said, "Whom will I make to know my doctrine? Them that are drawn from the breast and weaned from the milk." We wait for the truth from the throne room of GOD in reference to the great Battle of Armageddon and the mark of the beast. We await the greatest revival this world has ever seen. We await the power of GOD to come like a thief in the night. We await the decay of the works of man as it relates to GOD's Kingdom. We await the arrival of our Jewish brethren to make the family circle complete. We await our miracle. Do you hear what I am saying?

Let them that hath an circumcised ear hear what the spirit is saying. Let them that hath a circumcised heart gain an understanding prior to receiving the wisdom of GOD. Let them that hath a circumcised eye see into the realm of GOD's holiness. God has angels to send your way.

GOD has sent many visitors to our storefront church over the past years.

VISITING FRIENDS

We have had an impressive array of visitors over the years. One day a doctor from Tel Aviv came to our church services. He said, "When I get back home, I am going to tell my people that even in the little town of Appalachia we have people that love Israel." On another occasion a carnival came to Appalachia, and one of the carnival workers came to our church and asked if he could sing a song and he did a beautiful job. I could tell his life was rough and he was searching. GOD gave me a Holy Ghost prophesy for his life and one of the sisters in the church gave him her Bible to take with him. When the carnival left, he took the Bible with him. Some months later I got a letter from him. He was in California and said he was preaching on street corners. He sent us a love offering of $20.00. Time passed and he sent another letter and another love offering. This time he said he had a church and was now a pastor. We had other notable visitors.

Carson Howard a former member of the singing Crabb Family came to hold a three-night revival.

When he left our church, we heard that he died from cancer. He refused to go to a doctor.

GOD sent us doctors; we need to trust in them.

I trust in some way that you might have faith to believe in your angel, especially when you need the angel most, and then believing becomes seeing.

BELIEVING IS SEEING

Grandson Chris said to me one day, "Grandpaw, seeing is not believing but believing is seeing." We are told in the Bible that faith comes by hearing and hearing by the Word. The word is Adonai, Y'shua (Jesus). Read John chapter one in the King James Version of the Holy Bible. I want to tell you a couple more stories that bring this saying into focus.

I have already told you that I worked for Head Start for twenty-seven years. I only made an honorable salary for the last four years of my service to the community. I started out with an annual salary of $10,000. After my probation period of six months, the board gave me a $500.00 raise. We had no insurance in this program for the first eighteen years of my work. My wife and I never had much money at all.

We started a ministry at the rest home in Wise and for eight years, on each Sunday, we never missed a service. One day my wife said, "Bill, do you think we could stop and have a fish dinner at Captain D's when we go to the rest home on Sunday?"

I said, "Yes."

Well, when Sunday rolled around, we did not have enough money for gas and food. My wife said, "Well, I will take six cookies and we will get us a cup of coffee and have coffee and cookies." This made me think of the story of the six barley cakes that the high priest laid on the altar as a dedication offering unto GOD. We were doing the same thing.

We went on to the rest home at Wise and did not think any more about it. While I was going around and giving each patient of the rest home a hug, I continued preaching in service. As Freda was singing a song, a woman approached me and said, "I can tell that you love these patients, and they also love you." She placed something in my hand, and I never looked at it but put it in my pocket. After service I looked at what she had given me, and it was $20.00. I went to thank her, and she was gone. I asked the desk and they did not know what I was talking about. There was no such visitor answering the description. I said, "That is very strange." The woman at the front desk said, "Maybe it was an angel you saw." To my amazement I had remembered what GOD said: "Your needs I will supply." The twenty dollars gave us gas money and enough to stop and have a fish dinner. GOD sends ministering angels to us and sometimes we do not know they are angels. They often come and help us out of an impossible situation that we get ourselves into. They are always on time. My wife wrote and recorded a song, entitled "He Is Always on Time." Let me offer you another one of my angelic encounters.

My wife and I had been trying to sell a weight-loss program and other herbs to improve people's health. We did it to improve our health but to also earn some extra money if possible. Through the years we have learned to depend upon GOD for our finances.

GOD AND OUR FINANCES

I had my car trunk full of the weight-loss products and had $50.00 in my pocket. I was leaving Coeburn and going to Clintwood to meet a would-be customer. As I drove, I began to talk to GOD as I so often do when I am by myself. I distinctly heard him say, "Give and it shall be given back to you full measure, pressed down, shaken together and running over" (Luke 6:38 KJV). I asked, "What?" Then he said, "Stop at a house just down the road on the right and you will see a woman in the yard with children. I want you to stop and give her $50.00." I began to make up idle talk; I did not want to give away the last penny I had. As I drove and looked around, I did not see a house anywhere. My overactive imagination had caught up with me this time. I was to the end of the road and there was no house. I was relieved that there was none. Then, what was this?

I looked over to the right and there was a woman in a chair with five or six children playing and running. The house was not much to look at but the whole group looked happy. I stopped the car. I got out and walked over to the woman and said, “Here, GOD said you had need of this.” She asked, “Who are you?” I said, “I am a minister.” Teardrops filled both of our eyes as the children looked on with an innocent look. I got back in my car and went to Hardees in Clintwood to meet a potential customer for my weight-loss products. I did not have any money; I was planning to buy lunch for myself and my customer. I went inside and Buford was already there. The first thing he said was “Sit down; I am buying.” He insisted on buying my lunch. After lunch we began to talk and he said, “I want to buy all the weight-loss products you have.” We went out to the car and opened the trunk. I had $2,000 worth of products. He said, “I will take it and you can get me some more.” He gave me $2,000 in cash. He and his wife had a market where they resold the products.

I was quite happy with the arrangement, and I got into the car for the trip back.

People normally do what I did. Almost immediately I started to question if what I did was of GOD. I said, “Lord, if this is real, please show me a sign.” I was being a lot like the Jewish people. They required a sign in the olden days, just to know if it was really GOD in the arrangements.

As I neared my turnoff, I saw the woman and two of the children coming out of a nearby store with two bags of groceries in her arms. She was headed home to feed her family.

What a mighty GOD we serve. This old song says: “Angels bow before him. Heaven and earth adore him.” To obey his voice is to be blessed. The Bible is full of “Let him that hath an ear, hear.” I am talking about the deep-down-inside hearing of GOD’s word. I gave to someone in need, and I got a return on my obedience. Obedience is better than sacrifice. It appears my whole life I have been protected and blessed by angelic forces even to the point of the death fall.

THE FALL OF DEATH

Let me offer you one of my experiences of when I was about nine or ten years of age. As a young boy I had an angel break my fall from the top of a house. I called it the fall of death. Here is my story. Myself and five of my childhood friends chose up sides and engaged in a mudball fight. We had found a big mud puddle and we each made a whole bunch of mudballs. There was only one rule. If you got hit with a mudball, you were out of the game.

I found a lattice ladder running up the backside of a house behind the Borden Mill Village Recreation building on Pine Street, just across from Calvary Baptist Church. I placed my mudballs in an old tin bucket I found and proceeded to climb to the top of the house. While on the housetop my upbringing from my early church experiences clicked into my knower. My wife said we all have a knower. It lets us know when we are wrong. You may call it your conscious discipline.

I heard a small still voice say, "Go thy way and sin no more." Now I am sure that what I was doing was not a sin, but it was wrong, and I should not have been in this situation. My knower was talking to me with some good advice.

Just at that exact moment, I lost my footing and began to slide off the housetop. I can remember hitting flat on my back. As I hit, life left my body. I do not know how long I lay there. I heard Fred Jones, one of the older boys, say, "I believe he is dead." Fred was not throwing mudballs, but he came there to shoot basketball.

I opened my eyes, and all my friends were looking down at me. They did not know enough to call an adult for help. One of the boys, Charles Fannon, said my face was blue and I was not breathing. Once again, an angel had overshadowed the death fall to protect me. I never told my mother about this. I knew how much she would worry. Let me offer you another story of how GOD has had his hand upon me through life. I had a rescue angel.

THE RESCUE ANGEL

I was a sophomore in college at Lee's McRae College in Banner Elk, NC. Our football season was over, and we had just won the Western Carolina Junior College Championship. I and two other players had decided to go to Boone, North Carolina, and try out for football scholarship at Appalachian State College. Two young men from Saint Paul, Virginia, had come down to see Two-Ton McReynolds. Dewey was his real name and he had gotten them to agree to take us to Boone, NC, for the football tryouts. Johnny McCloud and I were in the back seat of the car. Dewey and his two friends were in the front seat. As the car was going around a steep mountain curve and slowed down, in front of us was a slow-moving truck. In the bed of the truck sat a Cherokee Native American all wrapped up in a blanket. He had a hat with a feather sticking out of his hat band.

The driver of the car started to pass the truck and as he did, we all began to do a Native American chant by bopping our hand to and from out mouth. As we passed the truck, an unexpected curve stared back at us. Quicker than time we plunged down the mountain. I blacked out as the car began to flip over and over, side to top to bottom. I did not know anything. When I woke up, I had been thrown out the back window of the car and the car was leaning upon two trees. I was directly under the car. I got to my feet and looked straight up the mountain. Dewey was climbing on all fours, trying to get to the top. I saw the Native American and the truck passenger standing and looking. Everyone crawled out one by one. We were all in shock. Cars were stopping with curious onlookers.

When we were all at the top of the mountain, the Native American said, "Just two weeks ago a car went over in this very same place and two people were killed." He looked at me and said, "Young man, if the trees had not caught the car, you would have been killed."

My head was filled with glass and Mr. Masters took me to the hospital to be checked. I often wondered, had my angel of life once again come to my rescue? This was another thing that I never told my mother. I told my brother Otis. He said I should have gotten some money from the insurance company. No one did except for Dewey. He got a new football letterman's sweater. His sweater had wrapped around the axle of the car and was torn up. Here is the follow-up on two of my football teammates.

Later a member of our football team, Gary Thompson was killed in a car wreck after graduation as he headed home. His car also went over one of those North Carolina mountains.

Dewey "Two-Ton" McReynolds was hit and killed by a truck as he stopped to help a woman fix her car. It was late at night and Dewey was the football coach at Rye Cover High School. There were several members of our championship team that ended up in the coaching profession.

I have shared with you information about the angels, I have told you about the six cookies. I also shared a story, give and it shall be given unto you. The fall of death was also a part of my testimony that I shared with you. Finally, I left on record the story about my rescue angel. Now the ball is in your court.

I challenge you to think back upon your life and count the times that you were rescued from danger just because your mother said a prayer. I remember these words from an old song: "When I am worried and cannot sleep, I count my blessings instead of sheep. I fall to sleep counting my blessings" (Irving Berlin, 1954). One of my blessings came in the writing of this book, and my first book Jews of Babylon the parable of Job.

I would like to share with you some valuable information about the dispensations of times. This is a necessary tool to help you understand the Biblical happenings I use in my writings. I will present this to you in the introduction, along with a brief overview of the story and its contents.

INTRODUCTION

This story will offer you an explosive mind-shaking story as Daniel brought the news of the Jews' release in the form of a decree signed by King Cyrus.

As Daniel addressed the remnant, he brought to their memory a horrid story of how King Nebuchadnezzar destroyed all that they held dear to their hearts in the Battle of Armageddon. He reminded them that all of this came about because King Hezekiah disobeyed the words of GOD.

After the death of Daniel, the remnant of the Jews followed his advice and began to keep records of their historical happenings through a series of notes, memos, and letters to tell their story.

The story of the Remnant will spark the understanding of your mind to connect with the wisdom of your heart, producing a new and exciting truth.

The letters and memos will produce a rich flavor of a diet that will have you wanting to eat the whole Torah roll. Your eyes will delight as the words placed before you will lead you to the true genealogy of the star out of Jacob.

The story will climax as you witness the tenacity of the Jews as they rewrite the Torah, put the Torah back into practice, repair the Western Wall and rebuild the walls and the city and finally solving the age-old secret of the star out of Jacob.

In the conclusion of *The Jews of Babylon: The Remnant Returns,* you will be asking yourself, why have I not heard this story before now? The end of the book will also offer you a timetable of charts and dates that will make the journey into the unknown enjoyable and anxious. This timeline was written and developed by me as the author as GOD shed his love upon me. It has been said that it is impossible to go back in time and develop a calendar that is accurate. Therefore, I developed my own timeline of historical events. All dates were developed by me, as a guide to establish dates in the books that I have written. The dates used will not agree in many cases with the dates you may find in your research.

All dates are traced backwards to the old law and forward to the present time from the birth of Y'shua (Jesus). What is the correct date of his birth?

GOD said, "I will bestow my blessing (Y'shua) upon you in the sixth year. It (My Blessing, Y'shua) shall bear fruit for three years" (Lev. 25:21 KJV). Y'shua was the blessing, and he brought the gift to mankind. That gift was the Holy Ghost. This was a ticket to his Kingdom. The Holy Ghost is the only way that Y'shua and the Church can stand together as one. GOD called it the great mystery in the book of Revelations. Blasphemy of the Holy Ghost is not forgiven: "Whosoever speaketh against the Holy Ghost it shall not have forgiven him in this world nor the world to come" (Matt. 12:32 KJV). Look at his birth.

THE BIRTH OF Y'SHUA

This date of 6 C.E. became the starting date for working backward and forward in writing events in the book. The book will reveal how the Jews have already survived the Battle of Armageddon. There is one way for us to accept the good news.

You as the reader should "study to shew thyself approved unto GOD a worker that need not to be ashamed, rightly dividing the word of truth" (2 Timothy 2:15 KJV).

In order to help you divide and conquer the word of truth, charts have been developed in the form of timelines for your understanding. These charts will challenge you to study for yourself and seek the truth about the Jews of Babylon as the remnant returns.

PUTTING TOGETHER THE PIECES OF A BIBLICAL TIMELINE

The challenges of putting together a timeline for the books I had written was a necessity. It could not be established anywhere that any person had never, nor could they ever go back into the creation of man and find a timeline that could ever make sense in relationship to our calendars. There were many dates listed for the birth of Y'shua, ranging from 3 C.E. to 5 C.E. Here is the established Biblical date in accordance with the Bible.

First, all time is recorded forwards and backwards from the birth of Y'shua. All calendars are dated backwards and forwards from the birth of Y'shua. I was blessed to use the King James Version of the Holy Bible as a resource. I have found that the Catholic Church lists the Holy Conception of this child as being in our month of December and the tenth day. This is correct according to my understanding.

Y'shua was born on Yom Kippur, the tenth day of the holy month of Tishri, or September for the Gentiles. This is just as the Catholic Church records it. Count nine months from the conception on dedication, December the tenth, to the birth on Yom Kippur, September the tenth, and you have the required nine-month birth cycle.

All Biblical events are covered in three dispensations of time. The three are given to us by the Hebrew of Hebrews, the Apostle Paul, in Romans, chapter five. The dispensation of death covered 2,000 years and reigned from the time Adam and Eve left the garden until Moses got the law. Then began another 2,000 years of the law that reigned from when Moses got the law until Y'shua completed his work. The last 2,000 years was the dispensation known as the dispensation of grace. It is well that people know that we have now entered a fourth dispensation of time.

This dispensation also came by way of Paul's writings. It is the dispensation of the fullness of time. This is the time for the great awakenings. These timelines are for you in the form of four charts following this writing. Prior to discussing the charts, I would like to take you back in time to the beginning.

The words in the first chapter of the Bible say, "In the beginning" (Gen. 1:1 KJV). What was the beginning?

There were millions of years before the dispensation of death arrived. In Psalms we read: "A thousand years in thy (GOD), sight is but as yesterday when it is past and as a watch in the night" (Psa. 90:4 KJV). Time is not reckoned with GOD. GOD only has to think and it is so, speak and it is steadfast. In Isaiah 55:8-9 GOD is quick to let us know that his ways are higher than our ways, his thoughts higher than our thoughts. There are two extraordinarily strong Biblical passages that offer much strength to this fact.

John said, "In the beginning was the word (Y'shua or Jesus) and the word (Y'shua) was with GOD and the word (Y'shua) was GOD: The same

(Y'shua) was in the beginning with GOD" (St. John 1:1-2 KJV). What exactly is the beginning?

The beginning was eternity, and the eternity was Y'shua the Messiah. The word "eternity" is only in the Bible one time, and it reads: "For thus saith the high and lofty one that inhabits eternity, (Isaiah 57:15 KJV). Y'shua was hid in Mother Wisdom before man ever had a being upon this earth. When it pleased GOD, He moved the little white stone and the waters of Mother Wisdom's womb brought forth the birth. Y'shua (GOD) in the flesh was the remedy older than the crime of the first man, Adam. He was in the world and the world was made by him and the world knew him not" (St. John 1:10 KJV). "All things were made by him, and without him was not anything made that was made" (John 1:3 KJV). No one can prove by any means known to man how old eternity is. Eternity is from everlasting unto everlasting. It was before the dispensation of death. The dispensation of death did not begin until Adam and Eve left the garden. Adam and Eve did not break any laws in the garden. The laws had not yet been set up. Here is what happened in the garden that got man ejected from the garden.

GOD made two trees in the garden. First was the tree of knowledge of good and evil. The fruit on this tree were 613 laws. This tree was for GOD and his angels. They knew which laws were good and which laws were evil. When GOD set these laws upon the tree, he said, "I the Lord GOD, I create evil. I do all of these things and no man can with stay my hand or say, what are you doing?" (Isa. 45:7 KJV). I can almost hear him say to Adam and Eve in a strong voice, "This is my tree. You stay away from my tree. If you eat of this tree, you will not know which of my laws are good and which are evil. If you were to eat of this tree, you would be guilty of breaking all my laws on this tree. Then you would die out to my love, and I would not walk and talk with you in the cool of the evening."

Then I can imagine GOD turning to the tree of life and saying to Adam and Eve, "This is a tree of life and there are fifty-three laws on this tree. Each law is good. There is life everlasting if you eat of this tree. It belongs to you." With this background information, here is what happened in the garden. Adam and Eve ate of the tree belonging to GOD, for Satan told the woman if they did eat of the tree they would be like GOD and their eyes would be opened to see into eternity. After they ate two things happened; the flesh of man betrayed the spirit of GOD. Adam betrayed the trust of GOD and then denied doing it. So betrayal and denial would follow them as they left the garden and began their journey upon earth.

"Whatsoever ye shall bind on earth shall be bound in heaven, and whatsoever ye shall loose on earth shall be loosed in heaven" (Matt. 18:18 KJV).

What was done in the garden would also have to be done upon earth, to restore man back to GOD. This was the law of balance between heaven and earth.

They could not hide from GOD because when GOD came to talk to Adam in the cool of the evening, he noticed the fruit of the fig tree lying on the ground. It was an untimely season for the figs to come forth. When Adam and Eve tried to make aprons of the fig tree, the great wind of betrayal took the place of the cool breeze and things would never be the same for the whole race. Now look at Timeline A: Dispensation of Death.

TIMELINE A: 2,000 YEARS OF THE DISPENSATION OF DEATH

"GOD ordered Adam and Eve to leave the garden in 4,027 B.C. and the dispensation of death began."

Man had now died out to the love of GOD and was dead, yet while he lived a new journey of resurrection into the things of the world would begin for all humankind.

He left with no laws to live by except for be fruitful and multiply and earn your living by the sweat of your face. After leaving the garden and traveling down through time, a new face appeared as an ancestor of Adam.

*This was Abraham. Abraham was born in the year 2,632 B.C. This was 1,395 years after Adam and Eve left the garden.

*175 years later, GOD gave Abraham a promise that he was going to set up new rules for man to live by. This promise was that the old law was coming.

*Abraham died in the year 2457 B.C. at the age of 175 years, after he got the promise. His last seventy-five years were spent in searching for a city made by GOD and not made by man.

*From the time Abraham got the promise up until the law was given to Moses was 430 years.

I have added three more timelines B, C, and D.

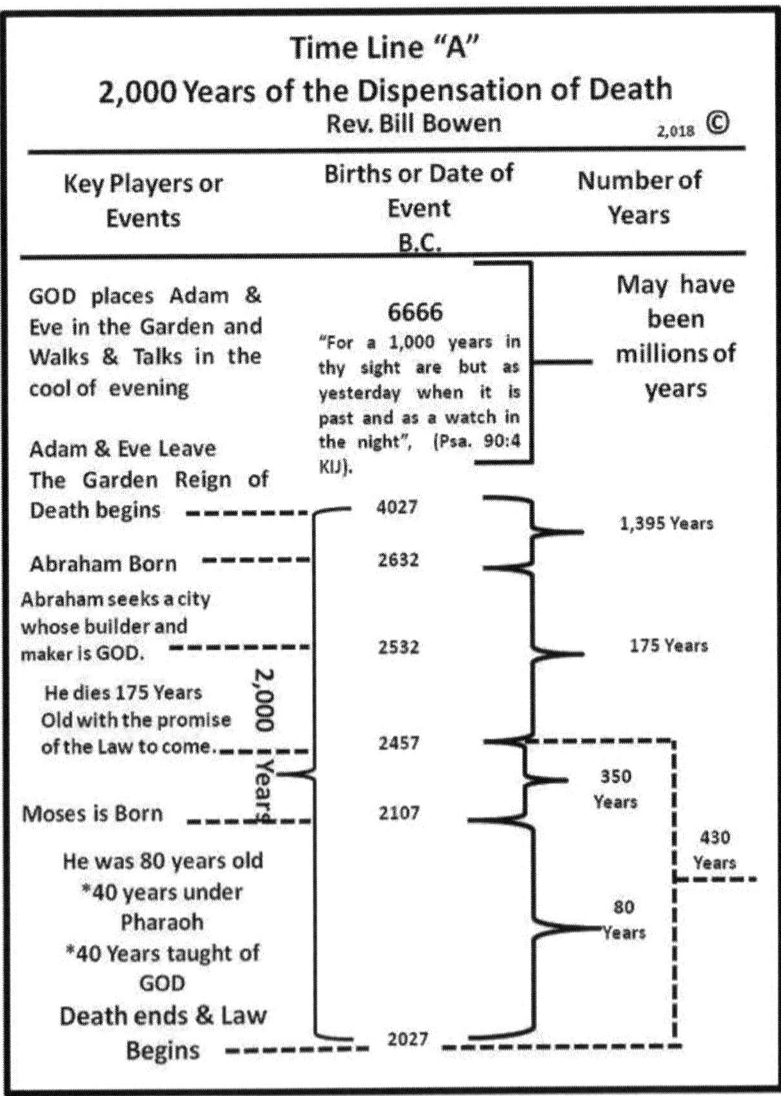
Time Line "A"
2,000 Years of the Dispensation of Death
Rev. Bill Bowen
2,018 ©
Key Players or Events
Births or Date of Event B.C.
Number of Years
GOD places Adam & Eve in the Garden and Walks & Talks in the cool of evening
6666
"For a 1,000 years in thy sight are but as yesterday when it is past and as a watch in the night", (Psa. 90:4 KJJ).
May have been millions of years
Adam & Eve Leave The Garden Reign of Death begins
4027
1,395 Years
Abraham Born
2632
Abraham seeks a city whose builder and maker is GOD.
2532
175 Years
He dies 175 Years Old with the promise of the Law to come.
2457
2,000 Years
350 Years
Moses is Born
2107
430 Years
He was 80 years old
*40 years under Pharaoh
*40 Years taught of GOD
80 Years
Death ends & Law Begins
2027

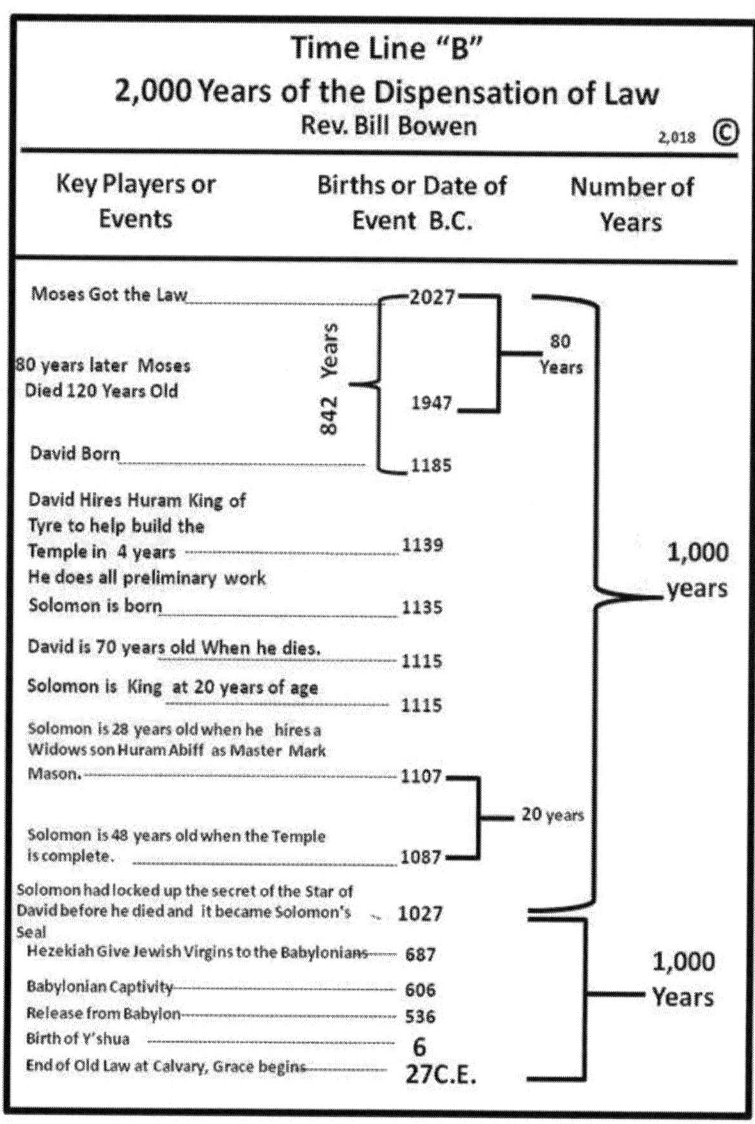

Time Line "B"
2,000 Years of the Dispensation of Law
Rev. Bill Bowen
2,018 ©

Key Players or Events	Births or Date of Event B.C.	Number of Years
Moses Got the Law	2027	80 Years (2027–1947); 842 Years (2027–1185); 1,000 years (2027–1027)
80 years later Moses Died 120 Years Old	1947	
David Born	1185	
David Hires Huram King of Tyre to help build the Temple in 4 years He does all preliminary work	1139	
Solomon is born	1135	
David is 70 years old When he dies.	1115	
Solomon is King at 20 years of age	1115	
Solomon is 28 years old when he hires a Widows son Huram Abiff as Master Mark Mason.	1107	20 years (1107–1087)
Solomon is 48 years old when the Temple is complete.	1087	
Solomon had locked up the secret of the Star of David before he died and it became Solomon's Seal	1027	1,000 Years (1027–27C.E.)
Hezekiah Give Jewish Virgins to the Babylonians	687	
Babylonian Captivity	606	
Release from Babylon	536	
Birth of Y'shua	6	
End of Old Law at Calvary, Grace begins	27C.E.	

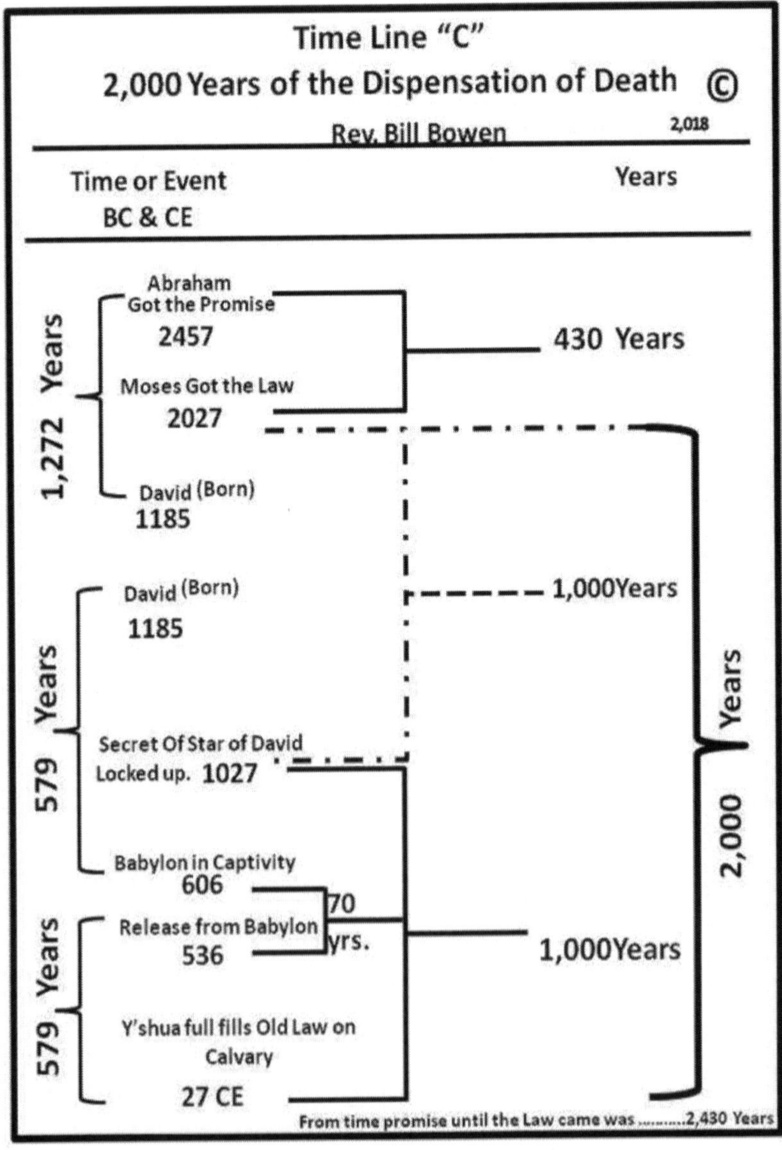
Time Line "C"
2,000 Years of the Dispensation of Death ©
Rev. Bill Bowen
2,018
Time or Event
BC & CE
Years
Abraham
Got the Promise
2457
430 Years
Moses Got the Law
2027
1,272 Years
David (Born)
1185
David (Born)
1185
1,000Years
579 Years
Secret Of Star of David
Locked up. 1027
Babylon in Captivity
606
70
yrs.
Release from Babylon
536
1,000Years
579 Years
Y'shua full fills Old Law on
Calvary
27 CE
2,000 Years
From time promise until the Law came was ....2,430 Years

Time Line "D"

A Readable Chart for Understanding ©

Rev. Bill Bowen 2,018

This is a helpful tool that places all of the Key events on one page. Events are from Time Lines , A , B, and C

Time Line "A" 2,000 years of the Dispensation of Death . This reign was from the time that Adam and Eve left the Garden up until the time that Moses got the Law.

*There was **1395** years from the time Man left the Garden until Abraham.

* There was a period of **100** years from Abraham until he sought a city whose builder and maker was GOD

* There was **75** years in which Abraham lived with the promise until he dies.

*There was **430** Years from Abraham's promise of the law until Moses got the Law and the Law began.

*There was **80** years from the birth of Moses until He got the Law.

TOTAL YEARS IN THE DISPENSATION OF DEATH WAS **2,000** YEARS.

Time Line "B" 2,000 years of the Dispensation of The Law . This reign was from the time that Moses got the Law until the time that Y'shua Died.

*There was **842** years from the Time Moses got the Law until David.

* There was a period of **50** years from David until Solomon was born.

* There **509** years from Solomon, as King, until the Carrying Away to Babylon

*There was **70** years from Babylon until their release. .

*There 530 years from their release until Y'shua was born.

TOTAL YEARS IN THE DISPENSATION OF THE LAW WAS **2,000** YEARS.

Time Line "c" The coming together of the 2,430 years

*There was **430** years from the Promise to Abraham until the Law.

* There **1,000** years from Moses getting the Law until The secret is locked up by King Solomon.

* There was **1,000** years from locked up secret until the law fulfilled and the secret of the Star of David was unlocked by Y'shua.

TOTAL YEARS IN THE COMING TOGETHER WAS **2,430** YEARS.

TIMELINE B: 2,000 YEARS OF THE DISPENSATION OF THE LAW

*Moses did not receive the law until the year 2027 B.C. He was eighty years old.

*Moses died when he was 120 years of age, in 1947 B.C.

*David was born in 1185 B.C.

*Solomon was born in 1135 B.C., when his father David was fifty years old.

*The Jewish people were carried away to Babylon in 606 B.C.

*The Jews were released after seventy years in 536 B.C.

Y'shua was born in 6 B.C. Now let's take a look at Timeline C.

TIMELINE C: A COMING TOGETHER

*1,272 years passed from Abraham down to David.

*There was a 579-year period from David until the Jews went into captivity.

*There was a 600-year period from the time the Jews were taken captive until Y'shua.

*1,000 years passed when Moses got the law until Solomon came and locked up the secret of the Star of David. Solomon called it Solomon's Seal. All the powers and principalities of darkness (Satan) were locked up for 1,000 years. Men of flesh could not understand the wisdom with which Solomon taught.

*Another 1,000 years passed until Y'shua came and unlocked the secret. Satan was loosed for a little season.

*These 2,000 years was the reign of the law. The law reigned from Moses until Y'shua brought an end to the law and established the grace period.

Look at Timeline D.

TIMELINE D: A READABLE UNDERSTANDING

*This is a helpful timeline for the dispensation of the 2,000 years of death.

*There was 1,395 years from the time Adam and Eve left the garden until Abraham was born.

*There was a one-hundred-year period Abraham was born until his call to search for a city whose builder and maker was GOD.

*There was a seventy-five-year period in which Abraham traveled looking for a city and holding tight to the promise until he died.

*430 years passed from the time Abraham got the promise that the law was coming until Moses got the law.

*Eighty years passed from the time of the birth of Moses until Moses got the law.

The reader should study these charts closely so that a solid picture as to the unknown is formed for your study. There are four charts listed for your learning.

Timeline A: 2,000 Years of the Dispensation of Death

Timeline B: 2,000 Years of the Dispensation of the Law

Timeline C: Coming Together Time and Events

Timeline D: A Readable Understanding in Summary

Immediately following the timelines, you will step into another dimension of history as Daniel arrives to deliver a proclamation of freedom to the remnant of the Jews.

DANIEL ARRIVES AND PROCLAIMS FREEDOM

Today is Tishra ten. It is the eve of Yom Kippur or Atonement. The significance of this day is not known to the majority of the Jews, who have been in captivity for seventy years. They have not had Torah Scrolls of the Law, to guide them. They have had no knowledge of how to practice the law if they had it in their hands. Only a selected few Jews have been taught about Israel's past history and the importance of the law. These were taught in secrecy by the Prophet Ezekiel.

The heads of the twelve tribes of Israel have assembled their fellow Jews together on this special occasion. The Jews were extremely excited.

Then Joash spoke to the gathering: "While GOD has confirmed this unto us, the leaders of the twelve tribes, we must keep it in house among ourselves and not let it leak out unto the masses of our Jewish population. Surely chaos will run rampant. We are not yet sure of how the new ruler, King Cyrus, would accept the word of GOD from our mouths. Also, a short while ago, a runner entered our camp, bringing us word that Daniel was now making his way toward our site and requests an audience with our council. Let us wait to receive the news he brings to us."

Joash had hardly gotten the words out of his mouth before Daniel was seen far off, coming their way riding a little white colt.

As Daniel rode into the encampment, he was easily recognized. The Jews had all but forgotten the historical symbolism of the law connected to the little white colt he was riding. The symbolism of the color of white was purity and the humbleness of the colt represented the patience of GOD. The message being sent was the one of freedom.

The price had been paid in full and freedom from bondage was now granted. While the Jews had lost much during their seventy years of Bondage, there were a few of the older elders that remembered the significance of the pose Daniel struck while sitting upon the white colt. It was the same

Mosan sign that Ezekiel had given them, to encourage their faith and trust in GOD. Moses had developed and used the sign language to communicate messages of hope to his chosen people without saying a word aloud. He did this because he had a speech defect. This Mosan sign was developed when two of the faithful servants of Moses helped to hold his arms up when Moses was tired and wanted to give up on Israel and give up on GOD.

Daniel sat tall on the white colt and thrust his head backwards, with his eyes toward the Heavens. The arms outstretched to the right and left, as from the East to West.

His body was facing toward the North, the inheritance of the tribes of a free Israel. His hands and fingers cupped like unto the knob and bowls of the Holy Candelabra. The significance was that a sign was given unto the people that all was forgiven and that after seventy years the promise of God was restored. The search for the long-lost *Light* was renewed as Daniel rode into the encampment and struck the Mosan pose of freedom. He sang the harp and told the story of the Jews of Babylon. He recalled his early years.

Daniel recalled as a boy of six, when Ezekiel carried him upon his shoulders and sang this song. The Jews were tempered by their Babylonian captors to sing them a song. The Jews said, "How can we sing a song of praise in a strange land?" They hung their harps on the willow tree and the branches hung low to the ground under the intense pressure. This reflected how the Jews felt in captivity.

The Jews were at the same place by the River Chebar, where Daniel and other prisoners had arrived in Babylon seventy years ago. Daniel began to sing this song as his Jewish heart beat true.

"We are a Nation of GOD's Prophesy. We are a people of destiny.
We are Israel in captivity. We are the Jews of Babylon.
We once had hope of the coming Messiah,
But now most hope has out stripped us and gone.
We sit here in chains by the River Che 'bar.
Wondering what happened to Jacob's Star.
We are a Nation of God's Prophesy. We are a people of destiny.

"We are Israel in captivity. We are the Jews of Babylon
Our Torah scrolls have been burnt,
They forbid that our children should ever learn.
Death, Hell, and the Grave will be our friends.
We are the Jews of Babylon.
We know we will suffer,
Loose daughters and sons.
But, one day, soon the Messiah shall come.
Then: faith, hope, and charity shall prevail
For the daughters of Israel.
We are a Nation of GOD's Prophesy.
We are a people of destiny.
We are Israel in captivity.
We are the Jews of Babylon.
We just got word from down in Egypt.
That Jeremiah out of prison has come.
He hath found the bright light of Jacob's Star.
What shall we do with our newfound hope?
We will draft our story in the parable of Job.
We are a Nation of God's Prophesy.
We are a people of destiny.
We are Israel in captivity.
We are the Jews of Babylon."

With the responsive singing ending, tears and sobbing from the Jewish heart filled the air. The Jews left their dwelling places and gathered around Daniel in like manner as their ancestors and mothers gathered around the tabernacle of Moses, when they received the law of GOD. Daniel wiped his eyes and cleared his throat. Then he began to address the nation of Israel.

"The song we just sang was a song that I heard my father, friend, and Prophet Ezekiel sing, as a cantor, to your fathers and mothers a long time ago, when I was just a boy of six years of age. We began seventy years under Babylonian authority on that day.

"As we have all heard, the song is one of hope. It is that hope we have held on to and kept close to our hearts for the past seventy years. With

Babylon falling into the Persians' hands. We have all wondered and have become unsure of what our future holds. I know that there are some among you who understood the meaning behind the royal white colt upon which I am riding. The meaning is clear; I bring you good news from King Cyrus. The new ruler has given me a decree and he has asked that I read it to you at this gathering."

A whisper fell across the crowd as Daniel unrolled the scroll, which he held in his right hand. This within itself was significant insomuch as King David had said, "If I forget Jerusalem, may my right hand its cunning loose."

Today for the first time the Jews witnessed a key figure of the Jewish people use their right hand to hold a royal proclamation while setting upon a royal white colt. The right hand to use was the one next to his heart. Quietness surrounded us, as the sound of the scroll unrolling echoed across the camp. Daniel began to read.

Official Document and Decree
Date: Tishri 10, 536 B.C.
By Cyrus King of all Persia and Media
This document is page one of two pages.

"In this, my first year as ruler over Babylon, I, King Cyrus, made this decree concerning the Jews and the house of GOD at Jerusalem. I have declared that the house of GOD be built in the place where the Jews of old offered sacrifices and I declare that the foundation of the house should be strongly laid. The height of the Holy of Holy should be three score cubits and the breadth there of be also three score cubits. Thus, according to scale by measure after the record left and documented by the Jewish Prophet Ezekiel.

"Furthermore, I declare that the sacrificial altar have three rows great stones. Also, let the timber and the expense of the house for this project come out of the king's house. I also decree that the gold and silver vessels of the house of GOD, which Nebuchadnezzar took forth out of the temple when he invaded Jerusalem, be returned.

"These are to be brought to Jerusalem and be restored again unto the temple, which is to be rebuilt. Let each item be returned to its place and place them in the house of GOD.

"Moreover, I make a decree that ye shall do nothing but good to the elders of these Jews that shall oversee the building of the house of GOD. I also commanded that a tribute should be paid to these Jews by those that dwell beyond the river. Let all expense be given unto these men and let not one hinder or interfere with their work. This which they have need of both young bullocks, rams, lambs, and such for burnt offerings to the GOD of Heaven. Let them receive it free of charge. I also command that they be given wheat, salt, wine, and oil according to the appointment of the priest, which shall be at Jerusalem. Let the priest receive this day by day without fail, that they make offerings of sacrifices of sweet savor unto the GOD of Heaven and pray for the life of the king's sons.

"Let the Jews, therefore, who have endured seventy years of hardship and tribulations under the Babylonians, go out as free men and women. Just as they left Egypt, let them go with their children, their cattle and all that they desire to take back to Jerusalem.

"Also, I have made a decree that whosoever shall alter this word, let the timber be pulled down from his house and being set up let him be hanged thereon, and let his house be made a dunghill for this. GOD has caused his name to dwell there to destroy all the kings and people, which shall put their hand to alter and to destroy this house of GOD which shall be at Jerusalem. I, Cyrus, have made this decree. Let it be done with great speed."

Signed, this day of Tishri 10, 536 B.C.

Cyrus, King of all Persia and Media

Great jubilation began as Daniel ceased to read and began to roll up the scroll.

There was spontaneous singing songs of praise and dancing filling the streets as Daniel turned to Joash and said, "What a wonderful day of joy."

The king had also set the groundwork for Zerubbabel and Jeshua to go immediately to prepare the building site for the temple and the city of Jerusalem. Daniel said, "It is good that I should rest. My journey has been a long and tiresome one."

It was then that Joash, of the tribe of Issachar, said, "Come, Daniel, it is preordained that we should talk. Spend the night with me and you can tell your story to the council tomorrow."

DANIEL ADDRESSES THE COUNCIL

Daniel began: "As we gather here this morning, we are all pleased with what lies ahead. It will be demanding work and will require total unity in our effort. Never forget that it was failure to obey GOD that brought us to this place seventy years ago. I was born in 612 B.C. and from the very beginning, Ezekiel became my mentor. He said it was King Hezekiah and his actions that betrayed the trust of GOD and got us into this condition of slavery. When GOD hands down his judgments, it rains upon the just as well as the unjust. Let us not forget that.

I was six years old when I first came here to Babylon in the year 606 B.C. Ezekiel said that Hezekiah entertained an envoy of strangers from Babylon and shared with them all of the sacred and secret things that were meant for only our people. He showed them all of our military secrets. He showed them all of our treasurers. He took them into the Holy of Holies and then he violated the law or the royal bloodline of inheritance. He gave virgin Jewish women from his harem to the Babylonians to take back to Babylon and to intermarry with his army.

It was this action by Hezekiah that brought us down into captivity. King Hezekiah had already died when the Babylonians invaded Jerusalem. The sons of the king were brought here to Babylon and made eunuchs. We know that some men were eunuchs from birth. Others were made eunuchs of men. Some were made eunuchs for the Kingdom of GOD's sake. This lot fell to me and others of our family. Thousands of Jews were killed or butchered as the army waged of war and destruction upon our city. With the death of King Nebuchadnezzar, we neared the end of our journey.

After the king died the brother of his wife came to the throne. You will remember him. He was Nabonidus. He kept me intact as chief counselor, then he ran off to idol gods and turned half of his throne over to his nephew, the son of King Nebuchadnezzar. Belshazzar came to the throne and if the truth be known I was closer to the king as a son than was Belshazzar. For the next fourteen years, I would serve him in a different capacity. I knew that things would change drastically because the first year that he came to the throne GOD gave me a dream about a ram and a he goat. I knew it would not be long until the Medes and the Persian armies would overthrow the government of the Babylonians. Belshazzar was an unstable ruler and he relieved me of my duty as a ruler and chief overseer. I lost my three friends due to his neglect. Shadrach and Abednego died after being poisoned. They became tasters for the king's food that was set before him. Meshach was murdered by an Asian. I was sad to lose my three first cousins that had ruled so wisely under my leadership. Belshazzar did nothing. He made fun of the fact that his heritage was part Jewish. One day his laughter and fun went a little too far with GOD.

A KINGDOM DIVIDED

King Belshazzar ordered that all the holy vessels, gold and silver alike, be taken out of his father's storehouse of treasurer. These were vessels that were taken out of the holy temple in Jerusalem and reserved for the high priest of the day. He said, "Since I'm part Jewish, I might as well use the things reserved for the Jews." He also said, "I'll let all of my wives and concubines drink from these vessels, seeing as how they are my family." He threw a party and a great feast and invited all to drink wine out of the holy vessels. They made fun of the Jewish GOD and drank and praised the fabricated gods of gold, silver, wood, stone, brass, and of iron. They sinned greatly.

That same hour there came forth a man's hand and it wrote over against the candlestick upon the plaster of the wall of the king's palace and the king saw the part of the hand that wrote. Everyone became afraid. The king's countenance changed, and his thoughts troubled him. His joints of his loins were loosed, and his knees smote one against another.

The king cried aloud to bring in the astrologers, the Chaldeans and the soothsayers as his father had done. Then the king told them, "Whosoever shall read this writing and shew me the interpretation thereof shall be clothed with scarlet and have a chain of gold about his neck. He shall be the third ruler of the Kingdom, ruling with myself and my uncle, King Nabonidus." The wise men could not read the writing nor make known the interpretation to the king. Now the queen, by reason of the words of the king and his lords, came into the banquet house and the queen spoke and said, "O King, live forever, let not thy thoughts trouble thee nor let thy countenance be changed. There is a man in Thy Kingdom in whom is the spirit of the Holy GOD and in the days of thy father, light and understanding and wisdom was found in him. Your father made him master of the magicians, astrologers, Chaldeans, and soothsayers. You have neglected asking advice of him even though he still resides in the Kingdom. He can interpret the handwriting for you. Your father gave him the same name which you have. He is Daniel, now called Belshazzar."

I, Daniel, entered the room. I had only saw the king a time or two. I was still considered a ruler by the counselors. The king said, "Are you the one that my father brought out of Jewry and into the way of the Babylonians? If so, I will give unto thee great gifts if you can tell the meaning of the handwriting on the wall."

I, Daniel, answered, "Let thy gifts be to thyself and give thy rewards to another. I will read the writing to thee. The Highest GOD gave unto thy father a Kingdom and majesty and glory and honor. Your father was a great ruler and what he said was obeyed without question. He humbled himself before GOD and made his home with the poor people for seven years and made his image of gold, which has brought great wealth to Babylon. More wealth than any nation has ever known. You have not humbled your heart as he did.

"You have brought the holy vessels and you and your lords, wives, and concubines have drunk wine from them. You have praised the small 'g' gods. You have not given praise to the GOD in whose hands thy breath is and whose all thy ways belong to. This GOD, of the Hebrews, has written with his own hand and has sent this message to you."

This is the writing on the wall: "Me-Ne, Me-Ne, Take's, U-Phar'-Sin."

This is the interpretation of the thing: "Me-Ne, God hath numbered thy Kingdom and finished it." Te'Kel: thou art weighted in the balances and are found wanting. Phar'-sin, thy Kingdom is divided and given to the Medes and Persians.

As I finished the reading, the vague faded image of the writing slowly disappeared from the wall. It was then that Belshazzar commanded that they clothe me in scarlet and put a chain of gold about my neck and make a proclamation concerning me that I should be the third ruler in the Kingdom of Babylon. This did not set well with the king's court. The enemy did not wish to see me, a Jew, return to the rule even a third part of the Kingdom.

In that same night, King Belshazzar was slain by his own servants.

GOD was true to his word and stayed not his hand. The same night that the king died, his kingdom fell. Then Joash interrupted by saying, "Daniel, Daniel," as he came back from the silent trip within the mind and memories of Daniel. "Perhaps you should get some sleep since you have to travel back for your council with King Cyrus tomorrow." "Yes!" said Daniel. "The king had not decided what position I should occupy in his Kingdom. Before I left, he told me he was considering setting up a Kingdom with 120 princes, each ruling over a part of the Kingdom. He said he would also have three presidents to whom the princes would answer. The king chose me for one of the top-three jobs due to my experience over the years. I am getting older, but I have achieved my lifelong ambition by bringing the word of freedom granted to my people, the Jews of Babylon, on this very night."

Daniel paused and then said, "Many of you are young and youthful and one day you too will be old like unto me, and GOD will use you mightily. I want to leave something with you. I want to leave with you all my writings and notes. Please share them with your young scribes as you begin to school them in our heritage and history. I see young Ezra is now twenty years of age, he can learn much from these writings. Here upon this parchment, with this pen, I will give you my last will and testament. When I die take this to the king and he will see that you receive all my belongings," said Daniel. He continued, "Do not ever forget that the family bloodline will always be the tie that binds the Jews together in strength.

"I ask this council to keep memos, letters, and all writings for the future of our people. Preserve them well and pass them on to your children and your children's children.

"Here is a collection that I have written that may better explain your coming to this night of freedom."

With that they each said their goodnights and looked forward to their meetings to help organize for the task that lay ahead.

The next morning Joash and the Grand Council began to study the writings that Daniel had left them. Joash picked up the first memo.

MEMOS

To: The file of Daniel

Date: Day 1 Elul 535 B.C.E. (August 1, 535 B.C.E.)

Ref.: On behalf of my brethren, the Jews of Babylon

I, Daniel, have entered prayer and fasting in this the Jewish month of preparation. Babylon has fallen to the Persian Empire. I will be appearing before King Cyrus to ask what he has in store for me. I also intend to petition him for the release of my people, who have been here for the past seventy years.

I do not know how he will take my request. Things are still unbraided as order is slowly being restored by the king's counselors. I trust in GOD and my fasting and praying for our release is encouraging. I will be in the king's presence on the 11th day of Elul (August 11) in the year 535 B.C. Our new year will begin on Tishri 1 (September 1), 536 B.C.

To: The file of Daniel

Date: Elul 11, 535 B.C. (August 11, 535 B.C.)

Ref.: Inside the palace of Cyrus, the king

Today I entered the palace walls of King Cyrus. Noise is taking the place of silence. The king's son, the prince of Persia, oversees making appointments for the king. He has finalized my paperwork and he is not pleased with my mission of seeking freedom for my people, the Jews of Babylon.

To: The file of Daniel

Date: Elul 21, 535 B.C.

Ref.: The prince has me on hold. I cannot go to have a conference with his father, the king.

The prince of Persia has held me at bay for the past ten days and nights. He has a belligerent attitude toward me. He has processed many other visitors to gain an audience with the king. I continue to pray and fast.

To: The file of Daniel

Date: Tishri 9, 536 B.C. (September 9, 536 B.C.)

Ref.: GOD Intervenes

The new year began nine days ago. Tomorrow is Tishri 10, the eve of Yom Kippur. It has now been one and twenty days since I first arrived here, and the prince of the kingdom of Persia has withstood me and kept me from seeing the king these twenty-one days.

Daniel paused and lay the memo down from which he had been reading and continued his story with a crackling voice.

"The day had passed slowly since morning light. Then when the sun became hot in the sky at twelve high, something happened. Lo, Michael, one of the chief princesses of the angels, was sent from GOD to help me and I immediately gained entrance into the presence of King Cyrus. I said unto the King, "GOD hath given me a vision of the future of your reign. I am come to make thee understand what shall befall thy people in the latter days of your reign, thee with a mighty army." As I spoke it was then that one touched my lips. It was the Holy Ghost, likened unto the similitude of the Son of Man. Then I opened my mouth and spoke of the spirit as it gave utterance. I said, "O my Lord, by the vision from my GOD my sorrows are turned upon me and I have retained no strength, for how I can as a servant of this my lord talk with my Lord?" Then no strength was in me.

There was no breath left in me as I stood still before King Cyrus. It was then that one like the appearance of man came and touched me again and strengthened me. Then said the great King Cyrus unto me, "O man beloved. Fear not!" The king continued, "Let my Lord Daniel speak. You have strengthened me also." Then the king said unto me, "I knoweth thou, wherefore I brought thee hence unto me. I will fight against my son, the prince of Persia, that kept you from seeing me. Afterwards I will turn my attention and focus on the prince of Grecia, which you say shall come against my Kingdom." Then said I unto the king, "I will shew thee, that which is noted in the scripture of truth. There is none that holds with me in these things, which I tell thee but Michael, your Prince of Peace."

Then I, Daniel, began to talk with the king and to tell him what would befall his Kingdom. I also gave prophesy and asked for the release of the Jews. I told him that GOD said the Jews were to be released after seventy years, which would come upon this very night of Yom Kippur. My ears beheld the king's words, which fell into the chamber of my heart as the oil of Hebron. The king said, "So let it be written and let it be done the sixth hour on this eve of Yom Kippur." I took the decree back to the Jews that were encamped by the River Chebar.

Joash said to the Grand Council, "As we read Daniel's memos, we realized the importance of keeping our records for our future generations. Zerubbabel and Jeshu had already left to go and clear the way for our rebuilding project. Here are some of the detailed writings that Daniel has left on record for us. Allow me to continue reading Daniel's story."

With all the writings and memos on file, we thought that surely this would be the last chapter of the Jews of Babylon. Then we found a story written by Daniel that brought new hope and more to life about our Jewish future.

DANIEL'S STORY

I, Daniel, take my pen in hand to draft my story of my coming into Babylon. I was born in 612 B.C. I knew Ezekiel was present, and I grew up under Ezekiel's guidance only knowing him as a friend of the family.

I was young when I came to Babylon. I came here in 606 B.C.

I rode upon Ezekiel's shoulders, and we arrived here by the River Chebar. We were greeted with sadness. Many Jews had arrived before us and the Babylonian soldiers were poking fun at them and said, "Go ahead and sing us a song while playing upon your harps as your hero, King David, did many years ago."

Then said the Jews, "How can we sing the Lord's song in a strange land?" Then one by one the Jews hung their harps on the willow tree, making its branches to hang their head in shame (Psalms 137:2 KJV).

We listened as the wind blew across the strings of our harps, making a gruesome sound of sorrow.

Then we remembered King Hezekiah and all that he did to anger GOD. He gave the Babylonians young Jewish girls from his harem to take back to Babylon and intermarry with the Babylonians.

GOD pronounced death upon him from the mouth of Isaiah, another of our great prophets. Word came forth that one day GOD would turn our country over to the Babylonians. Hezekiah repented of what he had done. He went to the western Wailing Wall with a broken heart and a contrite spirit and GOD heard his sincere cry and added fifteen years to his life. GOD turned the sundial back ten degrees when Hezekiah asked GOD to show him a sign. The time was at Yom Kippur, the day of atonement (I King 8:2 KJV), and judgment had been passed upon Hezekiah. He had received the death sentence in the holy month of Tishri. GOD reset the sundial back to the sixth month of preparation. The month of Elul (Neh. 6:15 KJV). Now Hezekiah had a fresh start on life as the shadow of the sun went back ten degrees. The hand of GOD moved the sun and the proof of his work showed upon the shadow upon the ground. The sign of the Messiah made its appearance in the patchwork within the circles.

It was the sundial of King Hezekiah that was to be the root of all evil. Surrounding countries wondered and desired to know of the sundial and its secrets.

This was what brought the Babylonians to our doorstep when Hezekiah was King, Ezekiel, told me many stories, but no one could pinpoint the sundial, how it looked or how it worked. Only GOD knew the secret thereof.

I prayed often unto GOD and desired to know of the sundial. Then came the vision unto me, by night.

THE SUNDIAL: A VISION

I went to bed with many thoughts spinning through my mind about the history of our Jewish past. I had searched out and written down many facts. I knew that King Ahaz, the father of King Hezekiah, was the one that drew up the blueprint for the sundial.

Ahaz was also known as Jehoaaz II. His father before him had chosen this name because of its meaning. It meant "Yahweh has held", (Biblestudytools.com). He trusted in GOD, the one unknown GOD. However, Ahaz became interested in idol worship and had many little “g” gods. It was this interest that stirred up his mind, as a genesis, to pursue building the sundial. He began to teach his young son Hezekiah and brought him into his planning sessions, along with all the wisdom keepers of his Kingdom.

I was beginning to realize from what I had learned that King Ahaz was interested in capturing all the knowledge and wisdom that the heavens had to offer and bringing it down to earth to rule his Kingdom. The stars, the moon, the sun, the constellations, and the planets would bring many secrets of the universe down to his level.

However, no one knew how the sundial made the ultimate connection. No one knew what it looked like nor how it worked. These were the thoughts that danced in my head as I lay upon my pillow by night. Then the vision fell hard within my mind.

THE VISION BY NIGHT

I saw many great stones fall from a great high mountain into a valley of many people. Many men of great strength and courage began to cut into the stones as they lay upon the ground. Then came an army of mighty men of valor from the tribe of Dan with many, many horses. These were too many to be counted.

The stones were numbered as was a great wall hidden within my mind. Many days, nights, and seasons passed and then I beheld a great circle within a circle and a hand from the Heavens above entered the circles and brought with it the stars, the moon, the sun, the planets, and the constellations. The hand laid these heavenly objects withing the circles upon the earth.

I saw meteors and fragments of stones of various shapes and sizes fall upon the great stones of high stature. The stones changed the weight of the great stones and caused the heavenly bodies to move from one position to another by casting shadows of dancing lights upon the barren soil beneath the stones.

A voice as it were of thunder said, "All numbers from the crying stones carry a message of hope to my people, Israel."

As I awoke the light from the moon and stars fell upon the floor by my bed. As I knelt to pray, I knew no knowledge would come of the vision, except it coming from GOD. A voice said, "Remember, Daniel, where much is given, much is required."

Afterwards, I worked and walked and thought upon my vision, but GOD sent no angel to my rescue. Then I turned my thoughts to what Ezekiel had taught me and my three first cousins with the dreidel game and the numbers. Suddenly the stones came to life and cried out to me with their hidden meaning. I was reading the stones just as with the dreidel game Ezekiel had taught me to play. My work on interpreting my vision now became a game to me and I was determined to play to win.

There were forty-two great stones, the same as the number of the chosen generations. These generations were promised to us by the law of

Moses, beginning with Abraham and coming on down to Our Messiah. We looked forward to seeing our Messiah. I knew truth must be established at the mouth of two witnesses. Who would witness for us?

None other than King Solomon. With his wisdom he placed forty-two rows of stones in the Western Wailing Wall. He had twenty-four rows above ground and eighteen row of stones underground.

The numbers played a wonderful song. There would be twenty-four chosen elders or prophets to sit with GOD as they judged Israel. Ezekiel told me the importance of the Ten High Holy Days as each true Jew revisited their past, present, and envisioned their future looking for a favorable judgment on Yom Kippur.

Then there was the number eighteen. Eighteen inches would be the length of the Jewish Messiah when he would break forth from his mother's womb in birth. He would come as the supreme sacrifice for our sins.

His height would be the same as a perfect Passover lamb offered for a sin offering for us. He would come as a lamb slain from the foundation of the world. Eighteen would become our perfect number and serve as a foundation for our giving. Now little by little, day by day, the vision began to fall together.

Forty-two great stones for King Hezekiah's sundial. There were two circles of twelve stones, each set up in a 360-degree circle. The larger circle had its twelve stones set up with angles of 45 degrees, which allowed the sunrays to travel the greatest distance, while the smaller circle set up within the larger circle had angels of 90 degrees. Ezekiel often talked of a wheel within the middle of another wheel. What about the eighteen remaining stones? These stones were laid on top of the upright stones. Twelve were laid upon the circle in this fashion. They were laid atop the upright stones with a space of six feet and six inches, underneath and between them. Here is the numerical meaning of the space.

The open space of six-foot-six represented the height the Messiah would be when he would come and grow into manhood. We knew this from the apparel of the high priest attire made to perfection for Aaron, brother of Moses and high priest. The attire had passed from generation to generation. No one had ever seen it, nor did we know where it was. Every high priest that had worn it was six foot, six inches tall. When the

Messiah comes, he will be measured twice as long as the Rod of Atonement, which was three foot, three inches long. The other six stones were moved to the smaller circle.

These six stones also were lain one at a time upon the upright stones. There were no open spaces as the stones lay touching one another as from head to toe. The anatomy of the Messiah was being told in the stones both in number and weight. All of the stones weighed 11,988 pounds. This was six stones each weighing one thousand nine hundred and ninety-eight pounds. The six was the anticipated year of the Messiah's birth as outlined in the writings of Moses. Again, the number eighteen, our toast to life, divided into the total weight of all of the stones together gave us the number six hundred, three score, and six. This 666 was the actual number of years of the chosen generations, which were carriers of the holy seed. There would be three segments of this number as it was chosen of God and hid in disguise for protection. They were known only to chosen men of GODs wisdom. There were fourteen generations of 666 chosen years from Abraham down to King David. There was another fourteen chosen generations numbering 666 years from King David down to the time we were carried away to Babylon. Now here we were, and we did not know but we anticipated the next fourteen chosen generations would bring us to closure of our 666 years with the birth of our Messiah. No man at this time knoweth the hour nor the day of his coming. It is known only to GOD and Mother Wisdom.

The lifespan of a person carrying the holy seed was to begin when the carrier turned thirteen years of age and would end when the seed was passed to the rightful partner chosen and preordained of GOD. Human knowledge could not account for these years. All we could do was to hope, pray, and wait with patience upon God. The stones brought us this wisdom and anatomy of the Messiah.

The Messiah would be born in the sixth year, he would weigh eight pounds and be eighteen inches long. This was the same as the perfected lamb raised and cared for by our temple priest at the Tower of the Flock, which was built by Jacob, until time for the sin offering to be made unto GOD on Passover. The Messiah would grow into manhood and stand as his ancestors before him. He would be six feet, six inches tall. Just as King Saul was from the shoulders to the head taller than any in Israel.

He would weigh 234 pounds. This divided by our base number of eighteen would give us the number 13. This was the number of attributes he would possess, distinguishing him from the flesh of earthly men. The high priest attire would be a perfect fit for him. He would only be able to do miracles or bear fruit for time, times, and a half of time or three and one-half years. Our expectations ran high every year in anticipation of getting to look upon him. I, Daniel, was able to piece this together in my mind with the help of GOD as I went about my daily chores. I never told anyone.

What about my dream and the meters and fragments of stones of various shapes and sizes? Suddenly it was like diamonds and words of wisdom falling from the lips of King Solomon. Then in my imagination, I remembered these stones of various shapes and sizes landing upon and becoming attached as a part of the larger stones. Then GOD showed it to me just as plain as the day I was now living in.

I visualized men of labor going to the Tigris-Euphrates River and bringing tons of clay back to the mudpits and mixing fine-cut straw with the clay to make a hard rocklike substance that could not be broken. The clay was used to adhere the smaller stones to the larger stones, forming the two circles as a wheel within a wheel. In the hands of skilled crafted freemasons, something supernatural, unseen by the naked eye, emerged upon the completion of the project. In the light of day, a shadow brough forth from the rocks by the sunlight cast the letters of the Hebrew language upon the ground. The message shown would change as the sun moved from one degree to another degree.

The smaller stones when adhered to the larger stones produced a guide to the pronunciation of the Hebrew words. These were the Jots and there were other stones also that helped in this great mission.

The smaller stones formed the crown points within the dancing shadows upon the letters, with extending edges. These were used to change meanings as if one would use a pen stroke to lighten the letter until it accomplished the intended meaning. These were the tittles, also called thorns.

I had learned all of this from my father and teacher, Ezekiel. Ezekiel invented the dreidel game and we used it right in front of our captives. They thought we were learning to gamble with the little stones and the spinning top. A game similar to what the king used and was most popular throughout the Kingdom at that time.

I was assured that the sundial, like the dreidel game, projected a far greater message to the Jewish people at that time than what is now known. GOD began to drop little stones like magic down into my spirit being. Then suddenly like a big splash out of my belly it began to flow like rivers of living waters.

The Sh'ma was the answer. A constant reminder of GOD's first commandment, that we should have no other gods before Him.

This was the commandment we ourselves had broken.

Ezekiel had told us that this was what Hezekiah said when he turned to the Wailing Wall to say the Sh'ma after the death sentence came from GOD, through the mouth of Isaiah, the prophet at that time. It was through his repenting at the Wailing Wall and saying the deathbed prayer, the Sh'ma, that made GOD have compassion upon him. GOD saw the bend in his heart like the bend in the Shofar and the call in his voice of repentance as the sound of the Shofar. GOD called this a broken heart and a contrite spirit. GOD added fifteen years to his life. Life and death are sealed up in the words of the Sh'ma. When a child is born and learns to talk, the first words its parents tutor the child is the Sh'ma. These are the last words spoken by a Jew upon their deathbed. That is why Hezekiah thought it important to share with his people the first and most important words from the mouth of GOD.

The larger stones had smaller stones, which were perfected in shape and size and strategically located in a position so at exactly at twelve high the words of the Sh'ma made their appearance in the middle of the small inner circle of the stones.

This was also the method used to bring down to earth all the secrets of the Heavens so that learned people of GOD's great wisdom might learn to communicate. The communication by these great craftsmen as freemasons was only known in a secret, yet sacred order. They were never made known to the public but communicated with one another by use of the Mosan sign language.

Ezekiel had taught me and only a few trusted friends to know the secrets and the method of communicating one to the other.

These were the elite elders and sages of GOD and men of valor, which created a daily log for King Hezekiah. He used this information to rule his Kingdom.

The men recorded what the sundial was able to bring down from the heavens in the form of shadows passing over the stones. Here is the information collected and chartered in writing for the king.

The watchers of time for use in military advantage over the enemy. The first watch, or the beginning of the watches, was recorded each evening from sunset and ranged until ten at night. The middle watch was recorded, to range from ten P.M. until two A.M. The last watch was the morning watch, or the Sunrise watch. This watch was recorded within a range from 2:00 A.M. until 6:00 A.M. As it is written concerning the watches, "are there not twelve hours in a day", (John 11:9 KJV).

The Babylonians changed these watches, and they became four watches rather than the three used by King Hezekiah. Much information was gathered by studying the heavens.

Data was collected on the rising and setting of the sun and how to use this information to make the Jewish Kingdom a much better place to live. The sun's developmental patterns on the stars and planets.

Also, the times of days and months of the year the high and low tides were scheduled to appear.

The current timing with great accuracy the occurrence of the pilgrimage festivals as connected to GOD's laws.

They recorded the arrival and correct timing of the month of preparation, Elul, and the feast of trumpets and the all-important month of Tishri giving way to the High Holy Days and the Day of Atonement. This was our anticipated birthday of our coming Messiah, although we knew not the exact meaning of the sixth year and the appointed time was not yet know to us. Other information had been collected and recorded.

The six seasons of the year with information on planting and harvesting, buying, and selling products, much information was collected on the constellations.

The shadows between the space created by the two circles were able to capture shadows that told how the constellations favored the Jewish people. The advantages of this information from the sundial set off curiosity seekers from other countries. They wanted to know how it worked. They wanted to learn of its secrets.

Each day, each hour of the day and night, each minute of the day and night and each second were recorded by the astrologers, scientists, priests, and prophets as they collected and recorded the changes made by the shadows from the stones created by the hand of GOD.

The information was constantly changing due to the light of the moon, stars, sun, and planets. No one knew how long it took the king to record or build all the parts of the sundial, but it was a lifetime achievement.

It was this lifetime achievement that brought the enemy to his door in disguise and landed the Jewish people in seventy years of captivity in Babylon. We as GOD's chosen people never seem to learn our lesson. Ezekiel taught me of the series of events leading up to the Egyptians and their rule over our people even before Babylon made its conquest a reality in our lives.

EVENTS FROM THE MOUTH OF EZEKIEL

Here are the words from Ezekiel. The period for these events centers around the reign of two brothers: Zedekiah and Josiah.

Josiah had two wives: Hamutal and Zebudan.

Zebudan was the daughter of Pedaiah of Ramah. Zebudan and Josiah had a son by the name of Eliakim. Later, his name was changed to Jeaoiakim. Josiah also had a son by Hamutal.

Hamutal was the daughter of Jeremiah and she and Josiah had a son by the name of Jehoahaz, later renamed Jehoiakim. Josiah became engaged in war with his enemy.

Josiah went to do battle with Pharaoh Nechoh of Egypt. The pharaoh had conquered the Jews and had made Josiah to rule over them. Josiah became dissatisfied with the pharaoh and went to battle to defeat Nechoh.

The two armies met by the River Euphrates at Megiddo. Josiah was killed. His body was carried in his chariot back to Jerusalem and he was buried. Pharaoh Nechoh came to Jerusalem and made Jehoiakim, son of Josiah and Hamutal, king of Jerusalem.

Jeaoiakim, like his father, was stubborn and rebelled against the king and refused to pay the required tribute of one hundred talents of silver and one talent of gold.

Pharaoh Nechoh only allowed him to rule for three months. Jeaoiakim was twenty-three years old when Pharaoh took him away in chains and put him in prison down in Egypt, where he died.

Pharaoh made Jehoiakim's half-brother, Elikim, to reign in his stead and occupy the kingship over Jerusalem.

Pharaoh changed Eliakim's name to Jehoiakim. He was twenty-five years old and reigned for eleven years as king over Jerusalem. He was king when the Babylonians came.

Then came Nebuchadnezzar, king of Babylon, and conquered Jerusalem. He took Jehoiakim and his son, Jeconiah, back to Babylon as prisoners. His uncle, Zedekiah, was made king to reign over Jerusalem. The prophesy of Isaiah had now come full circle.

King Nebuchadnezzar was fascinated by gold and was eager to find wealth that he heard the Jews possessed. He had heard these stories since childhood.

His great-great-grandfather had married one of the Jewish virgins who came from Hezekiah's harem.

Nebuchadnezzar tortured all the upper-class citizens until they died because they could not tell him the whereabouts of the Ark of the Covenant and the Golden Candelabra.

He had the eyes of King Zedekiah blinded by boring hot sticks of fire into and through his eyes.

Before losing his sight, Zedekiah looked upon his sons and descendants of King Hezekiah. These were put to death and some left alive and made eunuchs. All that Isaiah prophesied was followed up on by a series of letters written by Jeremiah. These letters show how GOD chose Nebuchadnezzar to be his servant.

Letters from Jeremiah
From: Jeremiah, Major Prophet of GOD
To: King Jehoiakim, son of Josiah
Ref. Jeremiah 27:1-7 KJV
Dear King:

The Lord GOD of Israel has spoken unto me and has told me to make three bonds and three yokes and to put them upon my neck so that you may plainly see them.

O King, as you can see, I have obeyed GOD. He has ordered me to send these yokes and bonds back to the messengers who are now upon their way here to Jerusalem to see your Uncle Zedekiah.

These messengers will arrive from Edom, Moab, Ammon, Tyrus, and Zidon.

I have been instructed to give a yoke or a bond unto each of them. They are to carry them back to their kings along with this message.

"Thus, saith the Lord of Host, the God of Israel. I have made the earth, the man, and the beast upon the earth. By my great power and my outstretched arm, I have given unto whom it seemed meet unto me."

Now I am giving all these lands into the hand of King Nebuchadnezzar of Babylon, my servant. All nations shall serve him and his son and his son's sons. Then I will send many great kings and nations to serve themselves of him. Until that time comes, all nations shall put their neck under the yoke and bond of the King of Babylon.

I have one yoke left, O King, and the last one is for you. You also shall submit your kingdom unto King Nebuchadnezzar of Babylon.

The word of the Lord by the mouth of Jeremiah has ended.

The letter is signed stained with my tears.

Jeremiah

Jeremiah, the Weeping Prophet

I now lay the yokes and bonds numbering six in all, at the king's feet. As the king looked upon the bonds and yokes, in walked the five messengers from Edom, Moab, Ammon, Tyrus, and Zidon.

To: King Jehoiakim and the Five Visitors

From: Jeremiah, the Weeping Prophet

Ref.: Jeremiah 27:8-15 KJV

Hear ye the words of the Lord GOD of Israel. If any nation represented here today refuses to put their neck under the yoke of the King of Babylon, that nation will I punish with the sword, saith the Lord GOD of Israel.

I will also punish them with famine and pestilence until I have consumed them by the hand of Nebuchadnezzar.

You will have your prophets, diviners, dreamers, enchanters, and sorcerers speak to your land. They will say, "This is not so. Ye shall not serve the King of Babylon."

I say unto you, believe them not because what they prophesy to you will be a lie. The nation that will follow GOD and put their neck under the King of Babylon and serve him, those will I allow to remain in their own land, saith the Lord. They shall till their own land and remain there.

If you do not as I command you, then you will die, thou and thy people as I have spoken. Harken not unto the words of your lying prophet, for I have not sent them.

They prophesy a lie in my name. If you follow them, then I will drive you out and you shall perish along with all these false prophets.

Done and Signed

Jeremiah

GOD is my witness, as I weep

With the closing of my words the mouth of Jeremiah, the prophet of GOD, is now silent.

To: King Jehoiakim

From: Jeremiah, the True Prophet of GOD

Ref.: Jeremiah 27:18-22 KJV

O, My Good King Jehoiakim, if you believe the false prophets that will come unto you. If you believe that they speak unto you the words of the Lord, then ask them to make an intercession unto the Lord of Host and say, "The vessels of gold and of silver that are now in the house of the Lord and those in the house of the King of Judah and those also in Jerusalem shall not go into Babylon." See if they can say these words to you. They cannot say these words to you. I say unto you, O King, all these vessels of which I have just spoken and the two pillows of Boaz and Jacin and the sea of molten gold and the bases and the residue of the vessels within the city shall King Nebuchadnezzar carry with him down into Babylon. Now, O King, these words will pierce your heart through. When the King of Babylon makes his first assault of your city he will take your son, Jeconiah, into captivity along with the nobles of Judah and the nobles of Jerusalem back with him into Babylon. All that I say shall happen and be so until the day that I will bring them up and restore them again unto this place, saith the Lord GOD of Israel.

I now make an end to the words from GOD.

Jeremiah

Yet I weep more for Jerusalem.

Years ago I, Daniel, wrote these letters down as I received them from Ezekiel. Ezekiel gave me these stories for such a time as this.

To: All that dwell in Jerusalem

From: Ezekiel, GOD's Prophet

Ref.: Ezekiel 21:21-23 KJV

Today I stood facing the gate to your city. I brought you a message from GOD. It is not a good message of favoritism but one of sorrow and trouble. I brought you a message of judgment. GOD is against you, O Israel, and my teardrops fall upon the ground where you stand. Every heart of every person in this city shall melt and every hand shall be feeble, and you shall not be able to grasp a weapon of defense. Every spirit within the walls of this city shall faint and all knees shall be as weak as water. It shall rain upon the just as well as the unjust.

Each of you have said, "We know of no evil coming our way. We are not weak in spirit." However, I say that GOD is sending a sword of vengeance upon this city. A sword that is sharp. The sword is polished so that it may glitter and shine. You will see it coming from a great distance. Even now the sword is in the hand of the slayer.

I raised my hand and smote it hard upon my thigh, and I said, "Do you hear that loud noise I made?" You listened even more, as I gave a louder clap of my hands and carried through with a great heave-ho over my shoulder and those that stood with me understood.

I then pointed my finger and said, "The Ark of the Covenant will do you no good after today. It will be seen no more." Upon hearing these words, the people sighed and gasped, grabbing their hearts. I told the people that the sword would double a third time. Three times the sword of slaughter will fall upon this city and each time it will double in strength. These are the three woes from GOD. All twelve gates of this city will be cut off and there will be no escape. The sword will fall upon the leaders and rulers of this city. Before your very eyes you will see the princes and king slaughtered.

The King of Babylon is coming with a mighty army. He will come by way of your inherited land to the North. He will come by way of Egypt to the South. He will come by way of the great sea to the west and he will come from Babylon by way of the East. His army will surround the city of Jerusalem. The king will arrive by way of the Great Sea to the west. He will step from the ship onto dry land. He will set up his post at the head of the way of the city, on the hill overlooking the fertile valley.

He will direct the battle as he faces the eastern gate. You will have no defense. You will hear a great clatter throughout the city of Jerusalem. The whoredoms you have committed with the strange Babylonians within your borders and the worship of your small "g" gods have become your downfall. You are now the great whore of Babylon, in the eyes of GOD. The city will be surrounded on all four sides and will be cut off from the outside world. GOD hath spoken and I have reported. My words for you will continue as GOD so ordains me to speak.

To: Notes to the file of Ezekiel

Ref.: Psychological Warfare

Here is an account of how King Nebuchadnezzar and his army conquered Jerusalem. After their five months' release of scorpions upon the people and the land.

He made the people think he had supernatural powers. There were Jews in the city that believed such things. He convinced them that he had a supernatural tie to their small "g" god. Idol worship was growing fast in Jerusalem. Over the years many spies had infiltrated Judah and Jerusalem, bringing this idol worship with them. Here are the three things the king did to take control of their city. First, he showed them weapons of destruction in vast numbers. Second, the king showed them a manner of worship. Thirdly, he showed them a horrible visual aide of death and destruction. Here is how he placed the weapons in view to the inhabitants of Jerusalem.

Nebuchadnezzar had a great love for gold. He was very wealthy and ruled much of the world. He made a journey to Jerusalem to steal all the gold that was known to be in possession of the Jews since the days of Hezekiah. He took much of the gold he already had in his possession and had his army dip their arrow tips and the blades of their swords in the liquid gold. The weapons were polished so that they gave off a great brightness during the day when the sun shone bright upon them. At night, the moonlight and the stars also shone bright upon them. The bright reflective light could be seen at a great distance.

The brightness of thousands of soldiers with their weapons could be seen day unto day and night unto night. This combined with the noise of the rattling of the arrows within the quivers was enough to drive the Jews into hiding and shake with much fear and trembling. Along with this the king displayed an unorthodox manner of worship.

He gave the people the impression that he had a supernatural connection with their little "g" gods. He brought many replicates of their god of stone and set it high and openly before them. In any direction that one would look they would see their god.

The king and his army would chant, bow, and worship before the little "g" gods of stone. This was the way that many of the Jews worshipped. They had gone a-whoring after false gods. They thought that there was a supernatural communication taking place between the Babylonians and their god. The king and his army proceeded to show them a horrible visual aide.

He brought out thousands of the Jews he had captured and lined the hostages up before the gods of stone. The hostages were lined up on the lefthand side of the gods of stone. This arrangement was very sacred to the Jews. This was the position and alignment of the sacrifices when they were offered unto GOD. This next move was horrible.

The army took the thousands of Jews and struck them through the liver with their swords of gold. All Jews received this same death at the same time.

There was a chilling call of death. The loud cries of pain and suffering filled the airwaves and could be heard for miles. This was a slow way of dying.

The sound was heard day and night for a prolonged period. This along with the bright glare of the weapons and the rattling of swords and arrows in the quivers was enough to drive anyone crazy. Then came the breaking point. He began tearing down the Wester Wailing Wall. King Nebuchadnezzar had his captains divided into twelve divisions and opened the mouth of the gates on all four sides of the city. They entered with battering rams and the war cries of victory. The army built mounts around about the city. The city was set on four hills. The mounts were built to great heights and control over the city was easily accomplished. The army built a fort for King Nebuchadnezzar on the highest mount. Nebuchadnezzar had his stonemasons cut the emblem of a skull on this site to use as another of his psychological warfare. He also built fires in the cavities, where the nose, eyes, and mouth were located. Executions of Jews from this Mount of the Skull was a constant reminder to the Jews day and night that death waited for them. The historical battle to be termed Armageddon, the apocalypse of disaster and destruction of Israel was underway from the Hill of the Skull. Information clerks went among all the Jews and gathered all the facts that they found. The clerks compiled reports for the king and his council.

The king was looking for the gold of which the Holy Candelabra was made and the Ark of the Covenant. These items were never found.

There were only a few Jews within the walls of the city that were faithful. Jews that knew the secrets had committed suicide as called for in the Vow of the Nazarene. Their vow of death was completed at the edge of the Tigers-Euphrates River. It had been rumored that GOD sent his four great Angels to watch over the blood of his Saints, Kings, and Prophets now hid in the waters of the river.

It was very well known from the teachings of the Torah that this would happen. They knew GOD was angry and this was his doing.

GOD said, "Because you have made your iniquity to be remembered, in that your transgressions are discovered, so that in all your doings your sins do appear.

You have come into remembrance before me and ye shall be taken by the hand of King Nebuchadnezzar. Your profane wicked prince, your king, shall be no more. The day of your prince has come. I will take away your crown and your diadem. You will be king no more.

I will make you to be in low esteem. I will bring in one, a child not yet grown, to take your place and to rule in your stead. I will overturn and overturn repeatedly.

Nebuchadnezzar will come against this city three times and reign until I bring forth this child, whose right it is to the crown, and I will give it unto him. These are my words and cannot be changed nor altered, for I the Lord GOD of Israel have proclaimed it to be so."

All things happened just as GOD said they would. However, GOD has never been left without a witness and so Ezekiel remained alive to carry with him in his mind and heart the great secret belonging to the once proud Jews now headed into Babylon.

King Nebuchadnezzar took Jeconiah, son of Jehoiakim, the King of Judah, captive. He left much of the city intact with much damage. He left King Zedekiah to rule over the people. Many of his own soldiers were left in the city to control issues that might arise. More importantly he left Jeremiah, the weeping prophet, behind for the people to look to for guidance.

Joash was one listening to this story and asked, "Daniel, tell us how you became the chief ruler over the Babylonians." Daniel was a little sleepy-headed when he answered, "My story is rather long so I will give you the most important happenings."

Daniel offered this story. "When I came to Babylon during the first invasion by Nebuchadnezzar along with my three first cousins, Hananiah, Mighael, and Azariah, Ezekiel had taken them to the outer part of the city and then he made his way back for me. He had me hide out in the king's quarters.

"My mother was killed during the invasion and Ezekiel took me upon his shoulders with my legs straddling on either side of his neck. He held me tight with his hands about my wrists, as my older cousins followed. Later, he told me that he had given me a sleeping potion and wrapped a blindfold about my eyes so that I could not see the pollution and mass killings taking place.

"Ezekiel took me to the wall, where he had already dug a hole under the wall. He placed me in the hole and brought me safely upon the other side. Here was the outer part of the city, where all the fruit trees and gardens to raise all the foods needed for survival. This was not an escape route. Ezekiel knew there would be no escape.

"This indeed was a GOD-given strategy of survival. No fighting would take place in this area because of its enriched supply of foods and cattle. Ezekiel found my three first cousins and escorted us safely to Babylon. We were hidden among the thousands of Jewish hostages.

"We had blended in quiet well with all the laborers of the field as we ended up by the River Chebar in Babylon. Ezekiel became our mentor. He taught us all the customs of the Babylonians in order that we might blend in well with their cultural as we grew older in this strange land, the greater part of his teachings would take place in secret meetings. I have mentioned this once, but it is so important, I will mention it again.

"Ezekiel knew the king's favorite game was a game in which he would gamble. Ezekiel chose to teach us a game of the dreidel with rocks or small stones. Each stone became a number, and each number had a deep Jewish meaning. We were learning the history of our people right out in the open.

"Our captors, the Babylonians, only thought that we were gambling and enjoying the king's favorite game.

"It was through the teachings of Ezekiel that I began to know more about Jehovah, our GOD. GOD began to visit me in visions and dreams. My diet was milk and honey. I became a student of learning, and I was able to rightly divide the spiritual from the natural. When I turned sixteen years old, and Ezekiel was now thirty-nine years old when the king began to make plans to invade Jerusalem for a second time. I was in the second year of my life as ruler over Babylon, when the king carried through on his invasion."

Jeremiah, the prophet, was left to help care for the Jews' spiritual wellbeing and began to preach to the people. He prophesied of destruction, famine, and death. He reminded them of the yoke and how they should submit peacefully to the King of Babylon. Then came forth a false prophet to King Zedekiah. His name was Hananiah.

Hananiah appeared in front of Jeremiah and King Zedekiah. He took a yoke made of wood and broke it to pieces before the king. Then he told the king that within two years this yoke of bondage that Babylon had placed upon him and Jerusalem would be broken.

Then Jeremiah spoke before the king, saying, "You have broken a yoke of wood and in doing so you have placed a yoke of iron upon the people of Jerusalem and Judah. You, Hananiah, shall die because you have prophesied a lie to the people of Jerusalem."

Zedekiah was in the ninth year of his reign. The King of Babylon cut Jerusalem off from communicating with the outside world.

Death, destruction, and famine were now a daily happening within the borders of Judah and Jerusalem.

Zedekiah and his army tried to escape but were overtaken on the plain by the great and superior army of the Babylonians.

Zedekiah was taken to Babylon and the last thing he saw before losing his eyes was the death of his sons. The Jews were forced to look by night and day upon the fire and torture on the Hill of the Skull.

Nebuchadnezzar brought back to Babylon the two pillars and sea of molten brass, the bases and all the vessels of the house of the Lord, and the post of Jacin and Boaz. He still could not locate the treasure for which he sought. Ever since he was a child, he had heard the story of the Jewish people and the gold they possessed.

His anger exploded within himself every time he thought of the great gold. He had a love for gold and vowed to possess all that was within his reach.

Later, I will share with you pages I kept from his war journal, his daily log of events and some of his writings of his memories, and his many visions and dreams, along with those collected from the kings long before him. Now I will read to you from my notes of my life in Babylon.

To: The File of Daniel

Date: 600 B.C.

Ref.: Notes on my life in Babylon, my Bar Mitzva

At the time of this writing, I am twelve years old. Ezekiel told me it was time that I became a man. Over half of my life at this point has been in bondage here in Babylon. Ezekiel had arranged for my Bar Mitzva to be done in secrecy with no one present from the outside. We could not yet trust our own people. Many betrayed trusts for some type of reward from the Babylonians.

Those present were myself, Ezekiel and my three first cousins: Hananiah, Mishael, and Azariah. There was no Torah to read from, only what I had learned in secrecy while playing the dreidel game.

Ezekiel informed me that in the past this day was Passover. We were now under the Babylonian calendar and no mention was ever made of the Jewish calendar. We were engaged in utilizing the dreidel game to complete my Bar Mitzva when six Babylonian soldiers barged into our room.

Their roughhouse tactics and loud voices disrupted the silence of the evening. They wanted to know what was going on. Ezekiel made them quiet down when he said we were playing the same game that King Nebuchadnezzar played. The soldiers were reluctant to give in. They took us all away.

Ezekiel was taken away, in chains. My cousins and myself were taken in the opposite direction. I did not know where Ezekiel was taken. He gave me the Mosan sign of deliverance as he was led away. He was taken in the direction of the River Chebar Prison Camp. My cousins and I ended up in the king's palace. We were taken into separate rooms to answer questions. Ezekiel had well schooled us. I was careful and in as many instances possible I answered a question with a question of my own. I was taught to pay high tributes to the Babylonians and to say good things about the Kingdom and the king.

After all the questions were over, all four of us were placed in a room together in the king's prison. We were teased constantly by the guards for not eating the king's portion of meat, served to us daily. We asked for morsels of vegetables. This became our daily diet. This was the same as the offering made unto GOD by Able, the brother of Cain. No one knew of my royal tie to the throne of Israel, which came through the bloodline of King Hezekiah. I guarded this secret well. I and the three Hebrew children, as they came to be called, were all blessed to be born within the sacred cycle and chosen of GOD.

Azaria was born on Pentecost. Mishael was born on Dedication. Hananiah was born on Sukkot. We had been in prison for a year when all four of us were summoned to stand in audience with the king.

MEETING THE KING

We appeared before the king. He was extremely impressed with our countenance and manner of respect we showed for his position on the throne. Ezekiel had taught us well about the Babylonian customs and their cultural. We were careful and hid much of what we had learned about the Jewish customs of our past. King Nebuchadnezzar was dressed in Babylonian attar of royal gold, purple, and scarlet.

The king informed us that he was changing our customs as well as our names. We were to have Babylonian names. The name change was written in the king's book of proclamations and records of deeds.

I, Daniel, was named after the king's youngest son. My name became Belteshazzar, meaning "Protect the king." Hananiah received the name Shadrach. Mishael took the named of Meshach. Azariah received the name of Abednego.

We spent much of the morning that day in the presence of the king. He sat the table before us and served us vegetables, milk, and honey, which we were accustomed to eating. We knew that GOD had blessed and found us highly favored to bring us before the king in this manner. Prior to our leaving the king announced that our living quarters was being changed.

We would undergo training to work in his harem. He was moving us into his palace and leaving the cold prison cell behind.

LIVING IN THE PALACE

In our new living quarters, we had great privileges and much freedom. We began a day-by-day training to get us ready to work in the harem.

The king had many beautiful girls and many of them were near my age, which was nearing fifteen years old. It was here that I met a beautiful girl. The girl was thirteen and she was being groomed for the king's harem. She had not been defiled by men. She was four years old when she came to Babylon. She and I talked daily. She told me the king was getting ready to change her name and to move her into the harem. This would become her new home. Her name was Sarah.

Sarah and I met in secrecy. I never told my friends, nor did she ever tell anyone that we were in love. We heard rumors that there was some mistrust brewing among the king's servants. The king was incredibly angry. Six months before my sixteenth birthday, all the king's workforce for the harem were gathered in one room. My three cousins and myself were set aside by Melzar.

Melzar had become our friend and was the chief overseer of the prince of the Eunuchs. Melzar was also a Eunuch. He informed us that arrangement had been made through the prince of the eunuchs and Ashpenaz, the master of the Eunuchs, for us to also become eunuchs. This was an effort to save our lives. Many in the room would be put to death.

Ezekiel had taught us that one day it would be our turn. We knew that men were made eunuchs from birth. Some men are made eunuchs by men and some men are made eunuchs for the Kingdom of GOD's sake. We knew our fate was in the hands of our GOD. We were of Hezekiah's seed and the prophesy of Isaiah was upon us.

After our surgery and recovery, we were moved into a more luxurious quarters. I was never to see Sarah again. She was carrying my child when Ezekiel smuggled her out of the country and sent her to Egypt. I knew in my heart that Sarah and my child would be safe, for it was of GOD's doings. GOD was working out of the sight of men just as he had done with Judah and Tamar in the olden days of our history. My mind was set to ease and then I learned of the king's troubles.

THE KING'S TROUBLES

I was favored by the king and walked with him daily. The king often inquired of me in matters needing understanding. He found more favor in me than he did in his magicians and astrologers. He was constantly seeking information from among the captives about the Holy Candelabra and the Ark of the Covenant. I did not know any information about these two great artifacts of Israel. This haunted him daily. He came to the breaking point.

The king was troubled, and he could not sleep. He had a dream, which he could not recall. He called all his astrologers, sorcerers, and Chaldeans into his council. He said unto them, "I have dreamed a dream and my spirit is troubled to know the meaning of this dream."

Then the chief of the Chaldeans spoke to the king in the language of the Syriac and said, "O King, live forever, tell thy servants the dream and we will shew the interpretation."

Then the king said to the Chaldeans, "The dream is gone from me, if ye will not make known unto me the dream, with the interpretation thereof, ye shall be cut to pieces, and your houses with all of your relatives shall be made a dunghill." Then he continued, "But if ye shew the dream and interpretation thereof, ye shall receive of me great gifts and rewards and great honor. Therefore, shew me the dream and the interpretation thereof."

Then they answered and argued again, "Let the king tell his servants the dream." The king became upset and said in anger, "You will only be stalling for time because you know the dream is gone from me. Therefore, there is only one decree for you. You must me destroyed." The chief spokesperson for the Chaldeans said, "There is no man on earth that can shew the king's matter; therefore there is no ruler that would ask such a thing of any magician, astrologer or Chaldeans. There is none other than can shew before the king except the gods whose dwelling is not with flesh." The king became terribly angry and said, "Destroy all the wise men of Babylon."

Therefore, a decree went forth that all wise men should be put to death. The guards went to the palace and gathered Shadrach, Meshach, Abednego, and me with all the other wise men and took them to dungeon to be put to death. Then came forth the captain of the guard.

Arioch, the captain of the guard, said to me and the Hebrew children, "The decree has gone forth," and he told Daniel of the whole matter. Daniel said, "Go and tell the king to give me a little time and I will show the king the dream and the interpretation."

The captain of the guard went to the king and told him of the matter. The king granted Daniel's request. Daniel, along with Shadrach, Meshach, and Abednego, were taken to their house, where they held hands up to their GOD in Heaven and prayed for this thing. Then Daniel said, "In a night vision the secret was revealed unto me, and I blessed the GOD of Heaven."

GOD THE REVELATOR

I, Daniel, said, "Sh'ma Israel, blessed be the name of our GOD for ever and ever, for wisdom and the mark are his. He changes the times and the seasons as he did for King Hezekiah. He removeth kings and setteth up kings. He gives wisdom unto the wise and knowledge to them that know understanding. He revealth the deep and secret things. He knoweth what is in the darkness (of the law) and the light dwelleth in him. I thank thee and praise thee, O thou GOD of my fathers, who hast given me wisdom and might and has made known unto me what we desired of thee, for thou have made known unto us the king's matter" (Daniel 2:20-23 KJV).

Then I called for Arioch and said unto him, "Tell the king not to destroy the wise men, for I will tell him his dream and the interpretations thereof." Then l was brought unto the king and the king called me by his given name unto me and said, "Belteshazzar, can you do this thing? Can you tell me the dream?" Then I, Daniel, spake unto the king. "The secret which the king hath dreamed cannot the wise men, the astrologers, the magicians, nor the soothsayers shew unto the king but there is a GOD in Heaven that revealth secrets and maketh known to the King Nebuchadnezzar what shall be in the latter days. Thy dream and the vision of thy head upon thy bed are these.

"As for thee, O King, the thoughts came unto thy mind upon thy bed. What should happen hereafter? He that revealth secrets maketh known to thee what shall come to past. But as for me, this secret is not revealed to me for any wisdom that I have more than any living. It is revealed for the sake of the lives of the people that came to thee from Jerusalem, which is why I shall make this dream and the interpretation thereof known to the king."

Then said I unto the king, "The GOD in heaven hath said the dream and vision upon thy bed are these (Dan. 2:28 KJV). Thou, O King, sawist and behold a great image. The image, whose brightness was excellent, stood before thee, and the form thereof was terrible. This image had a head of fine gold, his breast and his arms were of silver, his belly, and his thighs of brass. His legs of iron and his feet were part iron and part clay. Thou sawist till that a stone was cut out, without hands, which smote the image upon his feet, that were iron and clay, and brake them to pieces.

"Then was the iron, the clay, the brass, and silver, and the gold broken to pieces together and became like the chaff of the summer threshing floor, and the wind carried them away, that no place was found for them and the stone that smote the image became a great mountain and filled the whole earth. This is the dream and I will give the interpretation from GOD, before the king" (Dan. 2:31-36 KJV).

THE INTERPRETATION

"The image before thine eyes is the image of five Kingdoms. The first Kingdom is the head of gold. Gold stands for the glory of GOD. The head of gold is you, O Great King Nebuchadnezzar, for you are the glory of GOD's calling. GOD has made you the head and given unto you a great Kingdom, power, strength, and glory. GOD has made you ruler over all things, that peopled globe, the fowl of the air, and the beast of the field. Your great Kingdom is Babylon. You have already begun to bring about the captivity of the Jewish people as GOD has called you and set you high above Jerusalem and Judah. The second Kingdom shall be silver and silver is GOD's redemption. This Kingdom is inferior to you and is shown to you as the breast and the arms of this image. This Kingdom shall come with a mighty army armed only with sticks as a weapon. They shall strip your army down to the bear breast and beat your subjects down into submission with sticks as one would beat a dog. This is the army from Persia and Meade.

"This army will be mighty and will redeem the Jewish people from under your rule. The Jews will be released to pursue freedom after their seventy years of service under your rule. Yet you saw a third Kingdom of brass hidden within the belly and thighs of this great image.

"The third Kingdom is a Kingdom of brass brighten by the fire that burns within them. They will come as a great fire, burning out of hand. This army will burn up the Kingdom of sticks, which you saw as silver. While this Kingdom shall keep the children of Israel at bay while yet holding them under their control. Then shall arise a fourth Kingdom. This is the Greeks.

"The fourth Kingdom which you saw with legs made of iron. This Kingdom will be as strong as iron. It will break and subdue all the subjects of the Kingdoms before it. It will break all the people it comes into contact with. Innumerable number of soldiers will come as waves of the waters of the ocean. They will cover the land as the waters cover the sea. This Kingdom shall also hold control over the Jewish people. This Kingdom will weaken itself by dividing into ten subdivisions. This is the Romans.

"Whereas thou sawist the feet and toes, part of potter's clay and part of iron, the Kingdom shall be divided (Dan. 2:41 KJV). The Kingdom shall retain some strength but the subdivisions shall weaken the Kingdom. The people shall not cleave one to another. Each of the ten heads will have a desire to be a sole ruler over all the divisions. After this the GOD of heaven shall set up his Kingdom.

"Forasmuch as thou sawist that stone was cut out of the mountain without hands and that it breaks in pieces the iron, the brass, the clay, the silver and gold. The Great GOD hath made know to the King what shall come to pass hereafter" (Dan. 2:45 KJV). The stone is that which the builders of the other Kingdoms have rejected and is to become the head of all. The God of Heaven will set up a Kingdom that shall never be destroyed. The Jewish people will by the wisdom of GOD abide in this Kingdom as the first to enter thereby. This is a promise made by GOD when Jacob built the Tower of the Flock. This is the one Israel that GOD bought for the two tablets of the Ten Commandments.

Daniel said, "The dream is certain and the interpretation thereof sure" (Dan. 2:45 KJV). Then the king fell upon his face and worshipped me and made me and my cousins rulers over the Kingdom.

REUNION WITH EZEKIEL

I had last seen Ezekiel in 589 B.C., which was six years ago. I thought he might have been put to death. I held our very first planning session to get our leadership and authority established. Our first big task was to design and follow through on a census throughout the Babylonian borders. We hoped to find the names, nationalities, ages, and location of all races of people now in Babylon. We especially wanted to locate the remnant of the Jewish population. We advised our subjects to be aware of our efforts to find Ezekiel.

The census was in the third month when word arrived back to us that Ezekiel had been found. He was found in the encampment down by the River Chebar.

He had kept a low profile since his arrival at the encampment. He spent hours instructing handpicked Jewish people the Mosan sign language. Our awareness was catching on fast, without the knowledge of the Babylonians. As we awaited the arrival of Ezekiel at the palace, I left orders that he was to be bathed in oil and washed in water in accordance with our Jewish custom prior to meeting the king or a national ruler. This age-old Jewish custom was handed down from Queen Ester and now it was to be a custom among the Babylonians.

Ezekiel entered dressed in the royal attire of the king's court. I broke forth with tears in my eyes. My voice gave way to a quiver as I said, "May the eternal GOD of Heaven and Earth and the Great King of Babylon be blessed for returning you in safety to your people." Ezekiel immediately fell upon my shoulder and gave the newfound embrace as a prodigal son. "Daniel, Daniel, my prayers have been answered. I feel as though we have been ushered back into the hands of GOD". We did not have much time together until we heard footsteps headed our way from the Great Hall. Almost immediately we began to use the Mosan sign language, which came from our ancestor Moses. King Nebuchadnezzar and his entourage entered the room. At first, I was worried about Ezekiel and his ability to fit into and comprehend the proper demeter to use in the king's presence. However, Ezekiel knew just what to do and how to do it to please the king.

The king was more than happy to receive Ezekiel and to assign him to work in the guesthouse under my authority.

I was pleased, for it would allow us more time to continue to learn one from the other.

I had only held my position as ruler when King Nebuchadnezzar informed me that he was preparing to make another trip to Jerusalem. He was going to make a last-ditched effort to find the Ark of the Covenant and the Holy Candelabra. These items were not found. Their value was thought to exceed any item in the country of Babylon. Rumors were that they were still in Jerusalem. He was off on a treasure hunt.

TREASURE HUNT

I immediately sought council with Ezekiel. The captain of the guard told me that Ezekiel had left the palace and was on his way back to the encampment by the River Chebar. I mounted my little white colt, a gift from King Nebuchadnezzar. I arrived at the river and observed what was taking place from the hillside. As I overlooked toward the river, I noticed a crowd had gathered around Ezekiel. Ezekiel left the bank of the river and stepped down into the water. The water was up to his ankles. As he went farther into the water, it came up to his knees. Then, the water got up to his hips and then the water flooded up to his chin. It now became swimming water. I knew he was using the elements of nature to send a Mosan coded message to the wise elders that stood among the crowd on the bank. He came out of the water and began to tell a story of four beasts and a wheel that was in the middle of a wheel. Many left but those that knew of his message stayed. Once again, he was sending a message of hope to the captives of Israel.

I knew something very supernatural was being shared with the elders of our people. Ezekiel approached me and asked that I arrange a visit for him to come into the king's storehouse of treasurer while the king was gone back to Jerusalem. I did as he asked, based on the trust of my most loyal friends.

I met him early the following morning at the entrance to the storehouse of treasurer. This was the first time Ezekiel had been here. I had taken an inventory of all that was in the room for the king. The room contained gold, silver, rubies, emeralds, all the holy vessels from Jerusalem and many other items. I asked him, "What are we doing here?" His cutting remark was "The Ark of the Covenant is here." I was shocked and could hardly get words out of my mouth. "No one knows where it is; that is why the king went back to Jerusalem."

Ezekiel said, "It is not in Jerusalem. It is here in this room. Daniel, step over here." I very hurriedly came to corner of the room. He asked me, "What do you see?" I answered, "The two posts from the temple but they have been stripped of their gold and silver. They are of no value."

Ezekiel had me to step closer to the inner wall of the storehouse. I did as he requested. "This post is called the post of Boaz," he said. "What you do not know is that it is hollow inside and has an inner pocket especially made to hide the Ark of the Covenant." I was held speechless as he said, "We must get it out of here within the next two days. It must not be here when the king returns. We never know what information he might turn up with when he returns." I said to Ezekiel, "Two days from now will be my birthday." Ezekiel said, "That is good because I want to have a good birthday on Passover. Even though we cannot acknowledge it, people will long remember this Passover for years to come."

He proceeded to show me the Ark. I was overwhelmed with the pullies and leavers made to perfection by some master mark mason to hide GOD's treasurer. I was seeing for the first time what my ancestors of old looked upon with envy. No one had ever carried the ark since long before the Babylonian era began. Ezekiel told me to bring twelve of my most trusted servants for him to show them how to move it.

He quickly drew a sketch in the dust upon the floor. It was a map and as Ezekiel finished drawing the map, he pointed to an x mark and said, "This is where we will bury the Ark." He continued, "I will train the twelve on how to hold and how to move with the Ark. It will not take exceedingly long for this. I will already have the grave dug and the slaps of clay cut to go into place to hide and protect the Ark." Ezekiel continued, "I will have my most trusted friends there waiting to be of assistance to you once you arrive at the scene."

With our plans in place, we said our goodbyes as we awaited the eve of Passover to arrive.

THE EVE OF PASSOVER

The eve of Passover arrived, and I turned nineteen years of age. I had been here in Babylon for thirteen years and have been ruler for the past two years. I got twelve of my most trusted servants to aid me in moving the Ark. After our rehearsal and practice we moved the Ark. Many cried after looking upon the Ark for the first time. All was done in accordance with the law of Moses.

We arrived at the designated place in the North of Babylon. The grave to bury the Ark had already been dug by Ezekiel as promised. There were slabs of clay lying nearby. Two of Ezekiel's followers were standing close. We looked but did not see Ezekiel.

Suddenly, a figure gave way to the light of the moon as it peeked out from a top of the dark clouds. Ezekiel emerged from the shadows, and I was shocked. He was dressed in the Jewish burial attire. I thought this was a custom to be followed as the Ark was moved. But why? I did not know.

As he came near to me, he seemed to glisten and glow in the cool Passover night air. He was cleanshaven, and I assumed he had made a vow of the Nazarene in some sort of way.

He broke the silence and said, "Daniel, my son, I must talk to you in privacy." We walked to the side away from those who were ready to bury the Ark. I asked him what this was all about. He said, "Well, I want to give you this birthday present on this special eve." Then he said, "I whisper in your ear as I would whisper to a goat's ear, I know you will keep our secret. Happy birthday, son." He gave me a big hug and as he did, he whispered once again, "I'm your dad and sad to say but today I must leave you."

I was so shocked; I did not know what to say. He told me that Sarah and my child she was carrying were safe down in Egypt. He told me about my mother. He said that Isiah's daughter had married King Hezekiah. They had three daughters and he had married one of the second generation of one of these daughters. He was talking about my mother. She was killed during the first invasion by the Babylonians. I could not let it be known that I was your father. We would both have been put to death. It seemed like an eternity had passed as we concluded our conversation. He very quickly told me about his dress and as we both tried to hold back our tears he said, "You know what to do now, don't you, son?" I answered, "Yes, Dad, I know."

I questioned as we parted, are we the last of the generations of the Jews of Babylon? Were we the authors of *Jews of Babylon, The Final Chapter*?

Many years have passed, and the king has died, and I am in isolation under the new rule of his brother-in-law and his son. The agony of defeat laid heavy upon my heart and mind as I began to read the king's war journal and his memories, which he left in my care.

THE KING'S MEMORIES

I, King Nebuchadnezzar, was called of the Hebrew GOD to conduct his goodwill and pleasure and to clean up the bloodline much as King David was called to do many years ago. I have this day decreed that my constant companion and champion of the Hebrew GOD, who has no name, Daniel should be the recipient of my memories and my journal of the Babylonian war log.

The way for me to conduct GOD's calling in my life was paved for me to conquer many countries and to extend the Babylonian rule over these many countries. My father had conquered many countries and left them under my rule.

These were all the Kingdoms of the world upon the face of the earth (Jer. 29:36 KJV). There were over twenty-five of these Kingdoms under my rule. I will mention them by name later in my writings. Accepting GOD's providential responsibilities fell hard upon my shoulders. I was faced early on with the task of conquering Egypt and the Jewish people of Judah and Jerusalem. The jewel in my crown was to set my rule over the Jewish people. The groundwork had already been laid for me by my great-great-great-great-grandfather King Baladan.

King Baladan sent his son, Prince Marduk-Baladan, to visit the Jewish King Hezekiah.

When the prince returned, he brought with him all of the wisdom and secrets of the Jews in Judah and Jerusalem. It was this visit to Jerusalem that set up all of the strategic planning over the years that would make it necessary for me to conquer the Jews.

Our ancestors were always interested in conquering the Jews after hearing of the wealth and secrets they possessed.

Ninety-seven years before I conquered the Jews, my great-great-great-grandfather Marduk-Zakir-Shumi II began to divide the Jewish law from Moses and to make a detailed study as to why it was written to start with and to try to make sense of what to do to get it put into practice. He referred to the law as Sampson's Heifer. He found intense pleasure in parting the red heifer, this he said was called the Law of Moses. He had his scholars keep a daily log of his findings and their relationship back to living the everyday life.

It was my great-great-grandfather-Sargon II-Bel-I-Bni that succeeded him on the throne. This was in 722 B.C.E. He only reigned for seven years. He was the first to say that no foreigner could ever rule over Israel. The law was plain that the ruler over Israel had to be a native son of royal blood and could not be a foreigner (Duet. 17:15 KJV). We knew that if we ever conquered the Jews that one of their own homes' born sons must be left alive and set as a ruler over them.

My great-grandfather, Nabopolassar, began an operation that would plant spies behind the walls and within the city of Jerusalem and in the land of Judah.

These were men of great valor who were well trained to fit into the Jewish society and to become as one of the Jews.

Once we gained a foothold and became as a Jew, we began to smuggle beautiful Babylonian women into the Jewish villages. These women were also well trained and eventually began to intermarry with the chosen leaders of the Jewish people.

Before the Jews knew what was happening, we began to lead them away from their Jewish GOD, who had no name and introduced them into the worship of our many gods.

There was Enel, the deity that ruled the air. Shamash, the deity of the sun and power of the star. Next, we introduced them to know Anu, god of the sky. Finally, we persuaded many to seek after Marduk, the god of war, (Wikipedia).

Over the period of many years, the established belief of an underworld after death where people would suffer and be tormented for an eternity if they did not worship these many gods. From the time King Baladan sent his son, Prince Marduk Baladan, to visit King Hezekiah, the groundwork had been laid for the fall of Israel.

It was King Hezekiah's own ignorance that led GOD to call me out of the lineage of the Babylonian kings that would lead to destruction. Our spies that we had sent into the Jewish country and groomed began to take hold and to emerge in many positions of leadership. Some collaborated daily with King Hezekiah.

They offered him much misleading advice. He was encouraged to receive the diplomats from Babylon and to impress them with his Kingdom showmanship.

King Hezekiah began to fall. He told Marduk-Baladan all his secrets and gave him many Jewish virgins from his harem to take back to Babylon and have them intermarry with the Babylonians.

By the time my father, who was named after his father Nabopolassar took command of the throne he had married one of the descendants from a virgin. This was my mother, who was a descendant of a Jewish nobleman.

My father died in 612 B.C.E. I came to the throne at the age of thirty and began my reign as king.

MY REIGN

Prior to my becoming king, I studied all the military strategies of war and became a student of the Jewish way of life. My father told me that no king would go to war with another country without first studying and knowing all there was to know about that country.

I was six years old when I began to study the Jewish laws and customs of the Jewish people. I was taught at an early age that the Jewish GOD was the giver of many dreams and visions. Our line of kings became the recipients of this gift.

I was nearing the age of eight when I began to have visions and dreams. I was raised up outside of the calling that was upon my father, Nabopolassar.

My father was a visionary ruler and a dreamer of dreams. He was noted for having his advisory council translate his dreams.

My mother taught me the history of the Jewish people. She made me to realize they were the apple of GOD's eye and to be desired. She told me stories of the gold they had brought back out of Egypt. She often talked to me about the Jewish worship of just one GOD.

I could not comprehend this because my father taught me about the many gods that had made Babylon a great empire. He said this was now gaining lots of ground and expanding in the minds and hearts of the people now in Jerusalem. He said one day this belief would be of a great aid to us when the time came to conquer the Jews.

I was at my father's bedside when the death angel paid him a visit. Just before he died, he talked to me about becoming the next King of Babylon. He desired that I should rule over all the lands that he had conquered with much power. We introduced them to our way of worship, polytheistic, or worship of many gods. Ishtar was the goddess dedicated to love and war. He said I was the one chosen of the Hebrew GOD to rule over all the Jews.

He requested that I spend much time with the keeper of the Babylonian records, his faithful servant, Ramasel II. After my father's entombment, I prepared to spend much time with Ramasel II and the Babylonian records of the past.

Ramasel II had served four generations of the Babylonian Dynasty. He and his staff had gathered information on the Jewish people dating back to the years that Marduk-Baladan had returned with the many Jewish virgins and his report of the wealth and secrets in possession of the Jewish people. The documents mentioned the many valuable relics of gold in the possession of the Jews.

Two of the most prized possessions mentioned were the Holy Candelabra and the Ark of the Covenant.

I very carefully studied the list of all these valuable items. I became possessed with a desire not only to find them but to make them a part of the Babylonian treasurers. I also studied other documents.

DOCUMENTS OF INTEREST

I began to study the documents I had seen as a child. I dug into the deep-rooted beliefs of the law by which the Jews lived. It was this belief that brought the unity of strength to the Jews. I knew that strength of unity of the brotherhood between Judah and Jerusalem could be broken if we would destroy the strong belief they had in the Laws of Moses.

Our spies were brilliant in their work inside the walls and within every facet of the Jewish society using beautiful women to entice the men into forgetting their GOD. They should believe as the women and eat, drink, and make merry.

Here at home, and through the constant reports from our spies or the dark tribe, as they came to be known, we began to note weakness within the Jewish society.

The Twelve High Hour was a notable weakness. At this hour all the people would cease from their activities and work and bow to the ground in respect and worship of their GOD. It was their belief that the Jewish Messiah would come to deliver them at the appointed hour when the sun was high in the sky. It was just as in their past when King Saul first was made ruler over the Jews by GOD.

Saul used the law to unite the tribes of Israel. They then asked him when he would deliver them. He answered, "Tomorrow by the time the sun be hot, ye shall have help" (I Sam. 11:9 KJV). When the sun passed and the shadow was no longer under their feet, they would return to work.

They would once again cease work at the sixth hour. It was written within their law, "work while it is day, the night cometh when no man can work" (John 9:4 KJV).

THE NIGHT HOUR

The night hour ran from the sixth hour, 6:00 P.M., until the twelve low hour of midnight. This was a time for personal relationship with a one-on-one to GOD.

Each member of the four sects of Jews, each person belonging to any of the twelve tribes, each member of every family, and each member of the priesthood that came from within the families worked out their own salvation with much fear and trembling (Philippians 2:12 KJV).

For the Jews, it was their personal relationship with GOD through the law that became their first priority in their way of life. Then came the sabbath.

THE SABBATH

The Sabbath Day of each week provided an area of weakness within their military ranks. All their compatriots were in service to their GOD.

On this day at the sixth hour our findings showed the Jews' service to their GOD, even more so at certain times of the year. This occurred when their Sabbath Day was incorporated into their feast days. Their annual feast days occurred as various times during the year.

SABBATHS DURING THE ANNUAL FEAST DAYS

There were seven annual Sabbaths that occurred during their feast days. These were to the letter of the law. These days were in addition to their weekly Sabbaths. There were two in the spring, (Wikipedia).

One came on the first day of Passover, and one came on the seventh day of Passover. Another annual feast day came in the summer.

During the summer, the Sabbath fell on the eve of Pentecost. We also found that there were two in the fall.

In the fall, during the Holy Month of Tishri, two more Sabbaths were observed. Rosh Hashanah following the feast of trumpets brought Shabbaton. While Yom Kippur, the eve of Atonement, gave the Jews their beloved and yet dreadful Sabbath of Sabbaths. The last two Sabbaths came during Sukkoth. During the feast of Tabernacles, Sukkoth, the first Sabbath, comes during the first day of Sukkoth. The second one comes on the eighth day of Sukkoth, or Shim Chat Torah. We used all the information we gathered in our war council planning sessions. Our spies had gathered much valuable information.

OUR SPIES

Our spies brought us much valuable information from all the resources in Israel. Information came to us from people, places, and things within the country of Israel. From the highest point, at a sea level of over 2,500 feet was land that for years had been in the family of Adonikam. It had belonged to King David at one time and was a key military stronghold because the whole area around about it could be seen as an open book. A rich fertile valley lay around about this land and was enriched with soil that brought forth plants, herbs, fruit trees, and served as a site for raising all animals. The Jewish people had profound respect for this area and would not engage in types of military operations because of the life-supporting benefits derived from the foods in this area. This was our site we would select and secure for our base of military operations. This area would serve as our strategic military headquarters. Much food would be supplied for our troops from this enriched area. From all the information we gathered from our spies, we zeroed in on a time for our planned invasion of the Jews.

The planning and timing of the invasion was perfect. The invasion began on the day of the Sabbath of Sabbaths at precisely the sixth hour of 6:00 P.M. on Yom Kippur. The invasion would be swift and deadly. Our codename for the invasion and destruction of the Jews would be termed Armageddon, the apocalypse and destruction of the Jewish nation. This name, we determined, would forever live in the history of GOD's people, the Jews.

We would cut through the heart of the Jew, as prophesied by their own Jewish prophets from the mouth of GOD himself.

This invasion had been in the planning stages for years before I became king. My father was one of the greatest of these kings. He had a vision, wrote it down, and gave it unto my hands, saying it was for my eyes.

MY FATHER AND HIS VISION

My father had a vision of a revelation to come. He said that the Jewish prophet Ezekiel told of this vision and warned Jerusalem that a sword of the Babylonians would come against the city three times. He said each time it came it would double in strength. My father referred to this vision as coming in three great "woes."

He said, "The first woe came to me while I was in the last year of my reign. I had several visions and each vision had seven angels in the vision. Each angel brought unto me many words relating to the Jewish people.

"When I awoke, I could not recall all the visions. However, one such a dream stood steadfast within my mind, and I had to rise out of my state of slumber and write it down before it escaped my mind's entrapment.

"The words I wrote down were the words of the fifth angel. The fifth angel brought before mine eyes and dropped hard within my mind and heart the first great woe.

"I saw the angel sound upon his trumpet, a loud and horrible chilling sound. While he was yet sounding the trumpet I beheld, and a great star fell from the heavens. The star fell to the earth.

"The star had a key to a bottomless pit and a great smoke, like unto a furnace came out of the pit.

"The smoke was so thick that the sun, the moon, and the stars hid their light behind this dark smoke by day and by night.

"I saw scorpions as thick as the swarms of locusts, which plagued the Egyptians at the time of Moses the scorpions swarmed to the city of Jerusalem.

"The eyes of the Jewish people were troubled as they looked upon the scorpions. Their appearance and shape were like unto horses with crowns of gold upon their heads. Their face was as the appearance of a man. The scorpions had hair like the hair of a woman, and they had teeth like the teeth of a lion. They had breastplates as if it were iron. Their tails were like unto scorpions and their wings made noise as the sound of many horses running in battle.

"The scorpions had a king over them that named in the Hebrew tongue as A-bad-don. But, in the Greek tongue he was called Apollyon (Rev. 9:11 KJV).

"I thought the dream to be so strange and after I had written it down, I called a council my historians and my prophets by visions. Jadar, my chief historian, informed the council that such a scorpion as were, within my dream did exist, and were found on the dark continent of Africa, which lay to the west beyond Israel and across the great sea.

"Jadar informed our council that they were housed in the many volcanoes and were in a dormant stage due to the smoke from the volcanoes. These scorpions were awakened when the smoke would cease, and they would then find their freedom. They would often attack highly populated areas and places where fruit trees were grown, they could devour like locusts and sting like scorpions.

"Our historians noted to us that the King Hyrum, employed by King David and King Solomon, made many trips to this land, and every three years the ships returned to bring back 'gold, silver, ivory, and, apes' (Chro. 9:21 KJV).

"The scorpions could be controlled by having trained personnel man the hulls of the ships equipped with smoke furnaces, which kept the scorpions in a dormant stage until we would choose to awaken them. We created a whole new phase of our warfare.

"I had within my army a fearless general and leader of men. He was born a Greek and highly respected. I had changed his name, as was our custom. He became my choice along with his men to control these scorpions and have all the training supplied by the Africans. He would learn how to control and use the queen scorpion much as Solomon used his beekeepers in his day.

"I gave him a Greek name, Apollyon, which he loved. The Jews that were already a part of our society chose to call him A-Bad-don. They did this to appease me and to make a connection to the dream I had. All our enemies came to fear the name of Apollyon and he was nicknamed the King of the Scorpions.

"My council of prophets gave me this interpretation of my dream.

"The Great Star that fell from heaven to earth was the wisdom of the Jewish GOD. This wisdom was known to the Jews as Kabbalah, or the torta-ha-sol or the teaching of the secret. I knew this wisdom was given unto us, to use as an aid in conducting the Hebrew GOD's directions in conquering Jerusalem. The bottomless pit was the bottom of our six ships, where we stored the scorpions with our smoke furnaces and controlled the scorpions with their queen.

"The natives had gathered thousands of the scorpions and placed them in the cluster sac of the jungle green moss. This was the nest that our men learned to manage with great care."

I noticed my father's hand was growing weak to my touch as he said, "Son, this great first woe is in your hands. The GOD of Israel has chosen you as his servant to show forth his might and his power. Serve him well. You will have a vision of the other two 'woes.' GOD will send you an angel to guide you harken unto his voice. I love you much, now my journey here upon earth is finished."

Those were my father's last words, and now I began the preparation for what I was called to do. When I became king, I immediately prepared to conduct my first invasion of Jerusalem.

THE FIRST GREAT WOE: ARMAGEDDON

I, King Nebuchadnezzar of Babylon, had read repeatedly the prophesy given unto me by the great Jewish prophet Jeremiah. He wrote unto me: "Because Israel has not heard my words, I will send and take all of the families of the north, saith the Lord, and Nebuchadnezzar the King of Babylon, my servant, and will bring them against this land, and against the inhabitants thereof, and against all these nations round about, and will utterly destroy them and make them an astonishment, and a hissing, and perpetual desolations.

Moreover, I will take from them the voice of mirth, and the voice of gladness, the voice of the bridegroom, and the voice of the bride, the sound of the millstones and the light of the candle. And this whole land shall be a desolation, and an astonishment and these nations shall serve the King of Babylon, seventy years" (Jeremiah 25:8-11 KJV).

It was this prophesy from the Jews' own prophets that made me realize the importance of obeying the words of the Hebrew GOD.

I knew I must make a complete destruction of this people to please GOD. They had brought it upon themselves through disobedience. I learned that "it was a fearful thing to fall into the hands of a living GOD" (Heb. 10:31 KJV). I was very afraid of this Hebrew GOD with no name. I knew he could change his mind in judgment, just as he did with the Jewish King Hezekiah. We must be precise and do as he directed or we ourselves would be the ones to answer to him, rather than the Jewish people.

Our great general, the Scorpion King, Apollyon, chose the Greek name Armageddon for our battle. He said that the name fit the description of what we were planning. He told me that in his country the name meant a final or conclusive battle. When I heard this, I agreed to that name. It fit exactly where our army would set up headquarters.

Our headquarters would be set up on what had once been a stronghold for the Jews, it had been Megiddo to the Hebrews. From their past we knew it had once belonged to the tribe of Manasseh (Judges 1:27 KJV). Prior to that it had been a city belonging to the Canaanites (Joshua 12:21 KJV).

Presently it was Anathoth and belonged to Shallum of the family of Adonikam and was occupied by the members of the tribe of Benjamin. Our Hebrew interpreter translated it as being a mountain of troops for invasion. I understood that the Jewish King David had chosen this site for his city, the City of David. This was prior to King Solomon building his temple and watching the progress being made on the temple as he sat on this very site, where I had planned to be sitting and directing the battle. Jews believed that one day their Messiah would come to this mountain and die for their sin. This was the site chosen for our battle plan, the final and conclusive end of the Jewish nation.

STRATEGIC BATTLE PLAN

Our plan would be both psychological and physical. All our generals and all our troops were on the same page. There would be no weak showing. Our psychological warfare was most important. This began with our Scorpion King, General Apollyon. We would bring three ships with the bottoms of their hulls loaded with smoke ovens and thousands of times thousands of scorpion bags and queen scorpions to the great sea on the west side of the Jewish nation. We would also bring three ships with thousands and thousands of scorpions and scorpion queens to the east side of the Jews and dock on the Tigris-Euphrates River. This would be the beginning of our war as GOD directed us to do. We had taken captive six months prior to our invasion many Jews of important status. We placed the mark of the Jewish star upon these individuals and held them captive in the green grassy areas, for we knew the scorpions would not go to the greenery areas of the land.

For five months the scorpions would be released at various intervals and for five months of one hundred and fifty days, they would torment the people and destroy vegetation and foods. Nothing was safe from their army. Except those we had marked and the green grassy areas. As this part was playing out, we brought in our ground troops and equestrians. Our physical warfare was about to begin with a continuation of our physical strength.

We wanted the Jews to know of our strength, and we wanted to tie it into something they would be associated with. We chose to bring together eighteen countries under the Babylonian rule and to come against the Jews. Our codename for this phase was "The Great Surround."

THE GREAT SURROUND

The Great Surround was in the process of developing the whole five months of the scorpion invasion. Just as soon as Apollyon, the Scorpion King, recalled the scorpions back to the ship with the help of the queen scorpions and their keepers, our Great Surround began to emerge. We would bring 601,550 troops from eighteen countries from all directions surrounding the countryside of Judah and the city of Jerusalem. Why that exact number of troops?

Our research of Jewish history took us back into their past. This number of 601,550 was the number of Jews that came to their freedom out of Egypt when they left slavery behind.

We knew the value the Jews placed upon numbers, and we wanted to place before them the same number that came out free would now go back into captivity by that number of their enemy. How would they know of that number? We would offer them this picture.

Our troops would come from all four sides into the Jewish territory. We would bring them in numbers equal to the same number of Jews in each ethnic group that made their exit from Egypt.

From the North direction would come 62,700 of our troops. This was the same as the number of Jews in the ethnic group of Dan that came out of Egypt. From the Northeast would come 53,400 troops; this was the same number of Jews in the ethnic group of Naphtali that came out of Egypt from the Northeast.

From the Northwest came 41,500 troops. This was the same number of Jews in the ethnic group of Asher that came out of Egypt. Then came our troops from the South.

From the South came 41,500 troops. This was the same as the number of Jews in the ethnic group of Reuben that came out of Egypt. Then we had 57,300 of our troops come out of the Southeast. This was equal to the number of Jews of the ethnic group of Simeon that came out of Egypt. 46,650 troops entered from the Southwest. This was equal to the number of Jews in the ethnic group of Gad that came out of Egypt. Our alignment of troops continued in the East. From the East came our largest army of troops.

These troops numbered 74,600. This was the number of the highly respected Jews from the tribe of Judah. 54,500 troops emerged from the East. This was equal to the number of Jews from the tribe of Issachar. Joining them from the East also came an additional 57,400, the same as the number from the tribe of Zebulun. Next, we had an enormous number come from the West.

Our military troops from the West numbered 108,100. Of this total number, 35,400 troops represented the number of the tribe of Benjamin. The tribe of Ephraim was represented by our 40,500 troops. Finally, the tribe of Manasseh was represented by 32,200 of our troops. Now we proceeded to bring the picture alive in the minds of all the Jews.

We had taken control of the strategic operational point, known as the Mount of Anathoth, to the present Jews.

Our invincible elite guards and special forces had engaged in a skirmish and had taken control of this area without much incident, although the members of the tribe of Benjamin and the owner of the land Shallum resisted. We took all the leaders and priests captive throughout Judah and the city of Jerusalem and brought them to the Top of the Hill, which I had renamed the Hill of the Skull.

I, King Nebuchadnezzar, had my stonecutters busy cutting the image of a skull in the side of the hill facing Jerusalem, which lay to the East. As my captive leaders and priests stood before me, it was time for them to look below. From the hill where we now stood, they were able to view all around them at a great distance. Here is what they saw.

Our great armies from all the eighteen nations or provinces came together as one army. All our soldiers kneeled to the ground, and none were standing. Nothing was in view except for a bowed body of our troops. Then to the surprise of all, a great gallery of our musicians began to sound the shofar horn. The first sound was that of the Teki'ah.

When the one long blast sounded, announcing the coming of the Messiah, with that sound King Nebuchadnezzar trotted to the highest point of the mount on his snow-white horse, Purity. All eyes were upon him with his scarlet cape blowing in the wind. We had twelve soldiers, placed in a position as head of the twelve tribes. They arose from the ground and each one held the banner with the coat of arms of their respective tribe. Their armor shined like new gold in the hot of the sun. The Jews recognized this as the glory of their GOD. Then came the next sound, the Sheva rim. This was three short blasts as if the beating of the heart, anxious to be near their Messiah. This was a call to the heads of each of the families. We had our soldiers positioned as the Jewish families of old were positioned around the Tabernacle of Moses. Each head of the family arose from their position on the ground, and each raised their family standard with the family coat of arms. They each had armor shining like the silver of the Jewish Redemption.

The Jews knew that something supernatural was being played out to them as they began to cry with a broken heart and a contrite spirit. Then our musicians raised their shofars a third time and in unison they gave the sound of the Teruah. This was a sound of nine short blasts signifying time was running out and they had better hurry, or they would miss seeing their Messiah, the new ruler, King Nebuchadnezzar. As this sound ended, the rest of our entire army of 601,550 soldiers stood to their feet within the proper tribe and the proper family position. We had struck the inner man of each Jew present as they wept openly as to what they saw.

There before their eyes, as they looked down from the mountain into the valley below, was the perfect formation of the star out of Jacob, or the Star of David. It was the sacred emblem of the Jewish people. It was the sign of the Messiah and now had played into the hands of the Babylonians. Our soldiers had duplicated the very formation as did the children of Israel, around about the tabernacle of Moses, when they came out of Egypt. The sign of their freedom from Egypt was now becoming the sign of their bondage to the Babylonians. We released these leaders from the area atop of the hill and sent them back to their fellow citizens with instructions to tell them what they had seen and the enormity and power of our army.

Each was instructed to tell every citizen of Judah and Jerusalem that they were to lay down their arms and surrender peacefully or pay the price of being foolish with their lives and the lives of their families. We began to round up the Jews for their trials.

THEIR TRIALS BEGIN (II SAMUEL 8:2 KJV)

We set up many tribunal councils, six hundred and sixty-six tribunals in all, throughout Judah and within Jerusalem. As the prisoners were lined up, we explained to them that they were to be tried by their own laws and punishments to be conducted as did their King David of long, long ago. When King David tried the people, if some were found innocent they would be given strips on the back as a fool and left alive. King David had three horsemen, skilled in using a whip or a cat of nine tails, laced with barbed irons, just as a fisherman would use to catch fish.

The captive would be laid face down upon the ground and a lone rider with a writer's inkhorn would ride from the North and place the mark of the Jewish Star of David upon the left heel of the victim. The three horsemen in one line would then administer punishment by lashes upon the back and the pour them full of sea salt. The victim was then left alive as a fool. Next came the death sentence.

If the person on trial was found guilty, they received the death sentence, the person would be tied face up and stationed to the ground. A rider upon a white horse would come from the North. The North country was the inheritance area for Israel. This rider would have an ink horn and would place the Jewish Star of David upon the person's forehead and mark them for death. Then six riders upon white, black, speckled, and bay horses would take their place upon either side of the victim, forming two lines for death as King David had done. The riders administered their stripes to the front of the body and face of those sentenced to a death of horror, (2 Samuel 8:2 KJV).

THE DEATH OF HORROR

There were two deaths of horror. One was the sword through the liver and the other was the bashing in of a person's head. Many sites were set up on all sides of the city for the victims scheduled to die by having the sword thrust through the liver. I brought forth and set before the people gods of stone and metal. I wanted them to look upon what they had been worshiping. I encouraged them to call upon their gods for deliverance. Then within their voices I heard their hearts cry unto the Lord. They looked toward their Wailing Wall, the wall of the daughter of Zion. The wall born of wisdom. It was then that tears ran down like a river by day and night. I said unto the Hebrew GOD, "Give thyself no rest and let not the apple of thine eye cease" (Lam. 2:18 KJV). Then across the countryside at our sites of torture at the exact same hour, I called for all the hostages doomed for death to be brought forth. These hostages were arranged so that they stood to the left of the gods of stone and metal. This became a mockery before the eyes of the Jews. His army took their swords of gold and struck the hostages through the liver. This was a painful and long-suffering death. The bloodcurdling screams were as an echo across the desert and fell deep within the ears of all living. The cries and pleads for mercy went on day unto day and night after night. I looked and I saw them fallen by the sword. Slain in the day of my anger. I have killed and not pitied. In the day of the Lord, none escaped nor remained (Lam. 2:21- KJV). I had recalled somewhere in my studies that this was the way it would be when the Messiah would come. He would rule all nations with a rod of iron.

Just for a moment, "I used to think, I am the first and I am the last and beside me there is no God" (Isa. 44:6 KJV). Then again, I looked, and I beheld, "those that were wrapped in the swaddling band I have consumed" (Lam. 2:22 KJV).

Once again, my thinking was that when the Messiah comes the young children, wrapped in the swaddling band of their prayer shawl showing their birth record, would also be slain.

When my eyes beheld this sight, then prayed I unto the GOD with no name whom I knew not and I said, "Help me, oh Lord, GOD: save me according to thy mercy: that they, your people Israel, may know that this is thy hand of vengeance upon them and that thou O Lord has done it" (Psa. 109:26-27 KJV).

It was then that an unmistakable voice said unto me, "I will remove Judah also out of my sight as I have removed Israel and I will cast off this city, Jerusalem, which I have chosen and the house of which I said, My Name shall be there" (II Kings 23:27 KJV).

I lamented for the brotherhood that had been broken between Judah and Israel. I understood that no man can withstay the hand of the Hebrew GOD or say unto him, "Why are you doing this?" I returned unto myself and set about to bring the second great death to past. That night I had a troubling dream.

TROUBLING DREAM

That very same night after I had met with our military council and generals, I was very tired and had fallen asleep while sitting in my chair. As had been my custom when I awoke, I wrote the dream down. Here is my dream.

I saw a great lion sitting upon a golden throne with a rainbow 'round about his head. He held in his right hand a book from Babylon. The book was sealed with the royal wax made by the art of the apothecary by a special trained pharmacist devoted entirely for service to the lion.

The lion took the book in his paw and began to melt the wax and to open the book. When he had opened the book and loosened the wax, there was a great earthquake. The sun became black as a sackcloth made of hair.

I saw the paw of the lion take hold of a fig tree standing nearby. He began to shake the fig tree fiercely in his anger. The figs and the leaves began to fall to the earth.

As the figs fell, they became as Abraham's stars falling from heaven. The heavens opened as the Jewish rabbi would open the scroll of the law.

Then I beheld as the mountains and the rocks began to fall upon the stars and crush them to pieces. The stars became as people and ran but could not hide themselves from the face of the lion, who sat upon the throne. The lion said in a great voice as if the thunder would roar, "The great day of GOD's wrath has come and who shall be able to stand?" Troubled by this dream, I brought in my counsellors and wise men and prophets. I placed the dream before them, and they gave me the interpretation of the dream.

THE INTERPRETATION OF THE DREAM

My wise men said, "Thou O Great King, Nebuchadnezzar, art a descendant of Esau of old, the grandson of Abraham. Esau's father, Isaac, had no blessing for him but told him one day he would come into his dominion. You are the chosen seed, and the dominion of the Jewish nation is now before you to inherit. GOD of the Hebrews has chosen you to open the book of the genealogy. The rainbows around about your head are the many nationalities of people you have conquered, and they now worship your crown and are loyal to you. The revelation from the book to be opened by you will cause much confusion and darkness in your Kingdom and that of the Jews. God has chosen you as his servant to fulfill his promise. You are chosen to come into your dominion.

"The Jewish people, as the stars promised to Abraham, will try to run and hide as the stones that fall upon them will remind them of the laws they broke, and the broken promises made to GOD. They shall seek safety in the mountains and the caves, but they cannot escape your hand.

"Oh, King, this dream is given and is true to remind you of the task the Hebrew GOD has placed before you. You shall not fail in your mission."

The next few days my countenance changed. It was as if I became two different kings. This was most troubling to me and my peace of mind, and it began to interfere with my ability to think clearly. I knew I must get back to the task at hand, so I focused upon the second death.

THE SECOND DEATH

I had made preparations for the second death. My stonecutters had finished carving a huge human skull into the east side of the mound, where upon I stood directing the battle by day and night. The skull was visible to all in the holy temple and the city of Jerusalem. The stonecutters made large rooms inside of the skull's cavities, eyes, nose, and mouth. Our troops took great teams of horses and many, many laborers of our Jewish captives and forced them to begin to tear great stones from their Jewish western Wailing Wall. The people that refused were slain in front of their fellow Jews.

We took the stones and made torture tables out of them and placed them into the cavities of the skull. Huge fires were built to the rear of the cavities. These fires would burn both by day and by night to illuminate the scene of the second great death.

Our captives, appointed to die, were bound one to another. Our executioners took stone mallets covered with melted gold and smashed their heads upon the stones. The cries for mercy filled the airwaves and from one day unto the night and from one night unto the day the sound of death was heard.

Bodies of the slain were laid all around the city of Jerusalem. After many, many days a wall of dead bodies could be seen. These also included our troops. Blood was carried in golden pictures to the cistern outside of the gate and made its way into the Euphrates River to find the blood of all the Jewish ancestors of old. The bodies of the dead were burned and a great stitch of burned flesh filled the air.

After the bodies of the dead were burned, the ashes were loaded onto wagons and teams of white colts pulled the ashes to the Euphrates River, where they were dumped. The ashes were so many that they mixed with the red clay and adhered together and made a hardened surface. This is an ideal I took with me back to Babylon, where I joined the Tigers River to the Euphrates River for our own protection against future invasions. My engineers are also drawing up plans to make a wall around Babylon as the Jews have done here in Jerusalem.

Our armies spent almost three and one-half years here in Jerusalem and Judah. I have rounded up the valuable items of gold and silver, which I will take back with me to Babylon. I have also taken captive Jeconiah, son of Jehoiakim, the King of Judah. I have left behind a Jewish king to rule over the people; he is King Zedekiah and I have also left with the people a prophet by the name of Jeremiah.

I have left behind many of my soldiers and many people to aid the Jews in helping to rebuild and repair the damage we caused. They will always remember the Hill of the Skull, as it has now become a permanent landmark for the history books along with the Battle of Armageddon. I concluded the first great woe as prophesied by the prophets of old with the words from the mouth of the Hebrew GOD, will long be remembered.

I have often wondered about the two other great woes my father told me would come. My job is not finished and one day I shall return, but for right now I am happy to be back home in Babylon.

BACK HOME IN BABYLON

I have been back now for only six months. I spent three and one-half years in Jerusalem. It is now 602 B.C.E. My mind is still playing tricks and I find myself having a series of dreams.

This is the first dream I had since being back on my home soil. Here is the dream. I saw the lion upon his throne. I saw four great angels standing upon the four corners of the earth and holding the mighty wind tightly that the wind could not blow upon the earth, nor the sea, nor any tree. I saw a fifth angel, coming from the east; he had in his hand a seal and he said to the angels with the wind, "Do not dare hurt the earth, the sea, or the trees until I have sealed the servants of our GOD in their foreheads."

I saw the angel seal 144,000 Jews. There were 12,000 from each of the twelve tribes. Then I saw a great multitude of people and tongues and they took their place and stood before the throne, whereupon sat a great lion.

I looked and to my astonishment, the lion gave his seat of authority to a lamb. The people rejoiced.

The people were all clothed in white and took palms in their hand and said, "Salvation to our GOD, which setteth upon the throne and unto the lamb."

And all the angels stood around about the throne and I saw the elders and the four beasts as they fell before the throne on their face to worship God upon the throne. They said, "Blessings, glory, and wisdom, and thanksgiving and honor and power and might be unto God for ever and ever," amen.

Then a voice said unto me, "What are these which are arrayed in white robes and where do they come from?" I answered, "I do not know. Only you know." Then the voice answered, "These are those who have come through great tribulations and have washed their robes and made them white in the blood of the lamb. They stand before the throne of GOD and serve him day and night. He that setteth on the throne shall dwell among them." Troubled within about the dream as I always am, I called for my interpreters to stand before me and give the interpretation of my dream.

THE INTERPRETATION

After listening to this dream, my counsellors held a discussion among themselves. Then came before me Countstar, the spokesperson for my council, and said unto me, "Oh, King Nebuchadnezzar, your bravery has been noticed by the Hebrew GOD. Your mind has been wearied, and a rest is due you. God hath given you this dream. The four great angels which the king saw are four great rulers which God will send unto you to help rule your Kingdom. These rulers will take hold of the flesh of all men within the four corners of your Kingdom. These leaders will be faithful to you, and they will not allow the might wind, the breath of life to be taken from your loyal subjects. They will not allow rumors to establish a sea of doubt and unbelief in relationship to your Kingdom. The trees, which are your troops, will be held harmless by the wisdom of these four rulers.

"The fifth angel which sounded his voice is the voice of the Hebrew GOD, who guided you safely through your conquest and has brought you into your dominion.

"His voice advises that you choose out from among all the Jewish captives 12,000 from each of the twelve tribes of Israel. You are advised to set upon them the seal of your love so that they are protected from those within your Kingdom who are violent and who would love to kill all your captive Jews. The multitudes of people are those that have pledged allegiance to you as their ruler. To them you are the God in whom they have placed their trust and loyalty. You are the great lion who makes decisions just and true.

"Your decision is to share your throne with a yet unknown child; he is the lamb. He will be one of the four rulers and the wisdom of God is within him. When your Kingdom is divided among these four rulers, the people will applaud your leadership and shout salvation to our king.

"All the aged Jews that walk in your Kingdom will unite the four sects of Jews and your Kingdom will become twice as strong as it was. You will know of this ruler through a divine experience that will bring you into contact with him. Oh, King, the dream is sure and steadfast and much to the advantage of both you and your Kingdom."

Heaviness lifted from me and I proceeded to go about my task of ruling my Kingdom.

It was in the year 595 B.C.E., eleven years since I first invaded Israel, that I met the young boy Daniel, who was predestinated of GOD to be the lamb to sit upon my throne and govern with me. He and his three first cousins were to be a great aid to me in governing the Kingdom, just as the dream had been fulfilled.

Daniel gave the interpretation to my dream that none of my counselors could give. He gave me the dream and the interpretation, thereby dividing my Kingdom into three territories.

I became more restless in thinking about the gold that I had left behind in Jerusalem. No one seemed to know if a Holy Candelabra or the Ark of the Covenant ever really existed or was its imagination. I for one believed these items did exist because our Babylonian records had them listed and described them perfectly. Then I had another dream.

It was as if my dreams were a frying pan and were constantly frying my brain. I awoke one night in fright, as usual. After I had forgotten the dream which Daniel remembered, I had developed a habit of writing down my dreams. Here is what I wrote down on parchment.

MY DREAM

I saw four angels that stood before God; they each had a trumpet. Another angel came and offered prayer and burnt incense before the king, upon the altar. The prayers and incense became a sweet smell of savor unto God upon the throne.

Fire from the altar was cast into the earth. The seven angels prepared to blow their trumpets.

The first angel sounded, and hail and fire mingled with blood was cast upon the earth and one-third part of the trees and grass was burnt up.

The second angel sounded. It was as if a majestic mountain burning with fire was cast into the sea and one-third part of the sea became as blood. And one-third of the creatures of the sea died and one-third part of the ships were destroyed.

The third angel sounded, and a great star fell from heaven and fell into one-third part of the rivers and upon the fountains of the waters. The name of the star is wormwood and one-third part of the waters became bitter and many people died.

The fourth angel sounded, and one-third part of the sun was smitten. Also, one-third part of the moon and one-third part of the stars were smitten. The earth became dark, by day and night, and no light was seen. The voice thundered loud and clear, saying, "Loose the four angels that stand guard over the River Euphrates. For these will be prepared for a year, a month, and a day to slay one-third part of men." I looked and I beheld, and the number was 200,000 horses and the riders had breastplates of fire, jacinth, and brimstone. Their horses had heads of lions and smoke, fire, brimstone came out of their mouth and one-third part of men were killed.

The rest of the men repented not of the idle works of their hands, the idol worship of their gods, their murders, sorceries, nor fornications of thefts. Then I heard a voice say, "Woe for the judgments upon mankind have come up before GOD." Once again there came before me my chief counsellor, Countstar.

Countstar said, "Oh, great and mighty King that rules all nations with a rod of iron, God has sent unto you four angels to guide you into battle again. You are a vessel of honor unto GOD. Your army will once again advance toward Jerusalem and Judah. GOD hath called you to his altar. GOD will bless you.

"Daniel will bless you as you gather four of your top major generals and the elite troops of your army at GOD's altar of fire.

"After you have received the blessing and GOD has smiled upon you, go and prepare yourself for battle. The fire which you saw burning upon the altar is the fire of GOD's vengeance. This is the fire you will take with you to Jerusalem.

"Fire will be carried by all four of your generals and their armies to the four hillsides and four corners of Jerusalem.

"Your first major general will use oil to burn one-third of all the fruit-bearing trees and the fields of green grass. As the fire burns the darkened smoke from the oil will fill the air. No more fruit for food nor green grazing grass for the cattle.

"Your second army under the direction of your second major general will take many thousands of men and will cut down many trees and pile them high on many barges, soaking them in oil. Teams of great horses will be used to pull the barges down to the river's edge.

"The barges will be lit with the fire of GOD's jealously and set afloat on the waters. One-third of all the ships and boats upon the waters will be burnt and destroyed. The vessels used for fishing will be no more. Your soldiers will slaughter one-third of the men who occupy these ships. Their blood will be poured into the sea. Those that fish and feed the people will be no more. The fish will also die.

"One-third of the fish and all living creatures will die, from the blood poured into the waters. Fish to feed the people will be less and less. Now comes the plague from the third angel.

"The Star of Wisdom will guide your third general. The army under this general's command will bring ton after ton of wormwood to the city of Jerusalem and Judah.

"Wormwood will be dumped into the cisterns, wells, and river waters. One-third part of all the waters shall be made bitter and many people will die from the bitterness of wormwood. Behold the light of the fourth angel will bring darkness.

"The fourth angel will guide your fourth great major general in a different type of warfare. His army will bring oil. This oil will be twice as much as had been brought by your other generals.

"Many fires will be set and rage through the land. The black smoke from the burning oil will only allow one-third of the light of the moon, stars, and sun to shine through by day and by night. The darkness of death will be a constant companion to the people as they breathe and die from the smoke inhalation. Last of all your land army will be both physical and psychological. Death will be the call for all within the city of Jerusalem and in Judah, the smoke of the great whore of Babylon will be seen for miles. Two hundred thousand of your finest equestrian and horses will be made ready for this battle. Fear will be in all the inhabitants of the land as they look upon the horses.

"King Nebuchadnezzar, you shall have thousands times thousands and thousands more of your goldsmiths and your silversmiths and workers of fine metal prepare armor for your soldiers and the horses upon which they will ride. The workers of fine metal will design and make armor after the appearance in your dream. The horses and riders will have breastplates of polished silver. This will be like unto a mirror and will reflect the light from the burning fires all around them.

"The reflection will be the appearance of red from jacinth and burning fires of damnation of hell and brimstone. The heads of the armor of the horses shall cast fear upon all that look thereon.

"The armor for the horse's head shall be designed to look like unto the head of a lion. The bridle will take on the appearance of the teeth of a lion, set around about.

"The reflective appearance of the polished silver and gold shall shine and give the reflection of fire and brimstone coming out of the mouth of the horses.

"The armor that fits over the back of the horse shall have a sword in the appearance of a serpent and shall cut coming and going as the horse moves his tail. All that come close to the horse shall be killed.

"These riders will kill one-third of all the people that are still alive. Be not dismayed, oh King, to learn that a remnant of the people left shall 'not repent of their works of their hands, that they should not worship devils and idols of gold, silver, brass, and stone, and of wood, which neither can see nor hear, nor walk. Neither repented they of their murders, nor of their sorceries, nor of their fornications, nor of their thefts' (Rev. 9:20-21 KJV).

"I and my army returned home from Jerusalem for a second time. The streets were lined with Babylonians and other people of different nationalities who had lived well under my leadership. They greeted us with shouts, cheers, saying, 'The great whore of Babylon has fallen.' After settling in for a few weeks, I began to have second thoughts about the Jewish people and why they repented not of their fowl deeds against GOD. I thought that maybe I had called an end to the destruction too soon."

AFTER DESTRUCTION END

After time, times, and one-half time, I called for an end to the destruction. I did not spare, neither did I have pity. I repaid the people according to the ways of their sin and abominations I found during the invasion. The wrath of GOD had fallen upon the multitude of the people. The punishment was upon the innocent as well as the guilty. GOD had reached down to the third and fourth generations. I watched as they blew the trumpet and sounded the alarm for their army to respond and come to battle against our forces. No army could fight against the strong arm of GOD.

GOD had sent the sword without the great city to slay all within Judah. GOD had sent pestilence and famine within the walls of the city. I watched as many ran to the mountains like doves go to the valley. Every one of them was mourning for their own iniquity.

These survivors had hands that were feeble and knees that were as weak as water. Shame was upon their faces; although they had shaved their heads and beards confessing their vows as a Nazarene, it did them no good. It was a little too late.

They tried to bribe my armed men with silver and gold, which they threw into the streets at their feet. The strong, destructive hand of GOD could not stay with the works of the flesh. They had sewed to the flesh and now they were reaping corruption of the flesh.

I watched as the holy ornament and symbol of GOD's strength, the Star of David, was torn from all the flags that had been gathered from all of Jerusalem and Judah and set a fire upon Solomon's porch. Many soldiers from the many countries I had conquered cheered and laughed the people to scorn. This I stopped immediately as the smoke from the fire arose high over the porch.

The black smoke hovered over Solomon's porch and blackened the council chambers just above. All light from the sun was blotted out and the darkness was as thick as sackcloth made of camel's hair.

GOD had done just as the Prophet Ezekiel said he would do: "I have set my holy emblem, the Star of David, far from them and have given it into the hands of strangers for a prey and to the wicked of the earth for a spoil, and they have polluted it" (Ezek. 8:20-21).

Every day my commanders would come to me and say, "The people have had enough, and they are repenting and seek peace from the hand of their GOD." The people of Jerusalem sought a vision of deliverance from their prophets, but they were slain before their eyes and the laws and Torah scrolls were burned in piles throughout the city. The banners of GOD's love were burned also as the people looked upon the sight and cried openly before the face of their GOD.

I said unto the people, "Your GOD hath done unto you after your ways and according to the fleshly desires of your hearts. He hath judged you so that you shall know that besides him there is none other" (Ezek. 8:22-27).

I, King Nebuchadnezzar, rested from my obedience to the calling placed upon me by Daniel's GOD. I prepared to return to my homeland.

MY HOMELAND

I returned home for the second time and, with the help of Daniel, began solving the problems that my country and I were facing. Daniel took the lead role.

I fully restored Daniel's Hebrew name and took away the Babylonian name I gave him.

The name Belteshazzar was given him after my son's name. In helping to solve my problems, Daniel ended up in the lion's den. However, I placed the seal of Daniel's GOD upon the den of the lions. The seal of the Star of David must have pleased GOD, for Daniel's life was spared and the jaws of the lions were locked. One problem came after another, and I became restless and had another troubling dream.

MY DREAM

In this dream I saw another mighty angel come down from the heavens, clothed with a cloud. He had a rainbow upon his head and his face was as the sun and feet as pillars of fire.

In his hand he had a little book. He sat his right foot upon the sea and his left foot upon the earth. He cried with a loud voice as a lion would roar. When he cried, I heard seven thunders utter their voices.

When the seven thunders uttered their voices, I was about to write and I heard a voice from heaven say, "Seal up these things which the seven thunders uttered and write them not." The angel standing upon the sea and the land lifted his hand to heaven and swore by him who liveth for ever and ever, who created all things, that there should be time no longer. The voice said, "Go and take the little book from the angel." So I went to the angel and said, "Give me the little book." He said, "Take it and eat it up and it shall make your belly bitter, but in your mouth it shall be as sweet as honey."

I took and I did eat the book and it was sweet in my mouth but bitter in my stomach.

The voice said, "You must prophesy again before many people, nations, tongues, and kings."

Once again, I was confused as to the meaning of my dream.

I called together all the wise men of Babylon, the magicians, astrologers, Chaldeans, and the soothsayers. Then said they unto me, "The dream is far from our being. Call forth the Hebrew Daniel; he will say unto the dream and its meaning."

I said unto my chief advisor, "Call me Daniel."

Then came forth Daniel and he said thus unto me. The mighty angel which they saw, Old King, is the angel of death and he is clothed with a cloud as a glorious paradise of GOD. His feet are as fire to burn up the chaff of your Adam nature. The rainbows upon his head are the many nations and people that GOD hath brought before your throne for you to rule over. His face shines with the righteousness of GOD, which you have seen many times."

His hand did hold the book of life in which is inscribed the names of all men, which also holds your name.

He hath set one foot upon the land. This is the great country of Babylon and one foot upon the sea of doubt and unbelief, wherein you have lived a great deal of your life.

The cry is the cry of death, and it is as the cry of the Messiah for the Jewish people. The loudness of his voice will awake the voices of the seven sons of thunder.

You were given the names of the seven voices. Before you could write them down, you were ordered by the voice of GOD not to write them down. Therefore, the seven names are no more. The angel of death hath answered unto GOD and hath said that your life is near to an end and the great country of Babylon will fall.

The angel of death has directed that you take the book of your life and relive it within your mind. You are to eat it and, in your mouth, your life in the beginning has been sweet as honey but the latter end as your life's journey nears its end, your life has become bitter as digested food in the stomach.

However, before you are gathered to those that have outstripped you and gone on, GOD has called you to gather your many people under your rule and authority. The many nations you rule over will once again hear from your own tongue what should befall Jerusalem, as it is time for the third great woe to fall upon GOD's people and put an end to the Battle of Armageddon.

THE THIRD WOE, ARMAGEDDON'S END

I regained my strength and the courage of a lion returned unto me. I called for my captain of the guard, Nebuzaradan, and placed him in charge of all my command. All kings, armies, and people of war were at his command. I sent him forth for the third time in accordance with GOD's word to tear down the rest of the Jewish Wailing Wall so that not one stone would be left standing upon another.

He was ordered to raze and tear down every wall of the city and every building so that none was left standing, with the exception of the Tower of the Flock, built by Jacob of old.

I ordered him to bring back no captives and to charge not nor chase after those that escaped and ran to the mountains. So my story was nearing an end just as Ezekiel, the great Jewish prophet, has said.

"GOD is sending a sword of vengeance upon this city. A sword that has been polished so that it may glitter and shine and be seen. A sword that has been sharpened and it is now in the hand of the slayer. The sword will be doubled a third time. So all that the Jews once knew they know no more because they violated the first commandment of GOD, which said unto them, 'Thou shalt have no other gods before me' (Exodus 20:3 KJV). Their worship of the small 'g' gods brought destruction. As GOD hath said, 'All nations that forget me shall be turned into hell'" (Psa. 9:17 KJV).

So the great whore of Babylon hath fallen and shall arise no more. Never again shall the nation of Israel bow and worship the small "g" gods of the world. A lesson from their GOD has been well learned. GOD hath chosen them as his seed to be the first to enter into his Kingdom.

With the assignment that GOD gave unto me completed, I settled in to rule my Kingdom and to solve the many problems that would face me in the bitter end as prophesied by GOD.

Daniel was by my side when the death angel returned to pay me a visit. Here are the last words I said in the presence of Daniel and my counselors: "I lift mine eyes unto heaven and with my understanding I bless you, oh Lord Most High and God of Daniel."

I now say unto you as I repent, and you alone doeth according to your own goodwill and pleasure among the inhabitants of the earth and in the armies of heaven. None can stay your hand or say unto you, "What doest thou?"

I thank you for the time when you allowed my reasoning to return unto me. You restored unto me the glory of my Kingdom.

I am privileged with the last words of my breath to say unto you, "Thy Kingdom come, and thy will be done, in my earthly body of dust as your will is also done in heaven."

I remember when you returned unto me my brightness and wisdom of my mind. You added excellent majesty unto me and my Kingdom. It was then that all my counsellors and lords sought unto to me for leadership once again.

It is now that I, King Nebuchadnezzar, praise and extol and honor you as the king over heaven and earth. All your works are truth, and all your ways are judgments and all that walk in pride, you can abase or bring low. With these words I now close my eyes in peace and join you in the paradise of death, as within my mind and heart I cry out that Daniels GOD is GOD, Hear O Israel.

THE DEATH OF A GREAT KING

Babylon: King Nebuchadnezzar, the great Babylonian king, has outstripped his lords and counsellors and has gone to sit down with Daniel's GOD in the paradise of death.

He went through lifechanging experiences by living out his dreams and visions. His journey increased his faith and delivered him out of the sea of doubt and unbelief. His faith in GOD grew and his Kingdom flourished because of the Jews, whom he placed in charge of helping him to rule over his Kingdom. His Kingdom never departed from him during the many years of his reign. He came to the throne at the age of thirty-two in 608 B.C.E.

He was born in 640 B.C.E. and died in 561 B.C.E., making his stay upon this earth three score, ten and nine years. He was credited with leading three campaigns of war against the Jews. History records these as the three great woes. The war collective was known as Armageddon. The years of his invasion as recorded by Ezekiel, where the first invasion came in 606 B.C.E. The second came eleven years later in 595 B.C.E. and the final blow came in 581 B.C.E. He lived twenty years after his conquest of Jerusalem and Judah ended.

He died of natural causes. Those close to him said that he had a great desire to meet Daniel's GOD, the GOD with no name.

In his later years he became a firm believer in the power of GOD that Daniel's GOD possessed. His achievements were many.

He began his military career as a young soldier under his father's command. He defeated the Egyptians at Carchemish and brought Syria under his father's command.

In the year that he became king, he began to expand his empire and planned and conducted an invasion of Israel. They brought him fame and established Babylon as the wonder Kingdom of the ancient world. Among his ancient accomplishments was his completion of the royal palace. He also completed building an underground passage and a stone bridge connecting two parts of the city that were separated by the Great River Euphrates. He tripled the aligned walls around the city so that six horse-drawn chariots could run abreast around the city walls. This with other ideas he brought with him back from his invasion of Jerusalem. He restored the Lake of Sippar and opened the port of the Persian Gulf. He built the Mede Wall between the Tigris River and the Euphrates River to help protect his city against an invasion from the North (Wikipedia). His career was highlighted by another wonder of the world.

He designed and constructed the Hanging Gardens of Babylon and constructed eight gates leading into the city. His most elaborate gate was the Gate of Ishtar. Many say these ideals came from his study of the Jewish history and the feats that King Solomon had completed. He will long be remembered for erecting the golden image of himself. It overlooked the plain and could be seen by the many ships coming and leaving Babylon. The image was ninety feet tall and nine feet wide and was made from six hundred and sixty-six talents of gold.

His heritage by nationality was having a Babylonian father and a Jewish mother. He has left behind to mourn his passing Daniel, who was like a son unto him and his senior advisor in the affairs of the Kingdom. He also is survived by son Belshazzar, who became a ruler of one-half of his Kingdom, and his loving wife of Jewish descent.

His body was laid to rest in the peace and quiet of the Babylonian Hanging Gardens. His tomb was made of white marble and royal gold and facing the statue of himself standing on the plain and overlooking the river.

He asks that his tomb be sealed with the emblem of the Jewish Star of David and the Holy Candelabra, a relic that he was possessed with finding but never succeeded. Daniel saw that his wish was carried out and the emblems were made of royal gold. May he long be remembered as a faithful servant of GOD just as the prophets of old had written. "I am giving all these lands into the hand of King Nebuchadnezzar of Babylon, my servant. All nations shall serve him and his son and his son's son. Then I will send many great kings and nations to serve themselves of him. Until that time comes all nations shall put their neck under the yoke and bond of the King of Babylon" (Jeremiah 27:6-8, Ezekiel 21 KJV). He has helped to write *Jews of Babylon: The Final Chapter.*

Daniel completed his report and the Jewish people vowed that they would never let their people get into idol worship. There was much weeping and gnashing of teeth for their ancestors of old that had outstripped them and gone on. Joash said to the Jews, "As Daniel has noted to us, the keeping of records is a very important part of our heritage. We are from this day forward required to record all important aspects of our return. Zerubbabel and the children of Jeshu of the remnant have already begun the journey with many labors and skilled workers. They are taking the first steps of our renewed vow. We hope to hear of their progress before too long."

THE PROGRESS OF THE REMNANT AND THEIR RETURN

The following pages are a collection of notes, memos, and letters from the files of those who worked so hard and labored long to bring Israel back into line with GOD and his commandments.

One must remember that GOD bought Israel for the two tablets of the Ten Commandments. The commandments serve to remind Israel of the history of their marriage unto strangers and falling victim to serving the little 'g' gods of their strange wives.

Every Passover the holy words "Chad Gadya" are said by a child to remind them that GOD bought and separated them from the world with his commandments. Many tears will be shed as you read of the worries, fears, and struggles of the Jews as the remnant returns to rewrite their Torah, put the Torah laws back into practice, rebuild their walls and city, and trace the genealogy of the star out of Jacob, promised unto them by GOD. Their records began with a memo from Zerubbabel.

DATE: DAY 10 OF TISHRI: 534 B.C., SEPTEMBER 10

To: Ezra and the Council of Ekklesia called out to God's service
From: Zerubbabel, Jeshu and the children of the remnant of Israel
Peace of Our GOD unto you:

We are pleased to be back upon the soil and the site of our first great temple, built by King Solomon in the year 1087 B.C. After seventy years in Babylon, the feeling is most refreshing to be back home even though the work is extremely hard. The presence of GOD is with us, and the shout of a king is among us as we work. This morning we noticed a breeze stirring in the leaves of the mulberry trees. We hardly know where to begin for the formidable task that lies just ahead. This is the seventh month of Tishri, and two years have passed since we first left Babylon in the same month in the year of our release. Jeshu and I drew up the blueprint and the skilled masons built the altar after like manner of our father Abraham did on Mount Mariah. We recalled that Elijah did the same on Mount Carmel and so did Moses on Mount Hebron. We have followed the commandments by law from Moses in constructing our altar. We have set the altar upon its bases, for fear was upon us because the people on the other side of the river and around about us do not accept us.

We knew the altar of GOD had to be facing the right direction and had to be the perfect weight and shape in order for him to accept our offerings.

They want no Jews in this area! However, we offered burnt offerings, morning and evening. We have also kept the Feast of Tabernacles. We have offered burnt offerings by number according to the custom as the duty of every day required from the instructions given by Ezra upon the self-same night of our release. We do not understand everything we are doing. After this we offered the continual burnt offering at the new moons and all the set feast of the Lord. Everyone also offered a freewill offering unto the Lord, as commanded. The offerings began the first day of the seventh month of the Holy Month of Tishri. We did all of this before we considered laying the foundation of the Holy House. I will update you on our foundation progress at the next writing.

Master masons continuing to spend many hours in perfecting the plans for the house given unto our hands by Daniel and written by Ezekiel (Ezek. 40-44 KJV).

Shalom

From: The appointed for the remnant, Zerubbabel, master builder, Jeshu, assistant to the master builder and the children of Israel.

(Ezra 3:1-6 KJV)

Date: Day 2 of Hesavan: 534 B.C., October 2
To: Ezra, and the Council of Ekklesia, called out for GOD's service
From: Zerubbabel, Jeshu and the Children of Israel

Ref.: Temple Foundation Progress Report

Peace of Our GOD:

We have given money unto the master mark masons and to the master builders. We have also given unto them meat and drink and oil unto them of Zion and to them of Tyre as they make journey to Tyre to bring cedar trees from Lebanon by way of Joppa. This was done in like manner as King Solomon had done and in accordance with the grant that King Cyrus of Persia had furnished us from the file of Ezra 3:7 KJV). Thus, the progress of getting materials to rebuild the temple has begun in our second year of arrival. I, along with the these plans, was scaled in proportion to what the Messiah's temple of flesh would measure when he comes as a dwelling place for GOD. We trust that those of you with the council, who are in Babylon, will look over the copies you have on hand and catch a vision of what we are doing.

Zerubbabel, Mater Builder

Jeshua, Assistant, and Children of Israel

FORMER BABYLONIAN RULER AND JEWISH PROPHET DIES

533 B.C., BABYLON: The great ruler, Daniel, completed his work and is now gathered with his people on the first day of Passover (Nissan) at the sixth hour. He is now at rest and stands in lot of his days, which have now ended upon this earth. Making his stay here upon this earth, three score, ten, and nine years.

Having been born in Jerusalem in 612 B.C. during the reign of Jehoiakim, King of Judah, he came to Babylon at the age of six. He came from Jerusalem to Babylon upon the shoulders of his friend, father, and great prophet, Ezekiel.

The year of his entrance into Babylon was 606 B.C. Once in Babylon he grew into adulthood and at the age of seventeen he was made ruler over the whole providence of Babylon by King Nebuchadnezzar. He found favor in the king's eyes because of his GOD-given gift of dream interpretations.

The GOD of Heaven often revealed secrets and even the deep secret things unto Daniel. Daniel will long be remembered for the many things he did to make life better for the Jewish people during their seventy years in captivity in Babylon. Many of these things he set in writing with pen and paper by his own hand. History will record that just three years prior to his death, he secured the release of the Jews from Babylon captivity.

Daniel sought council with King Cyrus of Persia even though the king's son denied him council with the king for one and twenty days. GOD sent an angel to rebuke the prince and secured Daniel's council with the king. Daniel was preceded in death by his beloved mentor, teacher, and father, Ezekiel, and a host of Jewish friends that outstripped him in death. Daniel had no known immediate family yet living. Daniel became a eunuch for the Kingdom of GOD's sake. Daniel was in possession of a rod given to him by his father. Daniel's wish was that the Rod of Inheritance be passed on to Nehemiah. A host of surviving Jews mourns Daniel, many of whom are in Jerusalem on this day engaging in the rebuilding of the city. Daniel was buried with the burial of royalty and laid to rest in Babylon. His tomb has been declared a holy shrouded landmark by the decree of King Darius, King of all Mead, and Persia. The grave site was marked by the planting of a Pomegranate which was placed there by a unidentified woman from out of Egypt.

So let it be written that Daniel should sleep a restful and peaceful sleep until it pleases GOD to raise him up again in the Resurrection.

Date: Day 18 of Zif, 533 B.C. (April 18)
To: Ezra, and the Council of Ekklesia
called out for the service of GOD
From: Zerubbabel, Jeshua, and the Children of Israel
Ref.: Temple Foundation Progress Report
As Such a Time:

You will be pleased to know that we have received the coming of this year with extraordinary joy since our arrival. It is now the second month of Zif (April) and I, Zerubbabel, the son of Shealtiel and Jeshua, the son of Jozadak and the remnant of our brethren, priest, the Levites, and all others that have come out of captivity unto Jerusalem, are making great progress.

The blueprints have now been finalized. They have been translated to make sense unto us. Materials for the house are all finished and gathered in.

We have appointed the Levities from twenty years old and upward to set forward the work of the house of the Lord. Jeshu with his sons and brethren, Kadmiel and his sons and the sons of Judah have collaborated well with the sons of Headed and their sons and their brethren, the Levities, and the foundations are now complete.

With the foundation of the house of the Lord laid, we have now set the priests in their apparel with trumpets and the Levities, the sons of Asaph, with cymbals to praise the Lord. After the ordinances of David, former King of Israel, and after the historical documents furnished to us by Daniel prior to our coming here.

All have joined in and have sung together, by course, in giving thanks unto the Lord because He is good for his mercy endured forever toward Israel. The people with one voice have shouted with a great shout when they praised the Lord, for the foundation of the house of the Lord is complete. We have among us some of the older men, who were only children when they came into captivity down in Babylon over seventy years ago. They are now well into age and are serving as priests and Levities and chief fathers over us.

These ancient men saw the temple, which was built by King Solomon, when they were young. Now, seeing its new foundation laid again is a little much for them. They wept the loudest. They shouted with a voice of thunder and were overcome with joy until they could shout no more. The shouts of joy could not be distinguished from the noise of weeping. The sound could be heard far off.

Peace in Prayer, Zerubbabel, Master Builder
Jeshua, Assistant to the Master Builder
And the Children of Israel, from the Records of Ezra 3:8-13

Day 12 of Zif: 533 B.C. (May 12)
To: Ezra, and the Council of Ekklesia, called out for God's service
From: Zerubbabel and Jeshua
Ref.: Daniel's Death
Most Humble Reverence:

We received the news from you that Daniel, our great prophet and ruler, had died on Passover of last month. We held a memorial ceremony for him. I have placed his obituary throughout our camps, and we have also run it in our Jerusalem newsletter. We will be sending you more progress reports and update, as our work is ongoing.

Keep in Favor with GOD,
Zerubbabel, Master Builder
Jeshua, Assistant to the Master Builder
And the Children of Israel

Date: Day 27 of Elul: 533 B.C. (August 27)
To: Ezra and the council of Ecclesia, for the service of GOD
From: Zerubbabel, Jeshua and the Children of Israel
Ref.: challenging times
Request Your Prayers:

Remorse and sorrow have invaded our camp. While we had begun work on the house of our Lord, the adversaries came unto us. These are those that hated the descendants of Judah and Benjamin. They heard that we were building the temple unto the Lord GOD of Israel. They came unto me and unto the chief of the fathers and said, "Let us build with you, for we seek your GOD as ye do and we also sacrifice unto him, as we have done since the time of Esar Haddon King of as 'Sur, which brought us up hither."

We knew them to be of the dark tribe, those that say they are Jews but are of the synagogue of Satan. We knew them to be up to no good.

I, Jeshua, and the rest of the chief fathers said unto them, "Ye have nothing to do with us to build a house unto our GOD. We ourselves together as one man will build unto the Lord GOD of Israel as King Cyrus, the King of Persia, hath commanded us."

Now, because we have refused their help and turned them away, these intruders have weakened our hands and troubled us.

They have hired counselors and protesters to come in and go against our people to halt our progress. They have infiltrated our ranks. These crooked counselors are questioning everything we have in writing from Cyrus King of Persia even unto Darius of King of Persia.

They have begun a letter-writing campaign to Ahasuerus and to Artaxerxes. This is troublesome unto us and is a hindrance to our progress. We have established a plan to obtain copies of their letters, since they will not forward copies of their correspondence unto us.

We will stay connected with you and request that you offer prayers up unto GOD on our behalf.

Shalom

Zerubbabel, Master Builder

Jeshua, Assistant to the Master Builder

And the Children of Israel

Records of Ezra 4:1-8

Date: Day 20 of Kisleve: 532 B.C.: December 20

To: Artaxerxes King in waiting, son of Darius

From: Thy faithful servants on this side of the river

Ref.: Rebellion against the Throne

Most Honorable Artaxerxes:

Thy servants, the men on this side of the river and at such a time as this. Be it known unto the king, your father, that the Jews which came up from thee to us are building a rebellious and a bad city and have set up the walls thereof and joined the foundations.

Do you know that if this city is built and the walls set up again, they will not pay toll, tribute and custom and so thou shall be in endanger of losing the revenue of the king? Now, because we have maintenance from the king's palace and it was not meant for us to see the king's dishonor, we sent and certified the king that a search may be made in the book of records of thy father. Conduct this search and thou shall find in the book of records and know that this city is a rebellious city and hurtful unto the king and provinces. In times past, they had a reputation of moved sedition, for which their city was destroyed, many years ago.

We certify the king that if this city be built again and the walls thereof set up by this means, thou shall have no portion on this side of the river.

Signed, In Your Service

Rehum, the Chief Chancellor

Shimshal, the Scribe the Dinaites, the Apharsathchites, the Tarpelites, the Apharsites, the Arcievites, the Babylonians, the Susanchites, the Dehivites, and the Elamites. We speak as one man, and we stand together on this issue.

Records of Ezra 4:9-16 KJV

Date: Day 4, Tebeth: 532 B.C, January 4
To: Rebum in Symaria and beyond the river
Ref.: Reply to your letter
Peace and Prosperity:

The letter which you sent unto the king has been plainly read before the king. The king hath commanded and a search hath been made, and it is found that this city of old time hath made insurrection against the kings and that rebellion and deviation have been made within.

There have been mighty kings also over Jerusalem who have ruled over all countries beyond the river and toll, tribute and custom was paid unto them. I give ye now commandment to cause these men to cease and that this city be not built, until another commandment shall be given from the king. Take heed now that ye fail not to do this. Why should damage grow to hurt the king?

Signed, Artaxerxes, King in Waiting for Darius (Arsames)
c/c Jews, The Remnant of Israel at Jerusalem
Records of Ezra 4:27-22

Memo: To the file of Ezra
Ref.: Notes of Zerubbabel
Date: Day 18 of Tebeth: 532 B.C. (January 18)

I offer this as a matter of record. I have taken this from a note that Zerubbabel sent to me. It saddens me to record this writing.

Zerubbabel wrote unto me: "Now, when the copy of Artaxerxes' letter was read before Rehum, and Shimshai the Scribe and their companions went up in haste to Jerusalem unto the Jews to make them to cease their work by force and power."

Records of Ezra 4:23 KJV

Memo: To the file of Ezra
Ref.: Notes of Zerubbabel
Date: Day 18 of Tebeth: 532 B.C. (January 18)

I offer more notes to my file for future reference. These notes are from the writings of Zerubbabel.

Zerubbabel said, "Then the prophets, Haggi the prophet and Zechariah the son of Iddo, prophesied unto the Jews that were in Judah and Jerusalem in the name of the GOD of Israel, even unto them. Then rose Zerubbabel, the son of Shealtiel, and Jeshua, the son of Jozadak, and began to build the house of GOD, which is at Jerusalem, and with them were the prophets of GOD helping them.

At the same time came to them Tatna, Governor on this side of the river and Shetharboznai and their companions and said thus unto them, "Who hath commanded you to build this house and to make up this wall?"

Then said we unto them after this manner, and then they inquired, "What are the names of the men that make this building?" But the eye of our GOD was upon the elders of the Jews that they could not cause them to cease work till the matter came to Darius, and they returned answer by letter concerning this matter.

Records of Ezra 5:1-5

Date: Day 2 of Zif: 529 B.C. (May 2)

To: King Darius

All Peace to You

From: Tatna, Governor on this side of the river. Shethar, Boznai and companions the Apharsachites

Ref.: Refusal to cease work

Be it known unto the king that we went unto the province of Judea, to the house of the great GOD, built with great stones and timber laid in the walls, and this work goeth fast on and prospered in their hands. Then we asked those elders and said unto them, "Who commanded you to build this house and to make up these walls?"

We asked their names also, to certify thee that we might write the names of the men that were the chief of them and thus they returned us answer, saying, "We are the servants of the God of Heaven and Earth and build the house that was built these many years ago, which the Great King of Israel, Solomon, built and set up. But after our fathers had provoked the GOD of Heaven unto wrath, he gave them unto the hand of Nebuchadnezzar, the King of Babylon, the Chaldean. Nebuchadnezzar destroyed this house and carried the people into Babylon. However, in the first year of Cyrus the king, who conquered Babylon, issued a decree to build this house of GOD. The vessels also of gold and silver of the house of GOD, which Nebuchadnezzar took out of the temple that was in Jerusalem, were brought into the temple of Babylon. Search and see if there is a decree that was made by King Cyrus to let this house of GOD be built in Jerusalem. If such a decree is found, then let it be the king's pleasure to send us a copy.

Signed in Peace,
Tatnal, Governor on this side of the river
Shetharboznia and Companions Spharsachit
Records of Ezra 5:6-17

Date: Day 4 of Tammuz: 529 B.C. (June 4)

To: Tatna, Governor and Shetharboznal, and companions the Apharsachites

From: King Darius
Ref.: Decree by King Cyrus
All Peace Continuing

I have searched the Store House of Records at your request and have found and do hereby furnish you a copy of the decree you have requested. I hope this brings your mind to rest about the issue.

I ordered you to abide by this decree.

Signed,
King Darius, King of Mead and Persia
See the decree as an attachment
c/c to Jerusalem

STORAGE DOCUMENT #A120QZC LOT3CTPG 4-C
CONCERNING THE RELEASE OF THE JEWISH PEOPLE
Official Document and Decree Dated Ten, Tishri 536 B.C.
By: King Cyrus, King of Persia
This document is page one of two pages.

In the first year of Cyrus the king, the same Cyrus the king made a decree concerning the house of GOD of Jerusalem.

Let the house be built in the place where they offered sacrifices, and let the foundations thereof be strongly laid. The height there of threescore cubits and the breath there of three score cubits with three rows of great stones and a row of new timber and let the expense be given out of the king's house. Also, let the gold and silver vessels of the house of GOD, which Nebuchadnezzar took forth out of the temple, which is at Jerusalem and brought to Babylon, be restored and brought again unto the temple, which is to be built at Jerusalem. Let everyone return to its place in the house of GOD. Moreover, I make a decree what ye shall do to the elders of these Jews for the building of this house of GOD. Take of the king's goods, even of the tribute beyond the river, for with the expense be given unto these men, that they be not hindered and that which they need of both young bullocks and rams and lambs and burnt offerings to the GOD of Heaven, wheat, salt, wine, and oil according to the appointment of the priests who are at Jerusalem. Let it be given unto them by day without fail that they may offer sacrifices of sweet savor unto the GOD of Heaven and pray for the life of the king and his sons.

Also, I made a decree that whosoever shall alter this word, let timber be pulled down from his house and begin to set it up and let him be hanged thereon. Also, let his house be made a dunghill for this. Let the GOD that hath caused his name to dwell there destroy all the kings and people that shall put forth their hand to the alter to destroy this house of GOD, which is to be at Jerusalem. I, Cyrus, have made this decree. See that it is done with great speed.

Done and signed by the hand of King Cyrus

I, Darius, strongly endorse and support this decree.

Done and signed by the hand of Darius, King of all Persia and Meads

Original decree issued this, the tenth day of Tishri, 536 B.C. (Atonement)

Retrieved from the file of Ezra 6:1-12 KJV

Memos to file of Ezra, Scribe of Israel

Date: Day 17 of Ab: 525 B.C. (July 17)

Ref.: Ezra's notes (Ezra 6:13)

Then it became final. Tatnal, Governor on this side of the river, and Shetharboznal and their companions did according to that which King Darius had sent unto them. So they did speedily.

Date: Day 25 Ab: 520 B.C. (July 25)

Ref.: Ezra's notes (Ezra 4:24) written from Zerubbabel

The work of the house eased for these long years but now is in the second year of the reign of Darius, King of Persia and Meads, the work has resumed.

Memos to file of Ezra, Scribe of Israel

Date: Day 3 Adar: 516 B.C. (March 3)

Ref.: Ezra's notes (Ezra 6:14-17) written from Zerubbabel

The elders, the eyes of Israel, built and they prospered through the prophesying of Haggai the prophet and Zechariah the son of Dido, and they built and finished it according to the commandment of the GOD of Israel and according to the commandment of Cyrus and Darius and Artaxerxes, the King of Persia. The house was finished on the third day of the month of Adar, which was the sixth year (March 3, 516 B.C.) of the reign of King Darius. We all kept the dedication of the house of GOD with immense joy.

Memos to the file of Ezra

Date: Day 21 Tammuz: 513 B.C. (June 21)

Ref.: My request to go to Jerusalem

Today the GOD of Heaven placed it upon my heart to request and receive permission from King Arsames (Darius) to travel to Jerusalem. It has been twenty years in the making, and I only know what Zerubbabel has written to me. I will be pleased to see what progress has taken place. I will carry with me the Torah law, which I and the council have almost finished writing after these twenty years. The Torah and work on the house were finished in the same year. I am most anxious to share the written Torah with the remnant and to guide them as we put the law back into practice as we gather again as a nation. Zerubbabel finished the major work three years ago and the work continues on the wall and the city. I know he will be pleased to review the work I have completed. Together we will begin researching the genealogy of the remnant.

Date: Day 22 Elul: 513 B.C. (August 11)

Ref.: Delay in travel

My plans are on hold. King Darius (Arsames) has taken sick and is in grave condition. His son, Xerxes (Artaxerxes), although not yet crowned king, is overseeing all the matters for his father. I have an appointment to see him next month to discuss my travel arrangements.

To: The file of Ezra

Date: Day 10, 513 B.C. (September 10, Trisha)

Ref.: Great News

Blessed be King Artaxerxes, son of Darius who, on this the most holy day of Atonement, has completed what his father started.

He has shown favor not only to me but to all the Jews who wish to go with me to Jerusalem. This is the beginning of another new year and is the twenty-third anniversary date of the release and decree by Cyrus that allowed Zeruberral to go and complete his work. Now I will lead a caravan to join the remnant and see for the first time our old homeland. We are anxious and ready to go. We offer this copy of his letter written unto us.

Date: Day 10 Tishri: 513 B.C. (Sept. 10)

To: Ezra the Priest and Scribe of the Law

From: Artaxerxes, King for Darius

Ref.: Freedom to travel

Perfect peace and such a time:

I, King Artaxerxes, have upon this day make a decree that Ezra and all the people of Jewish descent and all the Levites residing within my realm are free to go to Jerusalem with Ezra.

For insomuch as thou art sent to the king and his seven counselors to inquire concerning Judah and Jerusalem according to the law of thy GOD, which is in thine hand.

It is for thee to carry silver and gold, which the king and his counselors have freely offered unto the GOD of Israel, whose habitation is in Jerusalem.

All the silver and gold that thou canst find in all the province of Babylon, with the freewill offering of the people, is given unto thee.

The priest shall take it willingly for the house of GOD, which is in Jerusalem. Take it so that they may buy speedily whatsoever you desire. Thy mayest buy offering of bullocks, rams, lambs with their meat offerings and their drink offerings. Take and offer them upon the altar of the house of your GOD, which is in Jerusalem. Do whatsoever seems good unto you and thy brethren with the rest of the silver and gold that seems well, after the will of your GOD. The vessels also that are given thee for the service of the house of GOD, which thou shalt have occasion to bestow. Bestow it out of the king's treasure house. Even I, Artaxerxes the King, do make a decree to all the treasurers that are beyond the river, that whatsoever Ezra, the priest and scribe of the law of the GOD of Heaven, shall require of you give it unto his hands with great speed.

Unto a hundred talents of silver and a hundred measurers of wheat and a hundred baths of wine and to a hundred baths of oil and salt for the sacrifices without prescribing how much.

Whatsoever is commanded by the GOD of Heaven, let it be diligently done for the GOD of Heaven. For why should there be wrath against the realm of the king and his sons?

We also certify you, that touching any of the priests and the Levities, singers, porters, Nethinims or ministers of the house of GOD shall be unlawful and punishable by death. It shall not be lawful to impose toll, tribute, or custom upon them.

Thou Ezra, after the wisdom of thy GOD, it is in thou hand. Thou shall set magistrates and judges who may judge all the people that are beyond the river, all such as know the laws of GOD and them that do not know the laws.

And whosoever will not do the law of thy GOD and the law of the king, let judgment of GOD be executed speedily upon him, whether it be unto death or banishment, or confiscation of goods or to imprisonment.

Done and signed this day by my hand,
Artaxerxes, Reigning King for my father, Darius
Retrieved from the file of Ezra 7:13-26

To: The file of Ezra
Date: Day 24 Kisleve: 498 B.C. (Dec. 24)
Ref.: Dedication of Books

We have gathered as one man and I have lain upon the altar a copy of the newly written laws of Moses. The altar was built in accordance with the altar Zerubbabel built as directed in the writings of Ezekiel.

The laws are in five volumes. I have spent the past thirty-seven years collaborating with my staff to redraft the books and to restore them to their original form. Seventeen years in research and twenty years in writing. Each time a mistake was made, we had to begin anew. I have rewritten the Torah from the information and written works left behind by Daniel and Ezekiel. My staff also interviewed over five hundred of the aged elders of Israel. Most of those gallant warriors have outstripped us and gone. The powerful spirit of GOD rested upon this Holy Book and all of Israel present at this dedication.

To: The file of Ezra
Date: Day 6 of Elul: 497 B.C. (August 6)
Ref.: Preparation before the High Holy Days

We have continually been depressed ever since my arrival. I have had an extremely tough time trying to teach the people the importance of the feast days and especially the ten High Holy Days and the Day of Atonement, which will soon be upon us. They know nothing! Going to the wall to make our vows seems to be just a new game to my people. This is the month of preparation and I have gathered the people, once again, and offered my prayer up to GOD for them. Here is what I prayed. "O my GOD, I am ashamed and blush to lift my face to thee, My GOD. Our inequities are increased over our heads. Our trespass is grown up unto the heavens." Since the day of our fathers, we have been in a great trespass even unto this very day. Our iniquities have been committed by us: our kings, our priests, and we have been delivered into the hands of other kings in strange lands. We have been delivered unto the sword, fire, and blown away by the wind of your breath. We have been made a spoil and confusion rest upon our face. Even today we struggle as a remnant that might be saved. Now, for a little space, your grace hath been showed from the Lord our GOD to have us a remnant to escape and to give us a nail as the heir of the royal seed in His holy place. As you, O GOD, said unto Isaiah, "and I will fasten him as a nail in a sure place and he shall be for a glorious throne in His Father's House." This, O GOD, has lightened our eyes and has given us a little reviving in our bondage. For we were bondmen. Ye, our GOD hath not forsaken us in our bondage but hath extended mercy unto us by using the sight of the kings of Persia to give us a reviving. The Persian kings have allowed us to set up the house of our GOD and to repair the desolations thereof. They have given us our Western Wailing Wall in Judah and Jerusalem. A wall that we may go to and offer, unto you, all that within us is. That we may be refreshed in your spirit. This, O GOD, I recalled from the oral Torah of GOD. Now, O Our GOD, what shall we say after this? For we have forsaken thy commandments which thou have commanded by thy servants the prophets, saying, "The land, unto which ye go to possess, is an unclean land and filthiness of the people of the lands are with their abominations." The people have filled the land from one end to another. They have filled it with their uncleanness. Now, therefore, give not your daughters unto their sons, neither take their daughters unto your sons. Do not seek their peace or their wealth forever. Refrain from evil. Be strong and ye shall eat the good of the land and leave it for an inheritance to your children forever. After all that has come upon us for our evil deeds and for our good trespasses, seeing that thou art Our GOD. You have punished us less than our iniquities deserve. Thou hast given us such a deliverance as this. Should we again break thy commandments and join in affinity with people of these abominations? Wouldest not thou be angry with us till thou have consumed us? If so, then there should be no remnant nor escaping. O Lord GOD of Israel, thou art righteous, for we remain escaped as it is this day. Behold, we are before thee in our trespasses. We cannot stand before thee in trespasses. We behold, cannot stand before thee because of this, so we bow humbly at thy feet." AMEN.

So I ended my prayer,
Ezra, the Chief Scribe of the Laws of GOD

To: The file of Ezra
Date: Day 6 of Elul: 498 B.C. (August 6); Ezra 10:1
Ref.: The people confessed their sin
and took the vow of the Nazarene

Meaning of the laws have been lost unto us of these many years and we are just now beginning to make sense of the laws of Moses and the conducting of those laws in practice as our ancestors of old did. We are now into the month of Preparation. The circle of life has started again. I have brought before the people the laws of Moses, which I have re-written for them. I have called before me a great congregation of Israel: men, women, and children. They have gathered as their family.

They have come family after family. All are weeping sore. After the gathering, one called Shechaniah came unto me. He is the son of Jehiel, one of the sons of Elam. Shechaniah answered me and said, "We have trespassed against Our GOD and have taken strange wives of the people of the land. Yet there is hope in Israel, concerning these things." Then he continued, "Now, therefore, let us make a covenant with Our GOD to put away all the wives and such as are born of them, according to the counsel of my lord Ezra and of those that tremble at the commandment of Our GOD and let it be done according to the law of the Nazarene as it is written." Then he said, "Arise, for this matter belonged unto you, standing here today. We also will be with thee. Be of good courage and do it."

After Shechaniah finished speaking, then I, Ezra, arose and made the chief priest and the Levities and all of Israel to swear with a vow of the Nazarenes that they would do according to this word, and they all did swear.

Then a proclamation was circulated throughout Judah and Jerusalem unto all the children of captivity that they should begin preparation to gather themselves unto Jerusalem on the first day of Tishri in the new year 497 B.C. and remain there until the tenth day, throughout Yom Kippur, the eve of our returning.

(Ref.: file of Ezra 10:1-9 KJV)

Proclamation, Hear Ye, Hear Ye

It has been thirty-eight years since our release in the year 536 B.C.

Hear Ye: all that dwell in Judah and Jerusalem and unto all the children of the remnant of the Babylon captivity era. You are hereby summoned to appear in Jerusalem no later than day twenty-seven of the month of Elul in the year 497 B.C. Both you and your wives and your children. All should gather, family by family, unto Jerusalem. Come to make your vow unto GOD. Come all, those that have taken strange wives and have children by these wives. Come and make a vow to give them up and send them back to be with their people. They will be well cared for financially. You must also prepare yourselves to enter the dedication and purification cycle as prescribed by law. On the 10th day of Tishri (Yom Kippur), the Lord Our GOD will pass judgment upon us. He sees us all as sheep gone astray. Those that do not come within the allotted time according to the counsel of the princess and the elders, all his substance should be forfeited and himself separated from the congregation of those that had been carried away. You have forty days to make your preparations.

To: The file of Ezra
Date: Day 13 Tishri, 496 B.C. (September 13)
Ref.: Atonement has come and gone

The radical Jews have chosen not to come and have forfeited their substance. All that came repented for two days. Afterwards we all sat in silence and remembered our past for the next seven days. We stood with much fear and trembling; on Yom Kippur, the tenth and final day, we waited for the voice of Our GOD and begged forgiveness. It was a time of returning.

We are now teaching our brethren and their families how to make Succoth booths as Jacob did for his cattle. We have learned that our booths should have been made during the month of preparation. We do not understand what we are doing or why we are doing it. I told the people we will never understand the ways of GOD unless we just do what he says for us to do. They all agreed that the best way to understand GOD is to do as he has commanded. At the end of Succoth, with our booths built, we prayed for rain and prepared ourselves to settle the issue of strange wives that was not openly before us.

To: The file of Ezra
Date: twenty-five of Kisleve: 496 B.C. (Dec. 25)
Ref.: Dedication

Time has rolled around, and we are coming into another dedication, but we still do not have the Great Candelabra in our temple. We are lost without its great light, the fire that consumes wherein GOD dwells.

I am mostly weary and tired. It has been a long-drawn-out and extremely grueling task, which we are still trying to cope with and conclude. Within the next few days, we are all gathering unto Jerusalem. People are sitting in the streets, and all are crying. Our prayers for rain have been answered and the rain is so much more than we expected. We are not able to stand in the rain. The people are crying and sitting in the streets and refuse to get up until GOD guides the people to make a right decision. This is being taken seriously and many others insist on trying to hold on to the strange wives in secrecy without confessing a wrong.

I think it will take more than two or three days to find these families that are illegally among us. We must find them to turn the fierce wrath of GOD from us.

To: The file of Ezra
Date: Day 4 Abib: 496 B.C. (March 4)
Ref.: Approaching Passover

It is yet ten days left unto Passover and unrest has settled at our doors. Some Jews that took the vow have already rebelled and we have within our ranks a civil war in the making.

To: The file of Ezra
Date: Day 10 Abib: 496 B.C. (March 10)
Ref.: Task Ending

The task is finally almost complete. We have singled out 358 families with many members of those families taking strange wives and each family with many illegal children, according to our laws. They number in the thousands. I have listed the family names in my census writings.

(Ref. Ezra 10:18-44 KJV)

MASTER BUILDER DIES BROKENHEARTED

JERUSALEM: Zerubbabel, the master mark mason and builder of the holy temple in Jerusalem, died as he slept of an apparent heart attack. He died on Kisleve, the 20th day in the year 496 B.C. (December 20th). He was eighty-six years of age. He had worked and directed the rebuilding of the temple for the past thirty-nine years. He first began his task in 536 B.C., after civil war broke out among the Jews. He saw all that he had worked for threatened to be destroyed. He was a man of constant sorrow.

Zerubbabel will long be remembered as GOD selected him to rebuild the house of GOD. He was born in captivity in Babylon in the year 582 B.C. He spent forty-seven years in Babylon, prior to coming to Jerusalem. This was his favorite place to spend quiet time in prayer. He would often walk the stairs into the construction site of the city of David.

He had no immediate family members. However, he left to mourn his death of the whole of Israel and his faithful servants. In history the Jewish people will long remember the name Zerubbabel.

To: The file of Ezra
Date: Day 1 of Sivan: 495 B.C. (May 1)
Ref.: The thinning out

The majority of the radical Jews have left but have sworn to return to take vengeance and cause more trouble to us. We are in a great straight as we observe the feast of the weeks.

To: The file of Ezra
Date: Day 10 Tishri: 486 B.C. (Sept. 10)
Ref.: Orders to return to Babylon

Years have passed quickly, and we have made progress in our goals of rewriting the Torah, putting the Torah back into practice, and rebuilding the wall and the city; we are still struggling with the genealogies. In days gone by, this would have been our year of jubilee. Strangers are among us, and our census cannot locate them. We have not found the star to come out of Jacob, which was promised unto us by our GOD.

I hope to study the records that Zerubbabel has accumulated and left behind for us to study. Today I received orders from the new King Xerxes to return to Babylon. This recall follows the death of his father. All Jews must return at various intervals to be recertified and to appear before the king. I hope to return soon. I have made arrangements to track the actions of the radical Jews while I am gone. I have left a plan of action in place to deal with them.

To: The file of Ezra
Date: Day 1 of Elul: 485 B.C. (August 1)
Ref.: Arriving in Babylon
Our days of preparation are upon us. Today I was pleased to see my longtime friend Nehemiah. We have many things to talk about in the wake of all that is taking place. We have a series of meetings set up just as soon as we meet the new king and see what his intentions are toward the Jews. I will also receive wages of royalty to be paid to me monthly. The king has also allowed me to assemble both the aged and young men of Israel to aid the cause of the rebuilding project still underway in Jerusalem. Our main concern is tracing the genealogy and finding the location of the Holy Candelabra, the Ark, and reestablishing the unity of our people.

To: The file of Nehemiah, son of Hachallah
Date: Day 1 of Tishri: 484 B.C. (Sept. 1)
Ref.: King's favor
Tishri 10, I will be seventy-four years old. I was selected by the newly crowned King Xerxes I to become his cup bearer. I will live a life of luxury in his palace. I will have my own servants and live in my own quarters. My main duty will be to sample taste all food and drinks, including the wine that comes to the king's table. This position offers more benefits. I will also receive wages of royalty to be paid to me monthly. The king has also allowed me to assemble both the aged and young men of Israel to aid the cause of the rebuilding project still underway in Jerusalem. Our main concern is tracing the genealogy and finding the location of the Holy Candelabra, the Ark, and reestablishing the unity of our people.

To: The file of Nehemiah
Date: Day 1 of Bul, 483 B.C. (November)
Ref.: Monthly Conference with the King

Today I went for my monthly conference with the king. I asked the king to give Ezra his traveling papers to return to Jerusalem. I also asked the king to give me permission to return to Jerusalem with Ezra so that I could give aid to the task of tracing the genealogies of our people. The king was pleased to give Ezra his release, but he wanted me to remain at court with him.

To: The file of Ezra
Date: Day 14: Heshvan 466 B.C. (October 14)
Ref.: Sukkot and the Torah presented at the temple

I have been back in Jerusalem for the second time since 482 B.C. Since then, I have completed the Torah. The first time I dedicated it outside, upon the plain, by the river. There I laid it upon the altar. This is much the same way King Solomon dedicated the Holy Candelabra before taking it into the temple. Today, I will dedicate the complete works in the temple.

Today is Sukkot and celebration has set in. I entered the temple for the first time with the restored Torah. The council and my staff have devoted over thirty years to the completion of this work. There was not a dry eye in the congregation. Everyone was crying, yet the tears were tears of joy. I entered and stood upon a pulpit of wood made from an almond tree. The same type of wood of the almond in which Moses saw the pattern divine. Beside me stood Mattithia, Shema, Anaiah, Urilah, Hikian and Maaselah. On my left hand stood Pedalah, Mishael, Malachiah, Hashum, Hashbadana, Zechariah, and Meshullam.

I opened the book in the sight of all the people, for I stood high above the people. When I opened the book, the people stood up. I blessed the Lord, the Great GOD of all the people. All the people answered, "Amen." All lifted their hands and bowed their heads to worship the LORD with their faces to the ground. We caused the people to understand the laws and they stood in their place as their ancestors of old did many years ago around the Tabernacle of Moses in the wilderness.

We are making plans of time to offer our Bikkurim (first ripe fruit) as the sacred gift to the temple priest. They read the book in the law of GOD. GOD distinctly gave sense and caused them to understand the reading. We are not content to read from the Torah only once. We are continuing to read it repeatedly and again. The elders and I have gone to the river to shave to show that we have fulfilled our vow according to the law of the Nazarene.

Those across the way, on the other side of the river, are waving their swords and spears at us in a threatening manner.

I will be writing and corresponding with Nehemiah, back in Babylon, over the next year. Our expectations are renewed, and our enthusiasm is high.

To: The file of Nehemiah, son of Hachalian

Date: Day 21, Kisleve: 465 B.C. (Nov. 21)

Ref.: Evil and darkness in Jerusalem

On the 20th year of my service to the king, in Shushan, the palace where I reside. On this day, Hanani and men of Judah came and talked to me about Jerusalem. They had just returned to tell me of certain men under my rule who had escaped from my servants' quarters and were on their way to Jerusalem. Hanani had met these men as he was coming back to Babylon upon orders from the king. I asked Hanani how progress was going with the Jews that were working on the construction of the temple and the city. Their reply brought tears to my eyes. Hanani said, "The remnants that are left of those that returned from captivity are in great affliction and reproach." I asked them, "Why are they under affliction?" Their reply was "Have you not heard? The wall of Jerusalem has been broken down and the gates are burned with fire. The Jews are at war, one with another. The dark tribe, those that have taken strange wives and refuse to give up their lifestyle, have joined forces with the enemy of Israel from on the other side of the river. They have infiltrated the ranks. The enemy is not readily visible, for they have blended in and are not known by name. Ezra is trying to continue, but his efforts are not enough. Civil war is raging within and without the city."

When I heard these words, I sat down to weep and mourn. Then I prayed this prayer: "I beseech thee, O Lord GOD of Heaven. The great and terrible GOD that keepeth covenant and mercy for them that love you and observe your commandments. Let thine ear now be alternative and thine eyes be open, that thou mayest hear the prayer of thy servant, which I pray before thee now, day and night, for the children of Israel."

As thy servant I confess the sin of the children of Israel, which we have sinned against thee. Both I and my father's house have sinned. We have dealt very corruptly against thee and have not kept the commandments nor the statutes, nor the judgments which thou commanded thy servant Moses. Remember, I beseech thee, the word that thou commanded thy servant Moses, saying, "If ye transgress, I will scatter you abroad among the nations, but if ye turn unto me and keep my commandments and do them, though you were cast out unto the uttermost part of the heaven. Yet will I gather all your people from thence and will bring them unto the place that I have chosen to set my name there."

Now these are thy servants and thy people whom thou hast redeemed by the great power and by thy strong hand. O Lord, I beseech thee, let now thine ear be attentive to the prayer of thy servant, who desires to fear thy name and prosper. I pray thee, for I am thy servant this day and ask that you grant unto me mercy in the sight of this, our great king. For I am the king's cupbearer, all to these years. Now let his heart be opened unto me and give unto me freedom to go unto Jerusalem so that I may be of service unto you, O great GOD, and unto the nation of Israel. Amen."

To: The File of Nehemiah
Date: Day 1, Tebeth: 465 B.C. (December 1)
Ref.: Before the King

In the 20th year of the reign of Artaxerxes (Xerxes –I), I came before the king to taste his wine. Thus, I have done for the past twenty years, least any try to poison him. I accepted the wine and gave it unto the king. I was sad before him and this was the first time he had seen me in this low estate. Wherefore he said unto me, "Why is thy countenance sad, seeing thou art not sick? This is nothing else but sorrow of the heart."

Then, I was sore afraid and said unto the king, "Let the king live forever. Why should not my countenance be sad, when the city, the place of my father's sepulchers, lie in waste and the gates there of are consumed in fire?"

Then the king said unto me, "For what dost thou make a request?" Then said I unto the king, "I have prayed unto the GOD of Heaven and he hath placed it upon my heart to ask of thee, O Great King, if it please the king and if thy servant have found favor in thy sight that thou wouldest send me unto Judah, the city of my father's sepulchers, that I may help build the city." Then the king said unto me, with the queen sitting by his side, "For how long shall thy journey be and when wilt thou return?" So I set the king a time that I should return, and he made his decision to send me. Moreover, I said unto the king, "If it please the king, let letters be given me so that they may convey me over till I come unto Judah." I also ask the king that he give me a letter unto Asaph, the keeper of the king's forest, that he may give me timber to make beams for the gates of the palace, which pertained to the house and for the wall and the city and for the house that I shall set up and enter for myself and my servants. The king granted me, according to the good hand my God placed upon me.

Official Correspondence

From Artaxerxes (Xerxes 1)

Given by My Hand This Day 1 Tebeth: 465 B.C. (December 1)

To: Sanballat the Heronite and Tobia, the Servant, the Ammonite, and Geshem the Arabian

I, Artaxerxes, king over the whole providence, do on this day of 1 in the month of Tebeth in the 20th year of my reign set forth my hand in writing by making a declaration that my faithful cup bearer, Nehemiah, the son of Hachaliah, be given all rights and privileges to come unto the holy city of Judah and in order to offer aid and resources unto his people, the remnant of them that are returned out of captivity to build up that city. Furthermore, I also declare that this thing be done with cooperation from my loyal subjects. All governors beyond the river are to convey safe passage unto Nehemiah, the son of Hachaliah, and all his escort with him. Let this be done under the signature which I offer by my own hand on this day one of the month of Tebeth in the 20th year of my reign.

Signed and Sealed

That it be done in haste,

King Artaxerxes (Xerxes I)

Official Correspondence

From Artaxerxes (Xerxes 1)

Given by My Hand This Day 1 Tebeth: 465 B.C. (December 1)

To: Asaph, the Keeper of the King's Forest

I, Artaxerxes the King, do hereby command that the following be supplied to Nehemiah, my faithful cup bearer, the son of Hechaliah:

#1 timber for the making of beams as much as should be required by Nehemiah.

#2 timber for the reconstruction of the gates of the palace at Jerusalem as much as should be required by Nehemiah.

#3 timber for the wall of the holy city at Jerusalem as much as should be requested by Nehemiah.

#4 timber for the private house and dwelling place for Nehemiah, as much as should be requested by Nehemiah.

Let all such beams and timber be cut and readied for use according to the blueprint, which may be provided by Nehemiah. So let this be done in haste and with much skill of craftsmen as may be required. Let this be done under the signature which I offer by my own hand on this day, one of the months of Tebeth in the 20th year of my reign.

Signed and Sealed

That it be done in much haste,

King Artaxerxes (Xerxes I)

To: The file of Nehemiah, son of Hachalian

Date: Day 22 Shebat: 465 B.C. (Jan. 22)

Ref.: The Death of King Xerxes I (Artaxerxes)

Wintertime has come early as I have just learned and am saddened to hear the news of the death of my master and king, Xerxes I (Artaxerxes). He did not get another wine taster when I left his service. The enemy did indeed poison his drink. However, at the age of ninety-four, I have been given permission by his son and successor, Artaxerxes II, to continue with the task which his father granted unto me. The new king has signed off on my travel papers. My caravan and I will leave at first light for Jerusalem.

To: The file of Nehemiah, Governor
Date: Day 1 Sivan, 464 B.C. (May 1)
Ref.: Arrival at the City

We have had a trying trip with many stops and explorations. We have gathered in the timber and supplies as we came. I presented my letters from the king as I made my journey in various stops. Those reading the letters were terribly upset and grieved that the king would send a man as well prepared as he had sent me to seek the welfare of the children of Israel.

Upon my arrival, the situation is worse than I could have imagined. After meeting with Ezra, I received worse news. Ezra told me that the actions of the dark tribe were informants with enemies on the other side of the river. The dark tribe were claiming to be Jews but were not. Ezra said they were of the Synagogue of Satan and were in every gathering of our people and we cannot locate them to destroy them.

They are in disguise while walking and talking openly among us. We cannot put our finger on them. Here are my observations as I inspected the city.

After three days I arose in the night and took two good men with me. These men were selected for me by our GOD. I told no one what GOD had placed in my heart for me to do for fear of the dark tribe. I went out by night by way of the gate of the valley. I could view, at a great distance, into the desert region, toward former sight of the leper camp as it had laid during the days of King Solomon. I gazed upon the sight even before the dragon well. I continued to the dung port, where the debris was being burned, and I came to a place where I could view the walls of Jerusalem. The walls that Zerubbabel had built when he first came here. Now these walls were once again broken down and the gates were consumed with fire and sweltering smoke. The enemy was causing chaos everywhere. Civil war was raging. I and my companions continued our journey until we came to the gate of the fountain and there we viewed the king's pool. I viewed the area that had connected back to the pathway of the leper camp, where the fruit trees grew. There was no place for the beast we were riding to pass through the rubble, so we turned back and ended our journey. We returned to the city and the rulers knew not whether I went or what I did. Neither had I yet told it to the Jews, nor the priest, nor the rest that did work. Only GOD and I knew what was developing.

To: The file of Nehemiah
Date: Day 9 Tibeth: 460 B.C. (December 9)
I was saddened today to learn that four years after my arrival, my friend of old, Ezra, died. He was ninety-six years old. Here is a copy of the news release about his death.

Ezra Sleeps with His Fathers
Jerusalem: The great Jewish prophet and master scribe fell to sleep in the arms of GOD on the ninth day of Tibeth in the year of 460 B.C. He was ninety-six years old. Having been born in 556 B.C. in the 50th year of the Jewish captivity, he had spent well over thirty years of his adult life researching and rewriting the Torah, which had been destroyed by the enemy of Israel in 606 B.C. He did extensive research in the genealogies of Jewish families. He was the presiding elder of the Ekklesia council. He was called out for service to GOD at an early age. Ezra guided the council in their research to gather information about Jewish history of years gone by. The original council members had out stripped him in death.

Ezra will be entombed in Babylon at the resting place called Selihah. He spent much of his time at this site, in seclusion, working on the Torah. A few close friends and nobles attended his graveside burial, leaving a acacia plant upon his grave.

To: The file of Nehemiah
Date: Day 11 Tishri: 459 B.C. (September 11)

Ref.: Genealogy on my birthday and appointment as Governor of Judah

I celebrated my 99th birthday yesterday, on Yom Kippur. It was the Day of Atonement. GOD has given me favorable peace of mind for the coming year. I have been appointed governor by the king and now my work is kicked into full speed. I studied the genealogy charts left to me by Ezra, the scribe. I became a confused scholar. I could make no sense from the records I reviewed. Then I said unto all Jerusalem, "You see the distress that we are in, how Jerusalem lieth waste and the gates are burned with fire and much has been destroyed. Come, let us repair and build up the Western Wall of Jerusalem. Let us do this so that we will have no more reproach to those beyond the river. Let us prepare a wall which we can turn our face to and talk to Our GOD as our fathers did in the days of old." Then, I told them of the hand of GOD which was good upon me. I told them the king also spoke words of encouragement to me and gave me his support. Then they said, "Let us arise up and build." So they strengthened their hands with fasting and prayer for this excellent work.

We had no sooner started, then came Sanballat the Horonite and Tobiah the servant and the Ammonite, the Ge'shem and Abaqbian and laughed us to scorn and despised us and said, "What is this thing that ye do? Will you rebel against the king by building a wall of prayer to another god, yet unknown to the king?"

Then I answered them, "The GOD of Heaven, he will prosper us. Therefore, we his servants will arise and build this wall of prayer as a memorial to Our GOD here in Jerusalem and wisdom will supply the blueprint for us to follow, just as in the days of King Solomon."

Prior to the building of our wall of memorial unto our GOD and laying it upon the underground foundation which Zerubbabel had unearthed, and which King Solomon laid the foundation years ago, we had to make many repairs to the gates and walls and other areas of the city, which the enemy had caused great damage. This we had to do before we even began on the wall itself.

To: The file of Nehemiah, Governor

Date: Day 1 Shebat: 459 B.C. (January 1)

Ref.: Repairs and new construction by the hand of GOD

Then the hand of the Lord Our GOD was mightily upon me. There was given unto me two goals to achieve: #1-Make the quickest and the best repair of the walls and the gates, #2-Weed out the members of the dark tribe as we worked. We redeveloped and polished up the Mosan secret sign language as a means of signal and sending messages. Moses developed this to help his people in dealing with the enemy. As a master mark mason, King Solomon also used it to great advantage in building the temple. We began a process of identifying the members of the dark tribe or the spies and removing them from our ranks without causing confusion. I chose out from among all of Judah and Israel forty-eight skilled men of valor upon which the hand of GOD rested. These were divided into four groups of twelve. Each of the twelve were assigned as head over a large group of overseers. The overseers were in command of a larger group of laborers and masons. As we worked, we would look for members of the dark tribe. They were lazy workers with an attitude to disrupt our progress. We spotted these individuals and our special forces proceeded to remove them and their families from among our ranks without arousing suspicions. Crews were assigned to work with three gates on each side of the wall. Here are the assigned work paths:

(1)-On the north side, crew #1 would work from the corner of the wall to the sheep gate.

(2)-On the north side, crew # 2 would work from the sheep gate to the dung gate.

(3)-On the north side, crew #3 would work from the dung gate to the old gate.

(4)-On the north side, crew #4 would work from the old gate to the corner of the wall.

(5)-On the west side, crew #5 would work from the corner of the wall to the valley gate.

(6)-On the west side, crew #6 would work from the valley gate to the fish gate.

(7)-On the west side, crew #7 would work from the fish gate to the fountain gate.

(8)-On the west side, crew #8 would work from the fountain gate to the corner of the wall.

(9)-On the south side, crew #9 would work from the corner to the garden gate.

(10)-On the south side, crew #10 would work from the garden gate to the beautiful gate.

(11)-On the south side, crew #11 would work from the beautiful gate to the water gate.

(12)-On the south side, crew #12 would work from the water gate to the corner of the wall.

(13)- On the east side, crew # 13 would work from the corner of the wall to the horse gate.

(14)- On the east side, crew #14 would work from the horse gate to the east gate.

(15)- On the east side, crew #15 would work from the east gate to the sheep gate.

(16)- On the east side, crew #16 would work from the sheep gate to the corner of the wall.

When we finished the wall, we should have weeded out the members of the dark tribe. These are the spies, those that say they are Jews but are of the Synagogue of Satan. We have chosen to put chaos from among our ranks. The crews would then finish the roads that ran on top of the walls and around the city itself and the temple. These roads ran six chariots wide, the same as the King of Babylon built around his city. He got the idea from Solomon's design of the first temple. The task would be hard, but the remnant of GOD is determined to succeed.

To: The file of Nehemiah, Governor

Date: Day 3 Bul: 458 B.C. (November 3)

Ref.: Progress and the Western Wall

For the past two years, progress is yet ongoing on the Western Wall. After we had completed much of the repair work, Sanballat heard that we had completed and repaired the Western Wall and he was worth and took great indignation and mocked the Jews.

Then he spoke before his brethren and the army of Samaria and said, "What do these feeble Jews want? Will they fortify themselves with this Western Wall? Will they sacrifice their lives for this Western Wall? Will they make an end in a day by praying here the Sabbath hour? Will they revive the stones out of the heaps of rubbish, which are already burned, to build this wall?"

Now Tobiah the Ammonite, who was with him, said, "Even that which they have built thus far shall come down. If we sneak up as a fox in the night, we shall break down their wall. Let them build on and we will bring it down again."

Then, in their sight, prayed I unto the Lord Our GOD this prayer:

"Hear, O Our God, for we are despised. Turn their approach upon their own head. Give them for a prey in the land of captivity. Cover not their iniquity and let not their sin be blotted out from before thee. They have provoked thee to anger before the builders. Now let the Lord GOD of Israel say, 'Arise, O Israel, and complete they work.'" After praying this prayer so that it fell upon the hearing of their ears, we continued our work without incident. We built and repaired the first half of the Western Wall, and all the other walls were joined together unto the half of it, thereof. We accomplished this because all the people had a mind to work. We were united men. We ask, is there not a cause? (Ref. Nehemiah 4:4-6 KJV

To: The file of Nehemiah, Governor of Judah

Date: Day 29 Kislev: 458 B.C. (November 29)

Ref.: work continues

Our work continued and we feared daily for our lives. I said unto the nobles and the rulers and to the rest of the people, "The work is great and large, and we are separated upon the wall, one far from another. Our walls are six chariots wide. In what place therefore ye hear the trumpet report ye thither unto us? Our GOD shall fight for us." Likewise at the same time I said unto the people, "Let everyone with his servant lodge within Jerusalem so that in the night they may be a guard to us and labor in the day." Neither I nor my brethren, nor my servants, nor the men of the guard who followed me, none of us put off our clothes. The only time we took off our clothes was for washing. (Ref. Nehemiah 4:19-23 KJV)

To: The file of Nehemiah

Date: Day 15, Tishri: 457 B.C. (Sept. 15)

Ref.: Building the second half of the wall

This day I continue to write unto you with my pen in hand. With more responsibilities added to me as governor, I must also work to complete what we have started. After we completed the first half of the Western Wall, our enemies were up stirred and angry.

When Sanballat, and Tobian, and the Arabians and the Ammonites and the Aphrodites heard that the walls of Jerusalem were made up and the breaches began to be stopped, then they were worth. All of them conspired together to fight against Jerusalem and to hinder it from being finished. Nevertheless, we made our prayer unto GOD at the Western Wall and set a watch against them, day and night. We continued our work and as we did one of our chief overseers, Judah, said unto me, "The strength of our workers that bear the burden of labor is nearing decay. They are worn out, for there is so much rubbish in our path that we are not able to complete the work as prescribed." Then he said unto me, "Our adversaries have said that we shall not know, nor will we see them, for they will come in and dwell among us in a far greater number than at the pace we are eliminating them. They will cause our work to cease. Upon ten separate occasions where we have been working too close to them, this has happened. Even now they have infiltrated our ranks." When Judah finished talking, then said I, "Be not be afraid of them, remember the Lord who is great and terrible. Arise up now and fight for your brethren, your sons, your daughters, your wives, and your houses. So long as your heart beats within your breast, fight for Jerusalem."

We continued our work with our weapons in our hands. They who build on the wall and they that bear burdens with those that labored, everyone with one of his hands wrought the work and the other held a weapon. For the builders, everyone had his sword girded by his side and so built. Also, he that sounded the trumpet was close by my side. We worked week out, and month, on month we worked.

To: The file of Nehemiah, Governor of Judah
Day: Day 22 Ab, 456 B.C. (July 22)
Ref.: Continued to solve our problems

We continue to solve our problems. We have continued to work as described in my last memo. It has been eight months past, and the people in the city were in vast numbers. We still have many of our people with strange wives and they are at war with their brethren. They are in vast numbers, and they said, "Since we are so great in number, we need much food and corn so that we may eat and live." Others among them said, "We have mortgaged our lands, vineyards, and houses that we might buy corn because of the dearth that is upon us." Yet others said, "We have borrowed money for the king's tribute to give unto him. We borrow this money upon our houses and vineyards." They said, "We have children by strange wives and have all mingled together within the bloodline and now our sons and daughters are in bondage, and we have no power to deliver them." I heard them beg and I set up an assembly and set them before the people. Then said I unto all the people for each to hear, "We have redeemed our brethren, the Jews, who were sold unto the heathen down in Babylon. Now ye are willing to sell and betray them again. Shall ye sell them unto us? Shall we buy back our own people?" Then they held their peace and gave no answers. It was then that I said, "What you do is not good. Ye should walk in fear of our Great GOD because of the reproach of the heathen, our enemies." I said, "Let us restore all unto the remnant: their lands, their homes, their vineyards, their olive yards, their hundredth part of their money, their corn, their wine, and their oil that ye have taken from them. Let us end this civil war from among ourselves. Let us do it now, for the last time." Then they said before the ears of the assembly, "We will restore them, and we will require nothing of them, and we will do as thou sayest for Our GOD hath forgiven us also." Then I took an oath of them before the priest to do as they had promised. In accordance with the custom of the law. I shook the apron of my lap and said, "So GOD shake out every man from his house and from his labor that performed not this promise, even thus be he shaken out and emptied."

All the congregation said, "Amen," and praised the Lord. The people did according to their promises and once again Israel sat as one man in peace and in strength. The unity had returned.

To: The file of Nehemiah, Governor of Judah
Date: Day 10 Elul: 456 B.C. (August 10)
Ref.: Sharing with the People

I was glad to see the unity restored to Israel. Even before I was appointed governor, there had never been unity. I nor my brethren had never sat down and eaten bread with the former governors.

The governors before me charged the people and took from them bread and forty shekels of silver. The governors even let their servants bear rule over the people. However, as governor, I did not do this for I feared GOD. I collaborated with the people, and I did not buy any land for myself. I also required my servants to work alongside of the people. I invited all to eat with me at my table. There were 150 of the rulers over the Jews, besides those that came from among the heathen to join us.

Daily, I had the following prepared for those that are with me: one ox, six choice sheep, fowls and all sort of wines and many other tasty foods. They all ate with me daily, and I charged them nothing because the bondage had been heavy upon this people. Then said I unto our GOD, "Think upon me, my GOD, for good according to all that I have done for this people, Amen."

To: The file of Nehemiah's days
Date: Day 25 Elul: 456 B.C. (Aug. 25)
Ref.: In another 52 days we finished

We finished the work of the city walls and built the Western Wall so that there were no breaches left therein with the exception for the crack and services for leaving our prayer request unto our GOD.

The work was completed on the 25th day of Elul, fifty-two days after we came into unity among our tribes. GOD sent an angel and blessed the stones, the work of our hands. The high holy days are drawing nigh, and we have not prepared as we should have due to our critical work we had to do to finish the task.

We had not set up the doors and the gates when Sanballat, and Tobiah, and Geshem the Arabian and when the rest of our enemies saw our wall complete they sent word to me, saying, "Come, let us meet together in a village on the plain of O-No." I knew they wanted to trap me and do me harm. I sent unto them, saying, "I am doing a splendid work so that I cannot come. Why should the work cease whilst I leave it and come down to meet you?" They sent back, four separate times, to try to get me to come and every time I sent them back the same message as before. Then Sanballat sent his servant to me for the fifth time with an open letter. Here is what it said: "It is reported, among the Heathen and Gashum said it unto me, that thou, Nehemiah, and the Jews think to rebel. For which because thou build the wall that thou mayest be their king according to these words. Thou hast also appointed prophets to preach of thee in Jerusalem, saying there is a king in Judah. I am going to report this to the King of Persia according to these words. Therefore, come and let us take council together before I report this to the king."

Then I sent him back words, saying, "There is no such thing. Come as thou sayest but you make them up out of your heart of hate for the Jews." Their tactics made us afraid, and they thought our hands would weaken from doing the work, but it did not happen, and GOD strengthened our hand even more.

To: The file of Nehemiah
Date: Day 18 Heshvan: 455 B.C. (Oct. 18)
Ref.: More lies continue

The threats and confusion have continued into the beginning of this another year. We finished the high holy days, and I came to the house of Shemaiah, the son of Delilah, the son of Methetabeel. Then said Shemaiah unto me, "Let us meet in the house of GOD within the temple and let us shut the doors of the temple, for they will come to slay you. Yes, in the night they will come to slay thee."

I said, "Should such a man as I flee? Who is there that would go up into the temple to save his own life? I will not go into the temple with you."

I perceived from his lies that Tobiah, and Sanballat had hired him. He was a member of the dark tribe all along and I knew it not until this time. He was a descendant of Shemi, who was a first cousin to King David, and their goal always was to cease control of the rule over the people. They had plotted together to make me afraid and to cause me to sin so that they might have matter of evil against me. I had Shemaiah removed according to these their works and the prophet Noadiah and the rest of the prophets that would have put fear into me. Thus, the matter was turned over to GOD. The letter writing came to naught.

To: The File of Nehemiah
Date: Day 24 Kisleve: 455 B.C. (Dec. 24)
Ref.: Dedication of the wall, complete with a vow

When the wall was built and the breaches sealed up, we prepared to take those lords, who were our elders and our overseers, and prepare them to conduct the completion of the vow of the Nazarene. They went to the river to shave their beards and their heads, which was a custom that had been restored under the law of the Nazarene. I and the 120 lords with me went to the river's edge and did so in accordance with the law.

Those on the other side of the river gathered and gazed, across the river, upon us. They perceived our message loud and clear. We had indeed completed the work and our vow unto GOD was recognized. They would have done us harm, but the hand of Our GOD was once again strong upon us.

To: The file of Nehemiah
Date: Day 1 Tebeth, 455 B.C. (Jan. 1)
Ref.: Additional Work

After the walls were complete, I sat up doors and appointed the porters, the singers, and the Levites as we prepared to put all phases of the law back into practice. I gave my brother Hananiah, the ruler of the palace, charge over Jerusalem. He is a faithful man and fears GOD. I said unto the people and the workers, "Let not the gates of Jerusalem be opened until the sun be hot in the sky at twelve high, according to the law. Then, when the gates are opened, let the people stand by them and let them shut the doors and bar them. Then appoint watchers of the inhabitants of Jerusalem. Let everyone have his watch over his own house." The city was great. We only allowed some people within because all the houses had not yet been built for all the families. Many families were still encamped outside the city walls. They camped in the gates and the villages and awaited to obtain their passports as we cleared them by genealogy to enter the city. We began at twelve high.

To: The file of Nehemiah
Date: Day 12, Adar: 453 B.C. (February 12)
Ref.: End of term as governor

It has been seven years since the death of Ezra. After his death all the genealogy charts of the Jewish people's family history were brought to me. I did not know what I would do with them, but I knew that I would have to be available to study and to try to make sense of them in one way or the other. I need to have quality time in seclusion for this project. The only way to have this is to give up my duties as Governor of Judah. I have held this position for the past twelve years. With my appointment ending this year, I have decided against asking the king to appoint me to another term. I plan to give the genealogy charts all my free time.

My objective is to find Jacob's Star, the royal seed. This seed has been promised to us for many years. I will be seeking one who is a native son and not a foreigner. I am sure the answer lies somewhere within these records. I am determined to devote the next several years to studying the charts and to make sense out of the numbers.

To: The file of Nehemiah
Date: Day 14, Nisan (Passover): 442 B.C. (April 14)
Ref.: Genealogy by Comparison

I have been making comparisons of the genealogies for the past eleven years. I have compared a list of all the Jews that came back with Zeruberral in 536 B.C. to a list of the families that made the trip with Ezra in 499 B.C. That was over fifty years ago. I have cross-referenced these files with the current up-to-date census of our current year of 442 B.C. I have listed the people into three columns by family, names, and number of children born into those families. I have noticed that most families have had many children born into their family. However, only one family had only one child born and recorded in the year 442 B.C. I thought this was very unusual. We had been concentrating on names instead of numbers. The family singled out by number from the file of Ezra was Bezai. By number comparison the family members numbered 323 on one chart and on the next chart the family numbered 324. Only one new name was recorded. That child was a girl, named Judith. We had been looking for a male child. While the child was a descendant of the holy priesthood of Aaron, our hope that the child would be the star out of Jacob was dashed. With our new research methods, we continued our search for a male child.

To: The file of Nehemiah
Date: Day 10 Tishri: 441 B.C. (Sept. 10)
Ref.: Six Months Later, a Call of GOD
I was in the spirit on the Lord's Day of Yom Kippur and the Lord said unto me, "Seek ye my face." Within my heart I answered, "Thy face, oh Lord, shall I seek!" Then said the Lord unto me, "What does the name Bezai mean"? Then said I, "I know not". The Lord replied, "Bezai means the shadow of GOD." There was a recall within my spirit when these words were spoken unto me.

An angel from GOD appeared unto me and gave me directions as he had done on the first day of Sivan, twenty-three years ago, when I first came to Jerusalem. Now I must follow my shadow back through unto the time to reach the substance of the goal, which GOD hath set before me.

I went out by night by the gate of the valley. I could view at a far distance into the desert region toward the former sight of the leper camp of the olden days. I gazed upon this sight and went through the dung hill until I came to a place where I could view the walls of Jerusalem. I went onto the pathway toward the leper campsite and just beyond I saw the grove of the fruit trees. This was a well-lit moonlight night, and the stars were twinkling bright. The stars reminded me of GOD's promise to Abraham about his seed becoming as the stars of heaven. As I came upon a rubble pile of stones, I was convinced that the little white colt I was riding could not go across the stones in the direction where the fruit trees were growing. I tied the colt and made my way across the field. There beneath an apple tree was a young Jewish girl. I became elated as I recalled the words from the Lord our GOD, which he gave unto his servant Solomon: "Who is this that cometh up from the wilderness, leaning upon her beloved? I raised thee up under the apple tree, there thy mother brought thee forth that bear thee" (Song Sol. 8:5-7 KJV).

I went to the aid of this young woman, Marykim, as she gave birth to her child on the eve of Yom Kippur. I found out that she was making her way out of Egypt, coming to join her family in Jerusalem. I asked her, "Who is your family?" She replied, "The family of Adonikam." I immediately said, "My Lord is risen!" My spirit leaped within me. Here was the star out of Jacob that we had been looking for, as it was written: "Out of Egypt have I called my son."

I placed the woman and child upon the white colt I was riding, and I sought shelter in the temple for the woman and the child. I wasted no time and went straight to the genealogy charts of the Adonikam family.

Upon examining the charts, I noticed that the family of Adonikam was recorded on the latest census charts as having six hundred and sixty-five children. This child would make 666 children born into this family. In accordance with the law, the head of the family was not to be recorded. The head is not counted in this number. Only one child was born. This child would go onto the charts with his name being recorded as Shemaiah. He was the last of sixty male children born into the family. It now became clear to me why Shemaiah, the son of Delaiah, the son of Mehetabeel, tried to entrap me and help Tobiah and Sanballat put me to death. He had everything to gain by stealing the genealogy place on the charts and making alternations and claiming the inheritance rights for his own family. I worked through the remainder of the night to correct the charts and to post them as official documents throughout the city as the people slept. I knew the morning would bring much rejoicing among the people.

To: The File of Nehemiah
Date: Day 11, Tishri: 441 B.C. (September 11)
Ref.: The Genealogy Charts Recorded

There was great jubilation, by anticipation, at sunup this morning. During the night I had recorded a new name upon the genealogy charts. This child, a descendent from King David and King Solomon, was the established bloodline of the promised Messiah we had been seeking.

This name, Shemaiah, from the family of Adonikam, was recorded opposite the child born six months earlier to the family of Bezai. One child was predestinated to follow in the shadow of the other; Judith, the daughter of the family of Bezai (in the shadow of God), would follow in the shadow of Shemaiah of the family of Adonikam (my Lord has risen). Judith was born six months to the day before our finding and recording the name Shemaiah on the genealogy charts. The shadow she would follow would one day lead us to the Messiah.

To: The File of Nehemiah
Date: Day 14 Nisan: 441 B.C. (March 14)
Ref.: The Holy Candelabra, the Mystery

It has now been one year and Judith of the family of Bezai, a descendant of the high priest, is one year old today. The child Shemaiah, of the family of Adonikam, is a descendant of King David and King Solomon and he is six months old. The unity of Israel has never been stronger. I just turned 118 years of age. GOD hath sustained me with good health. There is yet one task and a great mystery that lies before me. It is that of finding the Great and Holy Candelabra. Israel will never be the same until it is found and restored to its proper and appointed place in the temple and provide a resting place for GOD, in the highest flame, as a consuming fire. We have searched for over three score years, ever since our release from Babylon. Now, in my old age, I had decided to turn the task over to one of our younger elders until GOD placed it within my heart to begin a new study of the records of Ezra. I began searching Ezra's records and found among them writings of Daniel and Ezekiel. I also ran across a copy of the original decree from King Cyrus.

The decree by King Cyrus gave the scaled-down measurements of the room in the temple that would hold the Holy Candelabra. The room was scaled in contrast to the known facts about the star that would come out of the loins of Jacob. The room was built in accordance with his decree but as of now it sits empty without the Holy Candelabra. We have also a main operating room the full length of the basement. This is not known to the public. Only the chosen priest and skilled individuals have excess to this room. The golden pipes from the congregation of the holy empty the oil out of the candlesticks and it is carried back to where the Holy Candelabra will sit. The oil will cause the light to burn forever. We have erected a sliding wall and a moving floor. The engineers have erected pulleys and leavers to make all things work. The lights on each side of the congregation of the holy are burning dimly. These lights burnt as did our hope. At least we had hope.

We have lain tracks in the lowest level of the temple and have designed chariot-like carts to run on these tracks. The tracks lead from the Holy of Holies and run all the way to the base of the hollowed-out post of Jacin and Boaz.

We brought this post back out of Babylon when we were released. The post was repaired and is back to its original appearance. We use these two posts as vaults of safety, just as Solomon had them designed for that purpose.

I kept searching for the writings of Daniel and Ezekiel. The task seemed so extremely hard, and I have employed the scribes of youth to help me. We are burning the midnight oil to find any clue that might shed light to solve this age-old mystery. Where is the Holy Candelabra?

It was then that Michael the Archangel appeared unto me one night, as in times past, and said unto me, "Search the wisdom of Solomon and the leadership of Moses." Then said he unto me, "Renew your search again in Daniel and Ezekiel." He left quicker than he had come. I became more confused but was filled with a new determination to do as Michael had said.

I divided our scribes by scholars into three groups and made the following assignments. Group one would take the writings of Solomon, group two would take the writings of Moses, and group three would take the writings of Ezekiel and Daniel. We would study and take notes by comparisons. We would then report and discuss our findings.

To: The file of Nehemiah
Date: Day 24 Kisleve: 429 B.C. (Dec. 24)
Ref.: Reports on Progress Made

God has added twelve more years onto my life since this task began in 441 B.C. The following reports were offered to me as we met by the altar for dedication of the work we have achieved. Here are the reports from our groups.

GROUP #1: RESEARCH FROM MOSES

Moses gave instructions to Bez-a-leel, then son of Hur of the tribe of Judah, on how to make the candelabra for the Holy of Holies. Only three men were ever privileged to know how to assemble and disassemble the candelabra. There were twelve major sections of the candelabra: the base, the shaft, the branches, the bowls, the cups, the knobs, the flowers, the petals, the sepals, the wicks, the oil, and the flames. The highest flame leaped toward heaven to a height of eighteen inches. The candelabra was made of beaten work from royal talents of gold. The Holy Candelabra was set high on the plain. Its enormous design and height gave shade to the people during the day. It was hidden within the tent of the curtains and the heat from its flames burnt bright to give the heat and warm the people from the chilly air of the desert nights. GOD, as a consuming fire, dwelled in the highest flame. This was just as he did with the burning bush. Moses got the holy pattern for the Great Star of Abraham and the Holy Candelabra from the pattern and design formed by the branches and leaves within the almond bush. It was assembled as a great puzzle and could easily be taken apart and put back together again. It was an engineering feat of great wonder. We assumed the 1,198 pieces of this Holy Candelabra were in the shape of a triangular pyramid. We are not sure of how it fits together, and we could not determine its exact shape. The report from Solomon's research group may add light as to what we have reported thus far.

GROUP #2: RESEARCH FROM KING SOLOMON

King Solomon built his temple on the plain and dedicated the candelabra by the river before taking it into the temple for a permanent home. Solomon set the cap (corner) stone in the building so that it could be seen for miles. The cornerstone was overlaid with pure royal gold. This was a calling to the people to come into the temple and worship in the congregation of the holy. The cornerstone had a direct tie into the Holy Candelabra insomuch as they both weighed the same. The weight was 666 talents of royal gold. This weight of gold indicated that the candelabra weighed 99,900 pounds.

The research from the group studying Moses found the weight allowed by law to be carried by a man was fifty pounds and twenty-five pounds for the woman. A Jewish virgin, thirteen years of age, from Judah carried the highest flame, wherein GOD dwelled as consuming fire. Therefore, the committee has calculated there were 1,198 pieces of the Holy Candelabra and all pieces were within these limits as allowed by law.

The group that studied Daniel and Ezekiel will shed lighter on the height and width of the candelabra. Working hard, we may put the mystery behind us. Here are the results of the group's findings.

GROUP #3: DANIEL AND EZEKIEL

Daniel gave us clues in his writings. Daniel was only six years old when Ezekiel carried him on his shoulders into Babylon. Ezekiel taught Daniel many secrets in his formative years. These were secrets that Daniel was able to send to us in secretive writings of parables and riddles, such as King Solomon had done many years ago.

This was easily achieved by his position as ruler over Babylon. In secrecy Daniel described how tall and wide the Holy Candelabra was. He gave the measurements to King Nebuchadnezzar in order that the king might make his statue the same size. Daniel supervised the making of the statue for the king. The statue was set on the plain of Dura by the river just as Solomon and Moses before him had done. It was sixty cubits high (90 feet), and it was six cubits (9 feet) wide. It took 666 talents of royal gold to make it.

When we combined our group study results together, we produced a summary of what we were looking for. These are our results that applied to the Great Holy Candelabra:

*It was ninety feet tall.

*It was nine feet wide.

*Its weight was 99,900 pounds.

*Its substance was 666 royal talents of gold.

*Its number of puzzle pieces was 1,998.

*It had seven lamps.

*It was called the highest (largest artifacts of Israel).

*The highest lamp was called the Most High.

*GOD dwells as a consuming fire in the Most High. The flame was one cubit or eighteen inches high. GOD was the Most High flame, a consuming fire, burning in the Highest.

*It was dedicated by the river.

*It had a dwelling placed called the Holy of Holies.

*GOD gave the original blueprint to Moses. Moses passed the blueprint on to Bez-a-leel, the son of Hur of the tribe of Judah. Bez-a-leel was the architect who built it. Only three knew the secret: Moses, Bez-a-leel from the tribe of Judah, and Oholiab from tribe of Dan. With three you have the majority. With the majority you have the truth. While we have gathered this information, we still do not know the whereabouts of the Holy Candelabra. If we knew, we did not know if we could recover it. It is an age-old secret, yet to be found.

To: The file of Nehemiah

Date: Day 11 Shebat: 429 B.C. (January 11)

Ref.: We are learning of the location

We received a clear, yet complicated message from our former prophets. We dared not to broadcast our findings as we yet sought out the location of the Holy Candelabra. We began to review what we had learned in hopes of finding the location in the secret writings.

In studying the past happenings, we found that the King of Babylon made three separate trips to Jerusalem looking for the Holy Candelabra. He never did find it. He took out his frustrations upon our people. Coming back to Babylon, he continued to torture and kill our people to satisfy his own greed for gold. He claimed that he was only following the directives as given unto him by the Jewish GOD. We were blessed of GOD to have Daniel step into the leadership role as ruler over Babylon. Daniel appeased the king and took information he had accumulated regarding the candelabra and turned the king's attention from the candelabra and put it back upon the king and his interest. Daniel constructed the image of the king and placed it on the plain of Dura by the river as Moses and Solomon had done. Aside from showing the world how great the king was, Daniel brought a hidden message of hope to the Jews that looked upon the image. The image struck a pose that only the Jewish people cherished. It was the Mosan sign language betraying a message that the candelabra was safe and would one day be returned to the Jews. Only Daniel and Ezekiel knew the secret location of the Holy Candelabra and between the two of them, they left the secret for us to discern. The image of the king was a clue to the location of the Holy Candelabra. Its location on the plain by the river was the clue Ezekiel wrote in his file. Ezekiel wrote this: "Thus Ezekiel is unto you a sign according to all that he hath done, shall ye do and when this cometh ye shall know that I am the Lord GOD. I will send one unto you to cause you to hear it with your own ears. When this happens and you learn the secret, then your mouth will be opened, and you shall speak and be a sign unto them and they shall know that I am the Lord" (Ezek. 24:24-26 KJV). Ezekiel taught the Jews for years about the Holy Sign. It was known only to us as a sign, we knew it well, it was the star out of Jacob. Somewhere the answer was hidden in the secret language that Moses had revealed to a few of the wise men. We began to study Ezekiel and his writings, looking for more detailed hidden clues. Then we found the answer. Ezekiel preached his last sermon down by the river Chebar. He told about the wheel in the middle of a wheel and the four beasts. The royal seed was safe, somewhere down in Egypt. What about the Holy Candelabra? Then Ezekiel took the message a little farther. He waded out into the river waters up to his ankles. Then he went farther up to his knees and on out into the water up to his waist. Finally, the waters became waters in which one might swim. This was the answer we were looking for.

The Holy Candelabra was in the river water; it never left Jerusalem. It was still here right under our nose. But where?

Now we were left to wonder if we could ever find it and get it back into the temple. I called a meeting of the Jewish scribes to help find the answer. We were careful never to let any of this information flow back out into the community. We were locked together by a vow. GOD, through his holy oracle, had revealed his knowledge for his divine purpose. They found a book of the law of the Lord given by Moses. Once again, our trust turned to GOD.

To: The file of Nehemiah
Date: Day 2 Adar 429: B.C. (February 2)
Ref.: Pinpoint Accuracy

Within the next thirty-one days, our groups combined together and produced a pinpoint accuracy of the location of the Holy Candelabra. It was in the river Jordan. The river Jordan lay before me with the wilderness to my back. Our starting point was the place upon the riverbank where the Nazarenes were going to shave after they fulfilled their vows to GOD. We went back to our Jewish roots and the clue came from Daniel's writings. I got our master builder, Masada, and the book. Masada's great-grandfather had worked under Zerubbabel and secrets were handed down in the family for years. Masada brought with him his crew and the book and his trussell board for drawing. We found in Daniel's writings that there were two angels, one on each side of the river and another angel amid the river. This angel said, "God would scatter the power of his holy people and then he would finish his work." I said to the master builder, Masada, "GOD sure has scattered us and now he has brought us here to finish his work on his holy temple. It will not be complete until we bring the candelabra back to its proper place." Masada opened the book and began to run reference on the six cities of refugee. This was the river where the enemy was now encamped. On the East Side these are the cities that once stood: Golan was to the northeast, Bezer to the far southeast, and

Ramouth in the east. All these cities had stood on our side of the river. Then we gazed across the river and Masada pointed out the direction and location where the other three cities once stood. There was Kedesh to the northwest. Hebron was located far to the southwest and Shechem was to the far west.

Masada and his crew worked to calculate distances and produce a map on the parchment showing where the cities had been located. He began at Ramouth and connected to Kedesh on the northwest. Then across to Hebron on the southwest and then back to Ramouth. This was an equilateral triangle. We knew it to be a sign. It was then that I recalled from the law as rewritten by Ezra, which said, "And it shall come to pass, if they will not believe nor harken to the voice of the first sign, that they will believe the voice of the latter sign" (Exodus 4:8 KJV). The equilateral triangle was pointing back into our direction, telling us that man's voice was speaking unto us. There was a second sign yet to be found. Where? And what? I wondered as we stood looking from our side of the river. Three cities had once sat on this side of the river where we now stood and three on the other side of the river. The key to the secret was with us.

Masada drew a line from Shechem on the far west and came across the river to Golan in the far east and then went southeast to connect with Bezer and finally back across the river to Shechem. We were amazed at what we saw. The equilateral triangles lay across each other to form a perfect Star of King David, the symbol of Israel's strength. This was the second sign, the one we certainly believed in. We were looking at an image of what once had been Jacob's Star. It was a symbol of great power. Masada proceeded to pinpoint an area in the exact center of the star to be within the river. This was the position the angel took in Daniel's writings.

Then fell a beam of light from the Great North Star. The light fell a little to the median side toward Ramouth, where we were standing and where the lords would go to the river to shave. Then Masada said, "The Holy Candelabra is in the river waters, whereupon is the beam of light." We could hardly hold back tears. How would we ever retrieve it when we could not even see it? If we could see it, we wondered, what condition would it be in? It had been laying in the salt waters of the river Jordan for over two hundred years. Our faith, once again, began to dwindle.

Then said I unto the people that stood with me, "Our GOD is still the GOD of Abraham, and the GOD of Isaac, and the GOD of Jacob. He is still the GOD that parted the waters for Moses. He has delivered us again and He will restore unto us that which is his."

I began to chant the Sh'ma, and all the people joined in, for this was our prayer of a new birth. Then appeared an angel from GOD unto me and said, "Be of good cheer and stand still and see the salvation of GOD." The angel gave instructions unto me, and I instructed the people, saying, "Gather unto to me the twelve heads of the tribes of Israel. Let each leader bring with him 166 males over the age of twenty-one that have been set aside for service within the temple." I gave instructions to the six chosen men to go about the task within the next forty days.

To: The file of Nehemiah
Date: Day 14 Nisan: 429 B.C. (March 14)
Ref.: The Task Complete

Dateline, the first day of Passover. I took unto me the twelve chosen men of GOD. They had been instrumental in collaborating with me to uncover the truth in research and documentation. I brought them into the Congregation of the Holy and I read to them the story of our past. The story was about a man who had borrowed an axe and it fell into the river waters and was lost and a man of GOD came and retrieved it for him. Here is the story as I read it unto them.

"But as one was felling a beam, the axe head fell into the water and he cried and said, alas, master! For it was borrowed and the Man of GOD said, 'Where fell it?' He then showed him the place. The man of GOD then cut down a stick and cast it in thither and the iron did swim to the top. Therefore, the man of GOD said, Put forth thy hand and take the axe head. He put out his hand and took it." This is the story I read unto them, as it was recorded in 2 Kings 6:5-7 KJV. Then I opened unto them the law of Ezra, which he brought unto me before he died. Thus, I read, and Moses said, "Speak unto the children of Israel and take every one of them a rod according to the house of their fathers of all their princes according to the house of their fathers. Twelve rods and write every man's name upon their rod. Thou, Moses, shall write Aaron's

name upon the rod of the Levis. This shall be for the head of the house of the father of Levi. You shall lay these thirteen rods in the tabernacle of the congregation before the testimony is given and I, GOD, will meet with you" (Num. 17:1-4 KJV). Then said I unto the twelve, "This rod which I have for the Levis came from the Ark of the Covenant. It was given to me by Daniel. Daniel had gotten it from Ezekiel, his father. This is Aaron's rod, and it is a token against the rebels. The rebels are those that say they are Jews but are not. They are of the Synagogue of Satan. They are referred to as the dark tribe because once they infiltrate our ranks it is hard to single them out. Once they cometh near or bringeth anything unto the tabernacle of the Lord, they shall die. Then said I unto them, 'Let each man examine himself prior to taking up your rod, for you this day stand before GOD with much fear and trembling. It is a dangerous thing to fall into the hands of a living GOD'" (Heb. 10:31-33 KJV). As we this day have done, we are each held accountable for our actions. Then the twelve cried and said, "Amen, we are accountable unto GOD." Then said I unto the twelve, "Take each man your rod which GOD hath cut for me and pray each one of you for six hours, without ceasing."

Afterwards, we were joined by those chosen to come into the Congregation of the Holy. We told no man of our mission. We took the twelve sticks, and we prayed as we lay prostrate before the Lord our GOD for six hours. Then we were joined by those that were chosen to come in and join us. We gathered the twelve chosen, the twelve heads of the tribes and the six that ministered unto me. Our total in number was 1,998 men plus me. Here is what I said unto them: "We will meet at the river Jordan and wait for the time." The time is only known to GOD as Mean Sunset. No manmade device knows of this time. It was when the evening and the morning becomes a day and at that time the eventide is due in, and the gravity pull of the moon will cause the river waters to be troubled. The twelve men with the rods will touch the water with their rods and I will smite the waters like unto what Moses did with this rod now in my possession. GOD has assured me that when this is done in accordance with his word, the puzzle pieces of the Holy Candelabra will float to the top and be revealed. It will then settle, and the water will roll back and stand as a heap. Each man will walk forth on the dry shod and retrieve a part of the candelabra and follow the pathway back to the temple into the Holy of Holies and there the Highest will be assembled and the Highest light will be set in place by a thirteen-year-old virgin of the tribe of Judah, whom GOD hath chosen.

We did as we were commanded and GOD, with his mighty hand, rolled the waters back and the Holy Candelabra was set back into its rightful place.

To: The file of Nehemiah
Date: Day 15 Nisan: 429 B.C. (March 15)
Ref.: The Glory of GOD Restored

After all of these years, the gold shone as bright as the noonday sun. This was God's doings, and it was marvelous in our sight. It was there, in the presence of GOD, that the groups were sworn to secrecy by a vow before their dismissal. Each went their own way with a crackling voice and tear-stained eyes. The Levities were directed to make the holy oil by formula that the light might burn forever. The Holy Candelabra went together quickly, like a puzzle, under the direction of Modani. Modani used the secret offered him by the constellations and their placemen of the stars to complete the task. We began with the base and ended with the last bowl that sat in the center of the candelabra. The oil was poured into the two golden candlesticks in the Congregation of the Holy and ran through golden pipes into the Holy Candelabra. I climbed the stairwell to the top of the candelabra. A thirteen-year-old virgin of the tribe of Judah handed the top bowl to me. As the flame lit it shot forth to a height of eighteen inches, and in a soft voice I said, "The glory of GOD has returned to Israel." We felt prostrate before him, and his life of light was now complete within us. Israel at last was restored to greatness as during the reign of King Solomon. May we never falter and fall again. We planned a great celebration for this restoration during the last day of Passover. The power of Elijah was with us.

To: The File of Nehemiah
Date: Day 21 Nissan: 429 B.C. (March 21)

Ref.: The power of Elijah returns to Israel

The lords of Israel went to the river to shave. The notices were posted, and all the people took their places around the temple as they did in the days of Moses. The Shofar sounded one long blast, the Tekeiah, and the head of each one of the twelve tribes came to their assigned place in accordance with their inheritance by law. The Shofar sounded again, three blasts, the Sheavarim, and the head of each family within the tribes came to their assigned position. Then all the members of each family came to their assigned positions as nine short blasts, the Teruah, sounded the alarm. Moving even closer to the temple and stepping out from within the families were the ones to be numbered according to the burden they had to bear and the work they had to do. These were the Levites of the priesthood. A perfect formation of the ancient symbol of Israel, the Star of David, began to emerge. It was now time to present to Israel Judith, the daughter of Bezai. This was her Bat Mitzvah. She had now turned thirteen years of age. She came forth to read from the law prepared by Ezra. This was the first time a young girl had been selected to read before the congregation since Debra arose as a prophet in Israel.

After reading we brought forth Shemaiah before the Congregation of the Holy. Shemaiah was the 60th male and the 666th child born to the family of Adonikam. Shemaiah would within the next six months also celebrate his birthday, being thirteen years old on Yom Kippur. Here before us appeared the one we had longed to see, the star out of Jacob. This was the royal seed carrying the hope of Our Messiah. We had the dedication of Shemaiah (My Lord has Risen), and he made his way through the Congregation of the Holy and passed between the shadows of the two golden candlesticks and ended up in the Holy of Holies. Judith followed in Shemaiah's shadow that was thrown back to her feet from the well-lit room. She stopped at the entrance of the Holy of Holies. Shemaiah stood before the Holy Candelabra for his dedication. There was total silence, then the temple trembled with the voice of GOD as he said, "This is my beloved son in whom I am well pleased."

With the completion of the dedication, we quickly moved to the next level, which was that of protecting the identity of the two holy seeds that

GOD had revealed unto us. The Holy Ghost Power of Elijah had once again returned to Israel.

To: The file of Nehemiah

Date: Day 30 Elul 421: B.C. (August 30)

Ref.: Preparation ends, and we find complete rest

Here is my Report. Eight years have passed and we have completed our task. Upon hearing the voice of GOD, I directed the two seeds to go into seclusion in the desert, where we had developed an oasis upon the site that once served as the leper camp. We had circulated false stories of lepers with incurable and deadly diseases to keep the public at bay. The land belonged to the family of Bezai and lay a good thirty-day journey from the city by foot. The distance that one could travel to and from the camp was limited to the Nazarenes. Although isolated and secluded, it was modeled and laid out after the pattern of the city. There were three major parts: the entrance, the living area, and the outer area for growing fruit trees, vegetable gardens, and caring for the animals. No one knew the whereabouts of the royal seed except for their servants and guardsmen that accompanied them on their journey. At the time of this writing, the two children are now grown and have turned twenty-one years of age. They enjoy a healthy and safe life as this has become their home. The priesthood has been established in the temple. The Torah has been rewritten. The practice of the law has been returned. The temple walls have been rebuilt and the Western Wall has become our Wailing Wall, built upon wisdom. The stones hear our cries. The Holy Candelabra is in place and GOD dwells in the highest flame. The priest is directed by his consuming fire. The Ark was never found. However, I am in possession of the Rod of Atonement that once lay in the Ark. I look forward to celebrating my 139th birthday next month. Shemaiah turns twenty-two years of age the same month. Jerusalem is safe.

To: Nehemiah

From: Shemaiah, 60th son of the family of Adonikam, the last of 666 children

Date: Day 1, Tishri: 420 B.C. (September 1)

Ref.: the passing of my mother

Dear Nehemiah:

My father in Israel. I am sad to inform you of the passing of my mother, Marykim. She talked of you often and how that you found her giving birth to me under the apple tree and how you used her prayer shawl to trace our family genealogy. You brought us safely back into the city riding upon the little white colt. She told me many stories of your devotion and demanding work that produced the genealogy charts confirming that Judith and I were first cousins.

You will also be glad to know that Judith and I have created a partnership in administration for this oasis and we have agreed to share the ownership. Judith has given birth to her first child. She has chosen the name of Eliza for her child. We are keeping good genealogy charts of all who enter our encampment and any new births of children born under our watch. We are this day devoting our lives to caring for the sick and studying the law. Since my mother's death, we have developed new methods of healing for the lepers and specializing in the care and treatment of those that suffer from the dreaded disease of the mind often associated with people known as cave dwellers. King Saul had in the past been a victim of this, for he was a cave dweller. We would like to ask that you and the officials of the Great Council decree that all that are dwelling in the city with this sickness be sent to our site for their healing. Please send them to the priest and assign a care person to accompany them. Please have them to carry with them thirty sheets and thirty changes of garments of lightweight linen, in accordance with the law of the leper, as they will need this in their travel. We will accept them into our camp and care for them. One of our new projects was established as the result of my mother's death. It is the burial field and place of rest. We have a beautiful garden of rest for those who die. It is the Field of Blood. We chose the name because those that came here gave their lives and carried the hope of their blood, calling out to GOD from the ground in which they were lain.

In just nine more days I will be twenty-two years old. I am told that you also have a birthday on Tishri 10, and you will be 139 years old. GOD has blessed mightily.

We are continually developing more housing here on the west bank. We have a wonderful living quarter in this oasis of peace and love. Please furnish us a copy of your procedure for processing visitors to come to community.

Closing with my prayers,

Shemaiah, the Chosen of the family of Adonikam

To: The file of Nehemiah

Date: Day 10 Tishri: 420 B.C. (Sept. 10)

Ref.: Chest Pain

Today is my birthday. I am having unusual chest pain. I am going to lie down and rest after I write this memo. I am proud of the work we have accomplished. We will live to see the promised Messiah spring forth from the loins of Prince Shemaiah of the family of Adonikam. His whereabouts must be kept a secret. The genealogy charts must remove his name from among the living.

HOW THE MIGHTY ARE FALLEN: NEHEMIAH, FORMER GOVERNOR OF JUDAH DIES AT 139 YEARS OF AGE

JERUSALEM: Israel has lost a great historian and Judah lost a friend and former governor. The world has lost a wonderful friend. GOD has gained a servant. The Prophet Nehemiah died today. His death will be recorded on the Day of Atonement, Tishri 10, 420 B.C. He was found dead in his governor's mansion. His had laid his head down on the open Torah, which he had been reading. He was 139 years old. Nehemiah was born in Babylon in 559 B.C.

He served during the reign of five kings: Xerxes I, Artaxerxes, Xerxes II, Sogdianus, and Darius II. He was the cup bearer for the first two of the aforementioned Kings.

Nehemiah served as governor for twelve years. He served from 438 B.C. until 426 B.C. As governor he never taxed the people and always held a feast for them each year. He bore the burden of the expense himself. Nehemiah was loved by all and will be remembered for his great service to the nation of Israel and to Babylon. Under his leadership the following major projects were achieved: (1) He helped his good friend Ezra to exercise the rites of the laws of Moses for the Jewish people. (2) He was the overseer of the project that led to the repair of the walls and gates of the city of Jerusalem. (3) He rebuilt the Western Wall as a point of contact with GOD. (4) He, along with Ezra, traced the genealogy of the royal seed. (5) He returned the Holy Candelabra to the temple chambers.

GOD did not trust such feats as these to every man. Only Nehemiah was worthy of such tasks as these. In his later years, he worked with the energy of a young man and displayed the knowledge and wisdom of the Eternal GOD. This wisdom was given unto him without measure. His brothers died some years before him, and he has left to mourn him several nieces and nephews. He saw to it that his servants would be well cared for after his passing. His body will be entombed in the open garden of the governor's palace. He will be laid to rest in a white marble tomb built by the master builders of Babylon who served under his authority. The royal emblem of Jacob's Star, the Star of David, will be placed at his head. A team of his royal white colts will move his body to the burial site. How the mighty have fallen. The sound will be heard throughout eternity. Sleep on, sleep on, sleep on, O faithful servant of GOD and man. His last words were "So this chapter of Israel's growth ends. It is goodbye for now but not forever."

Source: *The Jerusalem Post*

To: The File of Judith, Family of Bezai

Date: Day 15 Elul, 409 B.C. (August 15)

Ref.: files delivered, as of this date I have turned over the following files to the daughter of Shemaiah:

#1: files dated Day 14 Nisan, 409 B.C. (March 14) – sad birthday

#2: files dated Day 1 Elul, 409 B.C. (August 1) – secret files

#3: files dated Day 10 Tishri, 581 B.C. (September 10) – confidential information

#4: file dated 579 B.C. – meeting the king upon his return

#5: file dated 579 B.C. – reading from his journal

#6: files dated Day 25 Shebat, 597 B.C. (January 25) – birth of my child

#7: the conclusion, a love letter to Israel

I have advised her to keep these files hidden. One day the Messiah will come, and our people will be able to close the book on the Jews of Babylon as a last chapter.

To: The file of Judith, Family of Bezai #1
Date: Day 14 Nisan, 409 B.C. (Passover, March 14)
Ref.: Sad Birthday

Today was my birthday, I am thirty-four years old. However, I am sad in mourning for my dear friend Shemaiah, who died today. He was of the family of Adonikam.

He had just turned thirty-three years of age only six months ago. We were looking forward to celebrating my birthday together. Shemaiah died by taking upon himself the disease of the patients he cared for. He died of leper's disease. He devoted and gave his life that they might live. His body is now laid to rest in an eternal tomb inscribed with the true meaning of his name. The words are "MY LORD IS RISEN."

These words offer hope of the resurrection of the bodies to all who pass by and gaze upon them.

He has a surviving daughter, who was named after his mother, Marykim. She is now staying with me and my daughter, Eliza.

We are doing well. The encampment has grown quite large and is truly a paradise for the sick. New people arrive every month. All the wisdom of Israel is here in the camp. We have physicians, lawyers, teachers, elders, and prophets. They have come here to learn and study. All are not sick. The quietness and terrain of the camp is healing for both the body and the mind.

To: The File of Judith of the Family of Bezel #2
Date: Day 1 Elul, 409 B.C. (August 1)
Ref.: Secret file found

Today I was going through the files that Nehemiah has left for Shemaiah in his last will. What I found was a letter from Daniel, the great prophet and ruler over Babylon. The memo was written in 581 B.C. Daniel requested that the memo be destroyed after his death. He requested that it should be read by the high priest and committed to his memory. Shemaiah never told me about this memo.

I will place this memo among his items and preserve it for history. One day, someone will know what to do with this information. I am attaching a copy of this memo from Daniel along with the rod, which Daniel carried. Nehemiah gave the rod to Shemiah just after he was born. A chest is also among his things.

The chest has a lock on it and has never been opened. It has the royal seal of the holy priesthood upon it. The seal is the Star of David, and it can only be opened by a holy priest, a descendant from the lineage of Jacob through David. I will keep these items safe for her until the daughter of Shemaiah is old enough to cherish the items.

To: To the File of Daniel #3
Date: Day 10 Tishri, 581 B.C. (September 10)
What I am sending: Confidential Information
What You Should Do: Destroy this memo after it is read
and recorded in your memory.

This is written on the night of the death of my friend and tutor, the Great Prophet Ezekiel. At the time of this writing, Ezekiel was seventy-nine years old, and I am now thirty-one years of age. We have been here in Babylon for twenty-five years.

I will long remember the happenings of the night, which I will share as I put forth my hand there unto this writing. Ezekiel brought me from Jerusalem to Babylon when I was a child of six years of age in 606 B.C. Ezekiel knew many of the temple secrets, which he shared with me and taught me as I grew into manhood. It was Ezekiel that guided me and helped me to find favor with the king. The story I am sharing with you must be put into your memory only. Please destroy this and all documents with it.

This is the end of Yom Kippur. I had arranged with Ezekiel to bury the Ark, knowing my authority as ruler over the providence of Babylon would be in question if we were caught. King Nebuchadnezzar was this very night in Jerusalem, for a second time, looking for the Ark and the Holy Candelabra. Ezekiel knew of the Ark as it came into Babylon. The Ark was hidden in the hollowed-out post of Boaz. Ezekiel said it was only a matter of time before its whereabouts would be known. He said we must bury it tonight. I put my life on the line along with my most faithful servants to bury the Ark. We moved it in the night to a secluded spot where GOD had directed us to bury the Ark. I did not know it at the time, but it was not only the burial of the Ark that we would be attending to. We arrived with the Ark under the cover of darkness as the clouds shielded the stars in the night sky. This was the night of the Atonement for Judgment. We came and found a pre-dug grave in which we were to place the Ark. I noticed there were several slats of thick clay, cut to precision. These would protect the Ark. Ezekiel had informed me to remove Arron's rod that budded and to take and keep it in safety. The rod is now in my possession and will remain with me until such a time as GOD would have me place it elsewhere. We were preparing for the ceremony as I glanced toward the East. Ezekiel made an eye-catching entrance as the moonlight hit directly upon him for a split second. The clouds passed and the moonlight gave us a view of Ezekiel. He was dressed in the Jewish burial attire. As soon as I saw him, I knew that our priorities had changed. I did not have time to talk due to the noise that came to our ears from across the sands of the desert that once had been silent. We heard at a great distance the rustling of soldiers' feet and the clanging of swords and spears. Ezekiel said, "What we must do, do it quickly." Ezekiel called me aside and quickly revealed to me that he was my father. We both cried and returned to the choir at hand. The soldiers were advancing closer. Suddenly, Ezekiel stumbled and touched the Ark of the Covenant and fell dead at my feet. He had violated the law of GOD to preserve the law of GOD.

It was then that I knew that GOD had prepared him for his journey into a paradise of the great beyond, in the valley of death. We quickly buried the Ark and laid the precut slabs of clay beneath it and a top of it to preserve it. It was well hidden, and no human eye could see it, only the darkness of the grave was visitable. We each took our place as the soldiers arrived to inquire what we were doing. I, Daniel, assured them that we were well within our rights and that we were preparing to bury our great prophet of GOD. They saw the body of Ezekiel and his burial attire and questioned us no more. They watched from a distance as we lay the body of Ezekiel atop the clay slabs, which were hiding the Ark of God.

GOD had assured me that the Ark would no longer be needed for the sake of Israel. The only item in the Ark at this point was the two tablets of the Ten Commandants, which were written with the finger of GOD. The Rod of Inheritance was taken from the Ark and was in my possession. It must be kept in safety. I kept it with me both day and by night. Those that looked upon it saw only a rod or a staff, which I carried for comfort. The grave is never to be disturbed.

Those in the future that would choose to disturb the grave shall fall under the curse of the rod which I now hold, the Rod of Atonement.

I will, with the king's permission, make sure that the grave of Ezekiel shall become and be preserved as a national memorial site. His tomb will be engraved with the emblem of the Holy Candelabra. No one will ever know that the Ark of the Covenant is lain beneath the body of Ezekiel, my father.

To: The file of Daniel #4
Ref.: Meeting with the king upon his return
Date: 579 B.C.

I have always made it a policy to be open and honest with the king.

Today I met with him upon his return from Jerusalem. I wanted to inform him of the burial of my father, Ezekiel.

He assured me that the burial site would be maintained and kept in safety.

He also informed me that this second invasion of Judah and Jerusalem had brought more destruction upon the Jewish people. He said that GOD, through the mouth of his Jewish prophets, said, "My people Israel have gone a-whoring and worshiping small 'g' gods. And I now give them to Babylon and they shall be known as the great whore of Babylon."

The king had only brought back a remnant of captives and placed the seal of GOD, the Star of David, upon their forehead as a sign of their protection. He forbids that any should come near to harm this remnant, upon who the mark was.

I was sad for this part of his report.

He had been writing in his journal and asked that I proofread it and file it with his records.

As he left the room, I picked up his journal and began to read from it.

To: The file of Daniel #5

Ref.: Reading from the King's Journal

Date: 590 B.C.

This reading from the journal of his return made me sad, yet I knew it was the hand of GOD that had acted. Here is a part of what I read these words the king had written.

"The Lord GOD of Daniel spoke unto me in a vision and said, 'I will remove Judah out of my sight, as I have removed Israel. I want you to cast off the city of Jerusalem, which I have chosen, and the house of which I said my name shall be there' (II Kings 23-27 KJV). These you shall reduce to rubble so that there is none left standing."

As I read, I had recalled these words from Ezekiel which he had taught unto me as a prophesy resulting from the things that King Hezekiah had done. I continued to read as tears stained the pages of the king's journal.

"I, the Great King Nebuchadnezzar, saw the young men and the old lie on the ground in the streets of that city. I saw the virgins and the young men fall by the sword. I slew them in my anger. I have killed and not pitied. In the day of the Lord's anger, none escaped nor remained (Lam. 2:21-22 KJV). Those wrapped in the swaddling band of birth, I have consumed.

Their hearts cried unto the Lord as they ran to the wall. Their tears ran down like a river by day and night. I knew I could not rest until the apple of God's eye was gone" (Lam. 2:18 KJV).

Reading about the young children wrapped in their swaddling bands of their birth hit home, hard, to my memory, for I too had a young child. I left the king's journal just long enough to look at the memo I had written and left on record about the birth of my own child.

To: The File of Daniel #6

Date: Day 25 Shebat: 597 B.C. (Ref.: Broken in heart and mind)

I have been in Babylon for nine years. I first came here in 606 B.C. with Ezekiel. I am now fifteen years old. I along with my three first cousins: Shadrach, Meshach, and Abednego, have been brought forth from the outer courts of the prison and called in service to the king. We will be in training to enter the king's harem and will be in service to him there. While in training I met a young girl who is now turning thirteen years of age. While being picked for the king's harem, she has not been defiled. I have fallen in love with her, and she is now with my child, having conceived on the 25th day of Tebeth (December 25).

Only Ezekiel knows of this. He has smuggled her out of Babylon, and she is on her way to Egypt. I am glad for her safety, but I miss her so very much. I know that I will never see my child after it is born. I have hopes of my child being called out of Egypt.

Shadrach has learned that within the next few weeks all four of us will be made eunuchs. We know it is not for the sake of man, but this is for the Kingdom's sake. This was prophesied by Isaiah because of what King Hezekiah had done. We will each take our place in service to the king in his harem.

I am alone, with GOD to comfort me, as I wait for the years ahead. I am sure on Yom Kippur His favor will shine upon me. Surely this is not the closing chapter of our Jewish people, here in captivity. We must pull it all together by some means.

THE CONCLUSION

To: My Son, Daniel

From: Your Father, Ezekiel

What I am sending: These are the last words I will write. It is a letter given to me by GOD.

What you should do: Keep this letter until our people, the Jews, are released from Babylon.

My Love, My Dove:

O, Israel, Israel, my one and only Israel. "Behold you are beautiful, My Love, you are Beautiful" (Song of Sol. 2:7 KJV). From the very first time that I walked and talked with Adam, my son, in the Garden of Eden in the cool of the evening, I knew that you would be forthcoming from within his loins. I knew all about you before you ever had a being in the earth. You see, my love, I have a desire for the work of my hands. My love became endangered, while we were yet in the Garden of Eden.

Lucifer, my firstborn by creation, was one of my three angels that were unto me as my sons. Lucifer was my angel of light and the beginning of my strength, the excellency of dignity and the excellency of power. He sat on my right hand. However, he is unstable as water. His wisdom was defiled by his beauty (Gen. 49:3-4).

The beauty I gave unto Lucifer, my son, I also created that beauty within you, yet while you were in the loins of Adam. It was I that formed the light or the beauty in Lucifer and it was I that also created the darkness within him (Isaiah 45:7 KJV). I gave him sovereignty over a portion of my power.

It was his power and principalities of darkness that you, as flesh, made from the dust of the earth, was not able to overcome. It was through your weakness that Lucifer was able to entrap you.

His desire was that you should become a part of him because of your beauty, which he also possessed. That is why I placed the tree of life in the midst of the garden for you. My laws on this tree were for your strength and eternal life so that you could overcome the wiles of Lucifer. Lucifer knew that if you ate of this tree of life that you could never become a part of his powers of darkness.

His diabolical plan was to have you for his own and to take control and rule in my stead. The only way to achieve this was to have you betray my trust and to partake of the laws on the tree of good and evil. This tree I had made for myself, my sons as angels, and Mother Wisdom. We knew which laws were good and evil, but you did not. If you ate of one law you would be guilty as if you had eaten them all and you would become subject to his command and be separated from my love I had for you.

He set his eye upon Eve, the mother of all men and women yet to come forth. She fell for the beauty that she saw hidden within him and his words of wisdom.

Lucifer enticed your weak flesh by saying that if you ate of this tree of knowledge of good and evil that your eyes would be open and you would be like unto me, to know all things.

The very instant that Adam and Eve partook of the fruit of reproduction, whose seed was within itself, the wild wind of betrayal shook the sacred fig tree, and its fruit was cast forth in an untimely season.

It was then that denial had followed betrayal and led to you trying to hide your guilt by wrapping the fig leaves about your naked body.

I could have cried a river at that time. The tears began to wash away my happiness and love I had for you. Once the words had gone out of my mouth and I said, "The day you eat of the tree of good and evil, that will be the day you will die out to my love, and you will have to leave this beautiful garden."

As you prepared to leave the shivering winds of distrust and sorrow were continually whirling about the leaves of the garden trees and animals were crying and hiding in fear. As I looked, you were shivering, and I knew that when you left the garden you would need some comfort and trust.

I brought fort the lamb, that had been predestinated by Mother Wisdom to come as a sacrifice before the foundation of the world had ever been laid (I Peter 1:20 KJV).

I called for the lamb to come and he said unto me, "Here am I." I took his fleece of comfort and trust, and made a covering to protect you on your journey. Then, I said, "One day the lamb will come to you and you must return his garment unto him. It is his pledge unto you and it is his garment in which he shall sleep" (Exodus 22:26-27).

As I made preparations for you to leave the garden, I turned to my son Lucifer, the first of my angelic creations. I had changed his name to Satan and I stripped him of his dignity but left him with a minimal of his power. I said unto him, "You wanted the beauty from my creation from the dust. I am going to let you have it. I will trade you, beauty for their ashes" (Isaiah 61:3). Your beauty has dulled your wisdom, as they leave the garden, you must go with them, and they shall be your dinner. You shall eat of the dust from which I made them all the days of your existence (Genesis 3:14) You shall become a fugitive and a vagabond, and thou shall be in the earth or the flesh of man (Gen. 4:12). You shall walk to and fro through the earth of man's flesh as a wandering Nomad. You will always be with mankind going to, and frow through his dust seeking to devour him (Job 1:6).

As for my love, Israel, which is yet to come, I will give them back their beauty and restore their garment of praise if they will mourn for me and shed tears as they would pour out the oil of anointing (Isaiah 61:3).

Then I said unto Satan, "I will put hate or enmity between thee and the woman, and between thy seed and her seed, and it shall bruise thy head and thou shall bruise his heel" (Genesis 3:15).

Since time, Satan has been, as a son, obeying my voice and going to and fro through the dust from which I made man. He is always looking for weakness and seeking whom he may devour (Job 1:7 and I Peter 5:8).

Although it hurt me, I kept a watchful eye upon you through the lattice window of eternity, the window through which I and Mother Wisdom looked through constantly.

I was overjoyed as you began to emerge and begin your travel back to me through the patriarchs of old, Abraham, and of Isacc, and of Jacob.

I kept a close eye on you as you made your way into Egypt and fell into slavery under the pharaoh.

Then I gave Moses my two tablets of the Ten Commandments and I said I will buy Israel back to me for the ten virgins. I wanted my virgins to accompany you on your journey and to supply you with warmth and companionship. I placed my name in the first five and related my name back to man. This was the oil. These first five virgins were wise. You wanted no part of the wise virgins.

The last five had no oil, for I had removed my name and replaced it with the names of man and man's relationship with other men. These were not welcome even though I told you that you could go back to my law and find the oil to make these five virgins burn bright. No, you would not.

You and your sister Judah chose to go your own separate ways and so you joined in and married with the Assyrians.

The Assyrians mistreated you and ate you as a cat would bite a child. I pleaded with you and I said return unto me and "remember the laws of Moses and I will send you Elijah, the prophet, before the coming of the great and dreadful day of the Lord. I promised to turn the hearts of the fathers to the children and the children to the fathers or else I will smite the earth, your fleshly bodies, with a curse" (Malachi 4:1-6). You would not obey my law.

I thought, "How often would I have gathered thy children together, even as a hen gathers her chickens under her wing and you would not" (Matthew 23:37 KJV).

I sent my prophets to you with my words of love for you. You chose to turn against my prophets, then said I, "Jerusalem, Jerusalem, thou that kills the prophets and stones them which are sent unto thee. Behold your house, the body in which you live, is left unto you desolate" (Matthew 23:38).

When I looked upon you, I saw you as a seething pot full of scum. I caught you looking toward the North, where you claimed your inheritance from me, and I decided that instead of your inheritance I would send evil to break forth upon you, from the North. I sent many kings of many countries, with King Nebuchadnezzar, and they set their thrones at the entrance of your gates of Jerusalem and the walls around about Jerusalem and Judah. I uttered my judgments against you and against the wickedness of you who did forsake me as your

GOD and you turned to worship the works of your own hands and to burn incense unto other small "g" gods (Jer. 1:13-16 KJV). I called to me my weeping prophet, Jeremiah, and I said unto Jeremiah, "Gird up thy loins and arise and speak unto them all that I command thee. Be not dismayed at their faces, lest I confound thee before them. I have made you this day as a defended city and as an iron pillar and brazen walls against the whole land. Everyone shall fight against thee, but they shall not prevail, for I am with thee to deliver thee" (Jer. 1:17-19 KJV). I sent Jeremiah and you rebelled against him, and you would have taken his life also as you did my other prophets, had I not protected him.

I tried again and sent another of my prophets unto you. I thought I must send a prophet that Israel can look upon and from seeing this prophet and seeing his condition, maybe they will know of my feelings for them.

I sent my Prophet Hosea to you, and I prepared him well. I wanted him to feel like I feel and once he understood my feeling, he would be able to express the disappointment and sorrow which I felt for Israel, my love.

I said to Hosea, "Take unto thee a wife of whoredoms and children of whoredoms" (Hosea 1:2). Hosea married a prostitute name Gomer. Nothing he did for her made her happy; she had children and none of the children were of the seed produced by Hosea. She left Hosea and the children. Her bad habits spoiled her. Her beauty bottomed out. She lost all of her physical attributes that would make her desirable. She ended up in the bottom of the bottom. She was without friends and family. She ended up as a slave and on the auction block to be sold to the highest bidder. A friend told Hosea that Gomer is on the auction block and is to be sold to the highest bidder.

Hosea said, "I know she done wrong and has lost her beauty, but I want to buy her back." Hosea got all of his bushels of barley and corn and what money he could take up and he went to the auction, and the total value of all of his goods was thirty shekels of silver. He purchased her back for thirty shekels of silver.

I told this story to show Israel that I was willing to pay the price to get her back into my arms. I said unto Israel, "All Nations have drunk the wine of wrath of your fornications and the kings of the earth have committed fornications with you" (Rev. 18:3 KJV).

I said, "O, Israel, thou hast despised mine holy things and hast profound by Sabbaths" (Ezekiel 22:8 KJV).

Then, "the Babylonians came to you into your bed of love, and they defiled you with their whoredoms and you were polluted with them" (Ezekiel 22:23 KJV). "You became their whore, the great whore of Babylon.

"I cast you into a bed with them, that commit adultery with you, and I cast you into great tribulations and I killed your children with death" (Rev. 2:22-23 KJV).

"This was my judgment upon the great whore of Babylon, who had drank from the golden cup full of the abominations and filthiness of her fornications and upon her forehead I wrote the name 'Mystery Babylon the Great the mother of harlots and abominations of the earth'" (Revelations 17:1-5).

My Prophet Jeremiah said unto Israel, "As a cage is full of birds, so are the bodies of the people, as the houses in which they live, they are full of deceit, and have chosen to become great by reputation and have chosen to become rich with the things of the world" (Jer. 5:27-29). I warned them, then I acted.

I caused it to be noised abroad, "Babylon the Great is fallen and is become the habitation of devils and hold of every foul spirit and a cage of every unclean and hateful bird" (Rev. 18:2 KJV).

Then when the history of promises was fulfilled and Israel came off the auction block and it was time for Israel's release from their seventy years in captivity, then I said, "Come out of her, my people. Let the remnant be not partakers of her sins and receive not her plagues" (Rev. 18:4 KJV).

The remnant came forth at my command and I placed my mark of protection upon them.

King Nebuchadnezzar took 12,000 from each of the twelve tribes of Israel and placed the emblem of my protection and power upon each of them. The sign of their Messiah to come, the Star of David. The 144,000, the remnant marched through the streets of Babylon and into their new home for the next seventy years. Then I commanded through the mouth of the king and he said, "Let no man come near nor harm any upon who is the mark." I said unto the remnant, "If you learn to fear my name, which I have placed upon the little white stone, then shall the sun of righteousness arise with healing in his wings, and you shall go forth and grow and you shall tread down the wicked as the ashes under your feet" (Malachi 4:1-6).

I say unto you as the remnant, "Blessed are they that do my commandments. That they may have the right to the tree of life and enter in through the gates into the city of my Kingdom" (Rev. 23:140).

For this was my promise through Jacob, if he would build me a Tower of the Flock on the hill of the daughter of Zion and call it the Tower of Migdal Eder, I would reserve the right for Israel to be the first ripe of the fig tree to enter my Kingdom, (Micah 4:8 KJV).

I will bring you to the night of my protection, "Leil Shimurim." You will be secure and none can ever harm you. This is as the same night I brought you out of Egypt (site Bible Gateway). This same night is the Lord's, vigil for the children of Israel throughout all ages" (Exodus 12:42). My promise to you is sure and steadfast.

"I shall come against you, Israel, as a great eagle not to destroy you but to protect you. I will come as a bird of the air and bring with me the voice of the mighty wind, the Holy Ghost. This is my fire which I will take to Israel" (Ecclesiastes 10:20). "I shall cover thee with my feathers and under my wings shall thy trust, and my trust shall be thy shield. Like unto King David, my shield shall bear the sign of the Star of David.

"This is the holy emblem. The sacred sign of GOD. The sign of the Son of Man.

"From this day forth, you shall say unto wisdom, thou art my sister and call understanding thy kinswoman that they may keep you from strange women" (Proverbs 7:6).

In closing, let me beg you, O Israel, to hear and remember my words of wisdom, which I say unto you.

Do not forget that "I created all things that are in Heaven and in Earth. This includes both visible and invisible, whether they be thrones upon which I alone set kings and rulers. I alone create principalities of powers of darkness. I create all things for your Messiah and your

Messiah is above and before all things and by him all things consist" (Colossians 1:16-17).

"Israel, lend me your ear and hear or let it be cut off through circumcision and let it again be placed upon your head that you may hear my words of wise guidance, which I leave with you. Hear, O Israel, the Lord our God is one Lord, and thou shall love thy GOD with all thine heart and with all thy soul and with all thy might, and these words which I command thee this day shall be in thine heart. And thou shalt teach them diligently unto thy children and they shalt talk of them when thou walks by the way, and when thou lies down and when thou rises up, and thou shall bind them for a reminder of the Star of David and place them upon thine hand and they shall be as frontals between thine eyes and thou shall write them upon the posts of thy house and thy gates" (Deuteronomy 6:4-9 KJV). Now, here are the words for your newly circumcised ear.

"Let us hear the conclusion of the whole matter: fear GOD, and keep his commandments: for this is the whole duty of man. For I, GOD, shall bring every work into judgment, with every secret thing, whether it be good or whether it be evil" (Ecclesiastes 12:13-14 KJV).

In closing let me say, "You shall not see me anymore until you say, 'Blessed is he that cometh in the Name of the Lord'" (Matthew 23:38). You shall receive my final word when the Jews of Babylon, the Final Chapter, will be opened to circumcise your eye to see into the realm of my holiness.

With Much Love,
Your Loving Husband,
The Shephard of Moses
The Great I Am

KNOW THE LAYOUT OF THE HISTORICAL EVENTS

In order to appreciate the information you will gain from my writings, I will offer you the following layout for each page of historical events. As you read keep in mind that this is my own personal series of events and may not agree with other authors you have been acquainted with.

First, I have a numbered column indicated by the symbol #, followed by a number. Each line will be numbered consistently, continuing through the number system. This will allow you to keep track of the order of events as they happened.

There is a year column. This column will offer you a date of the event when it happened. Note, there are three timeframes for historical happenings. They are B.C., C.E., and A.D. Look at their meaning. B.C. stands for "Before Christ." This captures all time events that happened before Christ ever came to earth. In my timelines, this includes 2,000 years of the dispensation of time known as death and 2,000 years of the old law.

Next is C.E., the Common Era, when Y'shua lived.

C.E. stands for "Common Era" and has come to be the time allotted to the life of Christ while he was walking upon the earth. I only show thirty-three and one-half years in this dispensation of time. To take the guesswork out of when he was born, I looked to the Holy Bible for the answer.

In the Bible I found that Y'shua, or Christ, was born in 6 B.C. The law was written, as GOD hath said, "Then, I will command my blessing (Christ – Y'shua) upon you in the sixth year and it (my blessing – Y'shua) shall bring forth fruit (do his work) for three years" (Leviticus 25:21 KJV).

There were only thirty-three and one-half years in the common era. Y'shua was not recognized as the Messiah for his first six years of his life. He spent five years in Egypt in the palace of Pharaoh. The C.E. period did not begin until Herod died, and the Holy Family were called out of Egypt.

For my own personal timeline, I have the C.E. begin in 1 C.E. After this era of time, we then have A.D.

A.D. was recorded after the death of Y'shua. It had a continuation through 2,000 years of grace. Although it has not been picked up by Bible scholars, there is another timeline recorded for our understanding in the Bible.

It is the dispensation of time known as the fullness of time and is recorded in Paul's writings. It is found in Ephesians, chapter one, and starting at verse eight. I will paraphrase what Paul wrote for our understanding.

Paul said, "GOD hath showed unto us through his wisdom and made us to know his mystery. GOD has chosen the dispensation of the fullness of time for this revelation to take place. He has had this hid within himself and will bring it to pass."

In this dispensation of fullness of time, GOD will gather all the things which are in heaven, and which are upon the earth. They shall be gathered in the body of Christ.

This body is his Church, and we have all obtained an inheritance from him.

He will bring us together in unity for the reading of his will to show us that we are predestinated according to his purpose. GOD will work all things together for the counsel of his own goodwill.

When we hear the reading of his will, then we will be the praise of his glory as when we first trusted in him as Christ the Messiah.

After we, as the Church, hear the good news we will know of his Gospel of Salvation.

The Gospel is the power of GOD unto salvation and that salvation is of the Jew. That Jew is Christ the Messiah. After we hear the inheritance he has for us, then we will receive GOD's seal of preservation, which is the Holy Ghost.

This is the prize of the mark of the high calling that hath been hid within Him. With our inheritance we will become the praise of his glory.

He prays that the Church will receive this wisdom and the revelation of the knowledge of Y'shua.

When this is received, then the eyes of our understanding will be enlightened to know of GOD's great glory and to receive GOD's great power, the Holy Ghost. Christ the Messiah is the head of all things to the Church, which is his body.

He gives the mighty power of the Holy Ghost to his Church in this dispensation of the fullness of time in which we are presently living. The Church will go forth to the fulfillment of GOD's own pleasure.

This is the times of great awakenings, and it has already made its appearance unto the children of Abraham.

The appearance is the Star of David, the eternal spirit of the Living God. Are you ready to receive this power of the Holy Ghost?

Remember, GOD wrote you a fortune worth more than silver and gold in his will. He signed it in his blood and sealed it with wisdom. As you study the charts, you will be excited and amazed at the wisdom GOD hath sent your way. The mantel of power, wisdom, and understanding has been thrown from the balcony of Heaven and the greatness of GOD's power will fall upon you as the power of Elijah. As you read you will find all things are in order. Here is a repeated summary for your understanding.

First there is a number, and all numbers are in a sequence of order. Next there is a date. Please note all the dates will be in B.C., or Before Christ. Later, it will change to C.E., the Common Era, when Y'shua lived. After a date there is an explanation of what took place in that date.

 # B.C.

1-6,666 (eternity): There were billions of years and more so than man can count before man shows his face upon the portals of GOD's great earth. The scripture tells us that one day is as a thousand years to GOD. "For 1,000 years in thy sight are but as yesterday when it is past and as a watch in the night", (Psalms 90:4 KJV). In the beginning or in eternity, GOD created all things in Christ Jesus (Y'shua). You make up your own mind but do not follow man. Always trust and follow GOD. The Bible tells us to try the spirits. The Bible only uses the word eternity one time: "GOD is the high and lofty one that inhabits eternity" (Isa. 57:15 KJV).

2- 4027: The reign of death begins as Adam and Eve leave the garden, where they were created.

3- 2632: Abraham is born.

4- 2532: Abraham seeks a city whose builder and maker are GOD. He is one hundred years old.

5- 2457: Abraham dies at the age of 175 years, with the promise that the law is to come.

6- 2027: Moses is born. He is an offspring and an ancestor of Abraham.

7- 2006: Moses got the law from GOD. He is eighty years old. He spent forty years learning under the Pharoah of Egypt. Then he wandered for forty years, where GOD beat all that man had taught him out of him. Then for the next forty years GOD teaches him about the law.

8-2006: The reign of death ends, and the reign of the law begins.

 # B.C.

9-1947: Moses dies; he is 120 years old.

10- 1185: David is born.

11- 1139: David hires Huram (Hiram), King of Tyre, to do all the preliminary work and get the temple materials ready.

12- 1135: Solomon is born. His father, David, is fifty years old.

13- 1115: David is seventy years old when he dies.

14- 1115: Solomon becomes king. He is twenty years old.

15- 1107: Solomon hires a widow's son, Huram (Hiram) Abiff to build the temple. He is the son of King Hiram.

16- 1087: Solomon is forty-eight years old when he finishes the temple.

17- 1027: Solomon locks up the secret of the Star of David and changes it to Solomon's Seal.

18- 812: Hezekiah is born.

19- 762: Israel is still under the reign of the law as Isaiah the Prophet to be is born.

20- 742: Isaiah becomes the lead prophet for Israel. He is twenty years old.

21- 742: Isaiah marries a prophetess.

22- 742: King Hezekiah is seventy-two years old.

23- 742-665: Isaiah has other children. He gives a prophesy of the coming of the holy seed. He is seventy-seven years old.

24- 740: Hezekiah had a harem of women. He is now seventy-two years of age. He has recruited young virgins.

25- 740: Isaiah had prophesied for years that the king must marry and give up the harem.

26- 740: Hezekiah becomes sick.

27- 739: Hezekiah receives an envoy from the King of Babylon. They bring him gifts and words of praise.

28- 739: Hezekiah falls into their trap. He shows them all his wealth. He shows them the Holy Candelabra in the Holy of Holies. No strangers should be here as GOD had commanded. He shared his military secrets. He shared with them the secret of the sundial, which he and his father made. They are free to look upon the Ark of the Covenant.

29- 738: Now Hezekiah is responsible for his own downfall when he gives young Jewish virgins from his harem to take back to Babylon and intermarry with the Babylonians.

30- 738: Isaiah prophesies that Hezekiah will die for committing the great offense to GOD. The king's sons are to become eunuchs in Babylon and Babylon will conquer Jerusalem for what he has done.

31- 738: Hezekiah turns to the Wailing Wall with a broken heart and a contrite spirit. GOD hears his prayers and adds fifteen years to his life.

32-738: Hezekiah asks for proof that this will happen. GOD offers him proof. He will turn the sundial back ten degrees.

33-738: Hezekiah and his father built the sundial, and he knows that it is impossible to turn it back in time. It only moves as does the sun.

34-737: It is Yom Kippur and judgment sets in as GOD turns the sundial back ten degrees and it stops at the month of preparation and Hezekiah has another chance at life.

35- 735: Hezekiah marries Isaiah's daughter. A daughter is born. The child is now a native daughter of Israel, and the bloodline now runs pure again.

36- 729: Isaiah brings the water in from the North and South and it goes inside the temple by way of the East and the West. The duct is complete as per GOD's request. Jews do not know why.

37- 722: Hezekiah dies. He had learned obedience is better than sacrifice. The reason for building the duct will come into play in the history of Israel and the genealogy of the royal seed as the future shall reveal.

38-666: Hezekiah has a great-granddaughter; she turns fourteen years of age. This young woman will give way to a carrier of the holy seed in due season.

39- 665: Isaiah ceases to be a prophet for Israel. He dies at the age of ninety-seven years old. He is at rest, for his eyes have seen the glory of GOD in his great-granddaughter.

40- 615: A new prophet arises in Israel. He is Ezekiel the prophet. He is now twenty-one years old. He marries a great-great-granddaughter of royal seed from the bloodline of Hezekiah and Isaiah's daughter. The girl is named Sarah. She is fourteen years old.

41- 612: Sarah and Ezekiel have a child in their third year of marriage. Ezekiel is twenty-four years old. The child is a boy. They name him Daniel.

42-609: For security reason and protection, Daniel begins his travel toward manhood without knowing that Ezekiel is his father. He only thinks he is a friend of the family.

43-608: A strong bond has developed between Daniel and Ezekiel. They spend a lot of time both in and outside of the temple.

44- 606: King Nebuchadnezzar of Babylon invades and overpowers the Jews in Jerusalem. Nebuchadnezzar is part Jewish. He is a descendant of one of King Hezekiah's wives, from his harem. Daniel's mother, Sarah, was killed during the conquest. Daniel is only six years old when the invasion came. Ezekiel takes Daniel upon his shoulders and walks to the hole in the wall and brings Daniel up on the other side. This is the outer part of the city, where the fruit trees and gardening and animals are kept. No fighting takes place here because all the things that bring forth food are respected.

45- 606: Ezekiel is now thirty years old, and Daniel is six years old as they arrive in Babylon and are held captive along with many fellow Jews by the River Chebar.

46- 600: King Nebuchadnezzar does not destroy the city on this first invasion. He tortures and kills many Jews. He leaves Jeremiah behind as a prophet for Israel and makes King Zedekiah the Jewish king. This is only the first woe!

47- 593: Daniel is now thirteen years of age. His three cousins are a little older. They are Hananiah, Mishael, and Azariah.

48- 593: Ezekiel teaches the boys about Israel's past relationship with GOD by inventing a dreidel game and using stones as marks. The game similar to the favorite game of Nebuchadnezzar. Soldiers guarding them think they are gambling. The stones count as numbers and each number carries a secret message.

49- 593: Soldiers arrest Ezekiel and lead him away in chains. Daniel and his three cousins are taken to the king's prison.

50- 591: Daniel turns fifteen and is now working in the king's palace. He interprets a dream for the king. The king has Daniel and his three cousins assigned to begin training to work in his harem.

51- 590: Daniel meets a young Jewish girl. She is now fourteen years old. She is being trained to be assigned to the king's harem. Daniel falls in love with the young girl, and she is with Daniel's child.

52-590: The young Jewish girl is named Sarah. Ezekiel arranges for her to leave the country and go into Egypt. Egypt is an ally with Israel.

53-590: Daniel and his cousins were given Babylonian names. Daniel carries the same name as the king's son. He is named Belteshazzar, meaning "Protecting the king." His cousins are renamed Shadrach, Meshach, and Abednego.

54- 589: Daniel is called to interpret another of the king's dreams. He tells the king that he is the head of gold, and he is the glory of GOD. Daniel is made to be the ruler over all of Babylon at the age of seventeen.

55- 588: Daniel is highly favored of the king. Daniel influenced the king to make his cousins each a ruler over one-third part of the Kingdom. Shadrach, Meshach, and Abednego settle in as rulers under the authority of Daniel.

56- 588: Daniel settles in to rule the Kingdom and do GOD's bidding. He knows that he will never see the love of his life nor his child again. He is a eunuch for the Kingdom of GOD's sake, as are his cousins.

57- 587: Daniel is now nineteen years old. In his search he finds Ezekiel and brings him to the palace to work under his supervision.

58-586: Daniel turns twenty-one years of age. King Nebuchadnezzar leads his army back to Jerusalem for the second time. It is 591 B.C.E. and the Ark of the Covenant and the Holy Candelabra become his passion. His part-Jewish mother has shared stories about these artifacts of Israel.

59- 586: Jeremiah hides in the hills and eventually makes his way to Egypt. Egypt is still an ally of the Jewish people.

60- 584: Nebuchadnezzar conquers Egypt and Jeremiah is thrown into prison.

61- 583: Jeremiah returns to the outer courts of the prison. There he meets a young boy who is six years of age. The child is a descendant of Sarah and Daniel. He is the royal seed. Jeremiah takes the child and his mother into his watchful eye of protection. Jeremiah also meets his cousin from Jerusalem that has a title to a piece of land. Jeremiah pays the full price. The land at one time belonged to King David. Jeremiah was born on this land.

62- 582: Jeremiah sends a runner to Babylon with the good news that Jacob's Star had been found again. He also sends the title to the land. The runner gets the document in the safe hands of Daniel and Ezekiel.

63- 581: Ezekiel shares with Daniel the location of the Ark of the Covenant. It is in the storehouse of treasurer of the Babylonian king. It has been hidden in the hollowed-out post of Boaz all these years.

64- 581: Daniel and Ezekiel know they must bury the Ark before the king arrives. They choose an isolated desert place in the northern part of Babylon.

65- 581: Daniel is now twenty-five years old, and Ezekiel is forty-eight years old. Ezekiel knows what he must do for the sake of his son Daniel and for Israel. He dresses in his burial attire.

66- 581: At the burial site they hear the soldiers coming. Ezekiel stumbles and touches the Ark and falls dead at Daniel's feet. They hurriedly place the Ark in the grave and cover it with slabs of precut clay.

67- 581: The soldiers come and inquire as to what was going on. They recognize Daniel as their ruler. Daniel tells them they have come to bury their prophet of old. The soldiers see Ezekiel in his burial attire, and they leave and watch from a distance as the body of Ezekiel is laid to rest atop the Ark.

68- 581: All at the burial site with Daniel are his loyal followers. They all take an oath unto GOD about their silence. Daniel places a marker on the site and seals it with the royal seal and markings of the Holy Candelabra.

69- 580: Nebuchadnezzar returns. Daniel tells him of Ezekiel's death and burial. The king decrees that the site is to be a holy shrine and never to be disturbed. He never knows that the Ark is in the grave.

70- 579: Daniel is now twenty-seven years old. He uncovers a plot among the king's royal court to assassinate the king.

71- 579: The king is aware of the unrest in his Kingdom and has a dream. No one can tell him what it means, and he is near a nervous breakdown.

72- 579: Daniel interprets the dream for the king and his endangerment is mounting with each passing day. Daniel retrieves the plans that have been on hold for some time. The plans are about making an image of a king out of gold. Daniel urges the king to go into hiding with some of his Jewish captives and begin the work on his image of gold. This will allow Daniel time to find those who would want to take the king's life.

73- 579-572: Daniel circulates a rumor that the king has left the country and begins to round up those that would betray the king. For seven years the king does not shave nor trim his nails as he works on the image of himself. Those that labor with him do not know him to be their king. He lives, eats, and sleeps for seven years among them. Daniel has rounded up and put to death or imprisoned those that revolted against the king.

74-570: Daniel turns thirty-six years old. He has been in Babylon for thirty years. He has ruled over Babylon for the past seventeen years. A plot emerges within the ranks of Daniel's followers. They seek to use the king's laws of the land and trap Daniel and his three cousins. The enemy would establish a strong foothold on Babylon if they were to succeed.

75- 569: The fiery furnace is maneuvered as a crafty scheme to get rid of the three Hebrew children as rulers. They escape the furnace and those who devised the plan are thrown into the furnace.

76- 568: Facing failure after failure, the enemy turns their attention toward getting rid of Daniel. They find an old law still active signed by the king. This law is used to have Daniel thrown into the lion's den.

77- 568: The king must obey his own law. He loves Daniel so much but cannot find a way out. He turns to his Jewish roots as taught to him by his mother. He seals the den with the emblem of the great Jewish kings of the past. He places the seal of the Star of David upon the mouth of the den and appeals to Daniel's GOD to save him. Daniel is spared as GOD locks up the jaws of the lions in the den. With Daniel's life spared, the king now throws those responsible for this into the lion's den and the lions devour them.

78- 566: Daniel now returns to the throne at the age of forty.

79- 559: Nehemiah is born in Babylon.

80-553: Daniel is now fifty-three years old. Nebuchadnezzar, the great king, dies. Daniel has him buried in the Jewish tradition. Six white colts pull a royal gold chariot and carry his body to an entombment at the foot of his image of gold.

81- 553: Daniel is removed as ruler over Babylon and fades into the background as an advisor to the new king. The Kings brother-in-law, Nabonidusk, now becomes the ruler. He decides to share half of his Kingdom with Nebuchadnezzar's son, Belteshazzar.

82-549: Daniel is fifty-seven years old and has become an inactive leader in Babylonian.

83- 549: The Kingdom is now under the leadership of the king's son, Belteshazzar. Belteshazzar decides to throw a big party and abuse the holy vessels taken from Jerusalem. He brings all the gold out of the king's storehouse of treasurer.

84- 549: A handwriting appears on the wall and none of the king's advisors or fortunetellers can read the message. The king in his anger prepares to kill everyone who cannot interpret the dream.

85-549: The handwriting will not go away. The king offers one-third of his Kingdom to anyone that can read the handwriting on the wall.

86- 549: Belteshazzar goes to his part-Jewish mother. His mother tells him about Daniel and how he interpreted dreams for his father. The king has Daniel to come and read the writing.

87-548: Daniel at the age of fifty-eight is restored as a ruler over one-third, part of Babylon by Belteshazzar.

88- 548: Daniel drops his Babylonian name of Belteshazzar and picks his Jewish name, Daniel, for the rest of his life.

89- 540: King Cyrus, King of Persia, conquers the Babylonians.

90- 540: King Cyrus, King of Persia, conquers the Babylonians. His son, the prince in charge of making all the arrangements of who is allowed to see the king.

91-539: Daniel is not well known to the new ruler. He seeks an audience with the king to secure the Jews' release from Babylon after seventy years in captivity.

92-536: The Prince of Persia denies Daniel access to see the king. This continues for twenty-one days. Daniel prays and GOD sends Michael the

Angel to confront the prince. The prince becomes afraid and grants Daniel permission to see the king.

93- 536: King Cyrus has heard of Daniel's fame; he invites Daniel to share prophesy with him. Daniel advises him that King Darius of the Meads is on his way to conquer his army.

94- 536: King Cyrus signs a decree and hands it to Daniel. The Jews were officially released from their captivity after seventy years. This is on Daniel's birthday, Yom Kippur. Daniel is now seventy-six years old.

95- 534: Almost immediately Zeruberral has prepared the first group of laborers, construction workers, and engineers to leave for Jerusalem.

95- 533: Darius becomes the King of all Mead and all Persia. He honors the decree by Cyrus as the Jews began to leave.

96- 533: Daniel, one of the first true Jews of Babylon, dies. He is seventy-nine years of age. GOD has let him live long enough to see his dream of freedom fulfilled. Daniel is buried in Babylon.

97- 533: Zerubbabel does not receive news of Daniel's death until a little over two months after he dies.

98- 533: King Darius sends Zerubbabel the blueprint from Ezekiel's files of how to measure and build the temple. This temple is by comparison to and in a ratio of the body, or the holy temple of the Messiah, when he comes.

99- 533: Zerubbabel reports trouble while trying to build the city.

100- 532: The enemy on the other side of the wall makes an inquiry to the king about the Jews' rights to build the wall and the city.

101- 532: King Artaxerxes sends word to the enemy that they must see that the Jews quit working until the issue is cleared up.

102- 532: Zerubbabel reports that the enemy has forced them to stop working. They have taken down our names of the Jewish leaders in charge of the restoration project.

103- 529: The governor searches the storehouse of treasurer and finds a decree signed by King Cyrus. The letter gives the Jews permission to build the wall and the city.

104- 529: King Cyrus signed copies of the decree on September 10, Yom Kippur. Copies were given to the Jews and the enemy on the other side of the river.

105- 520: July 17, Zerubbabel reports that the enemy has left them alone and they are free to resume their work.

106- 520: Zerubbel gives a progress report on the work.

107- 516: Zerubbabel reports that the work has been completed after twenty years of work.

108- 513: June 21, Ezra granted permission to leave Babylon and to go to Jerusalem.

109- 513: August 11, Ezra reports that his travel plans are on hold because the king has become sick.

110- 499: Almost fourteen years have passed, and Ezra now renews his plans to go to Jerusalem.

111- 499: Artaxerxes gives Ezra his traveling papers to leave Babylon.

112-498: December 24, Ezra gives an up-to-date report on the rewriting of the Torah, which he is taking to Jerusalem.

113-499: February 17, Ezra arrives in Jerusalem only to find much confusion.

114- 498: August 6, Ezra prepares the people for the Ten High Holy Days. The people have no idea of what the days are all about.

115- 497: August 6, Ezra convinces the people that they must repent before the all-knowing GOD.

116- 497: August 12, Ezra has a challenging time talking to the people about something they do not understand. He posts a proclamation for all the people to gather for GOD's judgment on the eve of Yom Kippur. The feast of trumpets is exercised and introduced to the Jews. They have no knowledge of what it is all about.

117-496: On the tenth day of Tisha (September), all have gathered to face GOD for judgment as did their ancestors of old.

118- 496: Dedication arrives; it is December 25.

119- 496: March 4, Ezra reports that there is much confusion as Passover draws near.

120- 496: Ezra separates and singles out 358 families that have taken strange wives.

121- 495: December 20, it is reported that Zerubbabel had died and buried in Jerusalem.

122- 495: 1 Sivan (May), Ezra begins to weed out the dark tribe, or the spies from within the Jewish ranks. These are those that say they are Jews but are not. They are of the synagogue of Satan.

123- 486: On Yom Kippur (September 10), Ezra receives his orders to return to Babylon. He is not sure what the meeting will be about.

124- 485: One year later Ezra is back in Babylon.

125- 484: 1 Tishri (September 1), Nehemiah, at the age of seventy-four, becomes the king's cup bearer. He puts his life on the line for the king. He tastes all the foods, wines, and drinks every day before the king eats or drinks. It was common for food and drinks to be poisoned when given unto leaders.

126- 483: November 1, Nehemiah request that the king let Ezra return to Jerusalem.

127- 466: Heshvan, October 14, Ezra returns to Jerusalem with the fully restored Torah that had been lost or destroyed.

128- 465: November 21, Nehemiah receives word that a civil war is being fought in Jerusalem.

129- 465: 1 Tebeth, December 1, Nehemiah asks the king's permission to go to Jerusalem. The king grants him permission to go because of his loyal service to the king.

130- 465: He displays his letter from the king giving him permission to go to Jerusalem. Those with authority would not cooperate with him unless they saw the letter.

131- 465: December 1, dedication is drawing near. King Artaxerxes writes a letter to the keeper of the forest to let Nehemiah have timber to repair the house and the wall in Jerusalem.

132- 465: 22 Sivan, January 22, King Artaxerxes (Xerxes I) dies.

133- 464: May 1, Nehemiah arrives in Jerusalem, amidst much confusion. A civil war is raging.

134- 460: 9 Tibeth, December 9, Ezra dies and his body is sent back to Babylon, where he is buried with honors.

135- 459: 11 Tishri, September 11, Nehemiah at the age of ninety-nine begins to study the genealogy charts left to him by Ezra. The stakes remain high as he searches for the star out of Jacob. The promise was made by GOD to the Jews as outlined in the law.

136- 459: 1 Shebat, January 1, Nehemiah begins a new construction project to repair the walls and the city.

137- 458: 3 Bul, November 3, Nehemiah reports on the progress made to repair the Western Wall.

138- 457: 15 Tishri, September 15, Nehemiah reports on the repair on the second half of the wall.

140- 456: 22 Ab, July 22, Nehemiah tries to resolve the many problems as they arise day by day.

141- 456: 10 Elul, August 10, during the month of preparations Nehemiah as governor invites all the people to eat at his table.

142- 456-25: Elul, August 25, nearing the end of the preparation days Nehemiah announces that the Western Wall is complete with 1,998 stones. These stones numbered forty-two rows. These were divided into three sections, with 666 stones in each section. This wonderful code was from wisdom. Forty-two generations from Abraham to Y'shua. There were 666 blessed years, showing the genealogy of the royal seed's generations from Abraham to David. There were eighteen rows underground, showing the 666 years as the blessed years of the royal seed's generations from David to the carrying away to Babylon. Not known at this time, these years would be the same number as the years, in the fourteen generations from the carrying away to Babylon until Y'shua the Messiah.

143-455: 18 Heshvan, October 18, Nehemiah writes about more troubles in the camp. The dark tribe, those that say they are Jews but are of the synagogue of Satan, from across the river are still infiltrating the Jewish ranks and it is a hindrance to our progress.

144- 455-24: Kisleve, December 25, is the month of dedication. The wall is dedicated with the vow of the Nazarene.

145- 455: 1 Tebeth, January 1, additional work plans were drawn up and in the first phase of being conducted.

146- 453: 12 Adar, February 12, Nehemiah's term as governor of Judea ends.

147- 442: 1 Nisan, it is now April 4. Passover has come and gone. Nehemiah has been studying the charts and he has found a descendant of the holy priesthood of Aaron.

148- 441: 10 Tishri, the feast of trumpets has ended. It is now September 10, Atonement. Nehemiah receives a holy calling from GOD.

149- 441-11: Tishri, September 11, Nehemiah records on the genealogy charts a seed from the lineage of King Solomon.

150- 441: 14 Nisan, March 14, Nehemiah searches out the mystery of the missing candelabra.

151- 431- 18 Zif, May 18: After ten years of research, the study of the missing candelabra is still a mystery. Nehemiah becomes exhausted. He is now 127 years old. GOD has promised not to call him home until he completes all the tasks assigned to him.

152- 429-24 Kisleve, December 24: It is December 24, the eve of dedication. Nehemiah brings a group sworn to secrecy to review the progress reports.

153- 429-1: Shebat, it is now January one. Nehemiah follows a lead from GOD as he searches for the location of the Holy Candelabra.

154- 429-2: Adar, it is now February 2, and Nehemiah and his master mark masons pinpoint the location of the Holy Candelabra.

155- 429-14: Nisan, March 14, the task is complete, and the Holy Candelabra is found.

156- 429-15: Nisan, Nehemiah announces that the glory of God has been returned unto Israel.

157- 429-21: Nisan, March 21, the power of Elijah has returned to the remnant, the Jews of Babylon, who have survived.

158- 421-30: Elul, August 30, Nehemiah seeks rest, and the holy seed goes into seclusion.

159- 421- 1: Tishri, September 1, Shemiah sends a letter to Nehemiah that his mother has died.

160-420: Tishri, ten, Yom Kippur. His vow completed; Nehemiah dies on the eve of Atonement. This is his birthday; he is 139 years old. Jerusalem is at peace.

161- 409-14: Nisan, it is now eleven years later and the important event in Israel continues. It is March 14, Passover, and Judith of the family of Bezai turned thirty-four years of age. She recorded that Shemaiah died today. He was thirty-three years and six months old.

162- 409- 1: Elul, August 1, Judith of the family or Bezai, reports the finding of secret documents and writings from the Prophet Daniel. They were in Shemaiah's files. I wondered if this is the final chapter of the Jews of Babylon.